BROKEN
FIELDS

Books by Marcie R. Rendon

THE CASH BLACKBEAR MYSTERIES
Murder on the Red River
Girl Gone Missing
Sinister Graves
Broken Fields

OTHER NOVELS
Where They Last Saw Her

BROKEN FIELDS

MARCIE R. RENDON

Published by
Soho Press, Inc.
227 W 17th Street
New York, NY 10011

Library of Congress Cataloging-in-Publication Data
Names: Rendon, Marcie R., author.
Title: Broken fields / Marcie R. Rendon.
Description: New York, NY : Soho Crime, 2025. | Series: The Cash
Blackbear mysteries | Identifiers: LCCN 2024042005

ISBN 978-1-64129-658-8
eISBN 978-1-64129-659-5

Subjects: LCGFT: Detective and mystery fiction. | Novels.
Classification: LCC PS3618.E5748 B76 2025 | DDC 813/.6—dc23/
eng/20240906
LC record available at https://lccn.loc.gov/2024042005

Interior design by Janine Agro
Printed in the United States of America

10 9 8 7 6 5 4 3 2 1

For Russell and Madelyne: potato pickers,
combine and grain truck drivers

BROKEN
FIELDS

Cash stepped out of the cab of her Ranchero onto the soft, black dirt of the field she was to plow under. The sun had barely risen, casting a gentle yellow haze over the Red River Valley. It was going to be a scorcher. The early morning heat and humidity made her thin cotton T-shirt cling to her back. This close to the river, the air was always heavy and moisture-thick. At least the mosquitos weren't out yet. To the west, cottonwoods, elm and oak created a green snake along the banks. A red hawk flew along the tree line.

Looking into the sun, her hand shading her eyes, Cash could barely see the slight rise of the ancient meandering shoreline of what used to be Lake Agassiz thirty-five to forty-five miles away on the prairie. The flat land of the Red River Valley with its deep rich soil was created by glaciers moving north thirty thousand years before Cash's time. As the glaciers melted, they formed a giant lake, larger than all the Great Lakes combined. When the Hudson Bay glacier melted, the waters of Lake Agassiz flowed into that bay, leaving behind the rich farmland.

Cash scanned the wheat and sugar beet fields spread out for miles along the horizon in both directions. When she looked to the east, her eyes stopped at a small farmstead way at the other end of the section of field she was to plow.

The small, white frame house, which even from this distance looked well worn, was owned by Bud Borgerud but was usually rented out to one of his field hands' family. This morning, it had a newer car sitting in the driveway. Cash saw a faint trail of exhaust from the rear of the car.

Cash lit a cigarette and blew the smoke softly into the air. She took a swig of coffee from her thermos. Another puff of smoke. Another drink of coffee. *I better get to work*, she thought. She tightened the cap back on the thermos, reached through the open window of her Ranchero and set it on the seat before walking over to the giant hunk of metal that was a Massey Ferguson tractor.

Bud Borgerud, or one of his other field workers, had left the tractor parked at the end of the field, the key in the ignition. Cash pulled her slight five-foot-two frame up onto the tractor. Even before she sat down, she realized she had forgotten the cushion she usually used to make the daylong ride a little easier on her behind. She climbed back down, retrieved it from the Ranchero cab and threw it onto the tractor before crawling up after it.

Once settled on the seat, she turned the key in the ignition, reached back for the lever to drop the plow into the ground and began plowing. As the tractor jounced down the field, Cash was grateful for the padded pillow cushion between her butt and the metal seat. As she neared the opposite end of the field, she noticed the parked car still running outside the white frame house. *Someone is wasting gas.* She turned the tractor and plow around in a wide, lazy circle and headed back the other way.

Back and forth, all morning. As the sun rose, Cash baked in its heat. She tied her dark-brown, waist-length braid into a knot at the nape of her neck. As she rode, her body jostled by the tractor traversing hard ground, she thought back on what occurred at the end of the past winter. When the flood waters arrived, there was the crazy woman and her pastor husband who kidnapped Native babies. Cash shuddered. The husband was dead. Cash, in sheer panic, had thrown a sharp paring knife straight into his neck. It had killed him. Cash's mind flashed on the knife thrower who performed every year at the county fair. That person had real skill. Her own throw was pure luck. The pastor was dead and she hoped his wife was still locked up in the asylum down in Fergus Falls. As far as Cash knew, the infants were back with relatives on the reservation.

Wheaton, the county sheriff, was always getting her into one mess or another. He had rescued her as a kid from an overturned car in a big ditch not too far from the field she was plowing for Borgerud. If she looked to the south, she could see the straight line of the gravel road where her mother had been drinking and driving and rolled the car. Cash had ended up in a series of foster homes, one nightmare family after the other until, in her late teens, Wheaton rescued her again and got her an apartment in Fargo, where she still lived.

Cash didn't know how or why, but she had developed sensibilities other folks didn't seem to have. A new friend, Jonesy, who lived in the tamarack over on the White Earth reservation, called them gifts. Cash wasn't sure about that.

4 · MARCIE R. RENDON

They seemed to come with the price of knowing too much about some other people's trouble and hurts. She could sense things other people couldn't. She out-of-body traveled in a near dream state at times, gathering information about crimes that weren't evident to others. Sometimes, she dreamt things that gave her true information; like when she dreamt the address to the house where some men were holding young women hostage in Saint Paul. That had been her first trip to the Twin Cities and she had no desire to return. She liked working the fields, not being a cop, but she felt she owed Wheaton and so when he asked for help, she helped.

He also wanted her to go to college. But it was summer and she had opted not to go to summer school. Killing a man, even a horrible man like the pastor, had messed with her concentration. Her grades remained good even though she skipped out on a lot of classes. She barely finished the spring semester. Given everything that had happened, she couldn't sit in a classroom without feeling claustrophobic.

Out here on the prairie there was room to breathe. And being able to see for miles in either direction created a sense of safety and security Cash had come to count on. She found some peace in the Red River Valley fields. When settlers had arrived in the Red River Valley in 1869, they received an allotment of a hundred and sixty acres of the most nutrient-rich soil in the world for an eighteen-dollar filing fee. Paupers from Scandinavian countries and Western Europe hit black gold. They grew children like corn. Some mothers gave birth to potential farmhands at the rate of one per eighteen months. Families would show up to church with eight to ten children, stepladdered from the tallest to the one on the hip.

It was their descendants Cash worked for. Her own folks, the Ojibwe, had been in this part of the world since the seventeenth century. Prior to the settlers' arrival, her people traded up and down the Red River with the Cree in Canada and the Dakota to the south. But they preferred to live in the forests by the lakes to the east, where deer and fish were plentiful. Cash, however, due to family circumstances and bad social policies, had grown up in the Valley. She had grown to love farm labor. She loved the quiet stillness of working the fields, driving the big machinery and trucks. There was the occasional broken machine or days of rain when one couldn't get into the fields. But as a farm laborer none of that was really her problem. The big farmers like Borgerud handled the problems. All she had to do was drive the tractor and get paid.

When the sun was directly overhead, Cash stopped the tractor by her Ranchero. She ate her tuna sandwich sitting in the shade offered by the big rear wheel of the tractor. There was a white wisp of a cloud in the sky, barely a wisp. She could hear birds talking to each other in the trees down by the river even though the river was a mile away. Looking to the east, beyond the little house with the car still running in the driveway, Cash could see cars driving down the highway two miles over, heading toward town for lunch at the drive-in or maybe to pick up machinery parts somewhere in Ada or Fargo. There were no cars driving the gravel roads out here where Cash was working. A few sections of land over, field dust was rising from another farmer plowing, but that was all that seemed to be moving in the Valley. Cash relished the peace. Sandwich. Coffee and cigarette. She was ready to get back to work.

Climbing back up on the tractor seat, she looked down the field again at the car in the yard. Several hours and it hadn't moved. She hadn't seen anyone come in or go out of the house. Cash felt a familiar tingle at the back of her head, just behind her left ear. *No. Just go to work*, she told herself. She turned on the tractor and started plowing. The closer she got to the house, the greater the tingling sensation at the back of her head got. At that end of the field, she shut off the tractor. She could hear the soft hum of the car engine running. *Not your issue, Cash. Get to work.* She started the tractor again and headed back to the other end of the field.

Cash made about four more rounds before she knew she'd have to check it out. Someone might leave a car running to go inside for a quick errand but no one left a car running all day. And that tingle told her *something* was off. When she got back to that end of the field, she shut the tractor off and hopped down. She brushed the field dust off her jeans and shirt as best she could. Slicked back the loose strands of hair that had escaped in the summer heat. As she walked up to the house, she ran different scenarios through her mind before settling on just asking for some water. She could always say the heat had gotten to her.

Cash came into the yard from the field side so she walked right up to the car in order to turn toward the house. She glanced at the house windows. Sheer white curtains were open and no one was peering out. No farm dog announced her presence. Cash took a quick look into the front seat of the car. It was a soft, bluish-gray Chrysler model. The key was in the ignition. The leather seats were clean. No papers strewn about. A neat and tidy car. Tire tracks indicated at least one other car had recently been in the driveway.

Cash looked again at the house. Still no movement in the windows. The back of her head started to vibrate as she walked closer to the two wooden steps that led to a screen door. Through the mesh of this outside door she could see inside the entryway, where another all-wood door was ajar. She knocked on the outside door. No answer. The door creaked on its spring hinge as she opened it. The thought ran through her mind that it was like the screen door at the Casbah bar. When she walked into the Casbah after a day in the fields the hinge would bring the door slamming shut right behind her, almost, but never quite, catching her long braid.

Cash stepped up into the entryway. Denim work jackets hung on nails on the wall above a pair of worn field boots. "Hello?"

No answer. The air where she stood was heavy.

"Hello!" she called again before pushing the inside door open and stepping into the farm kitchen.

There was a dead man lying in the middle of the kitchen. Blood congealed on his back and the floor around him. He faced away from Cash. Across the room, a .30-30 Winchester deer rifle looked as if it had been thrown and lay where it landed, against the base of the kitchen cupboards. Empty shells were scattered on the floor by the body.

Cash took deep breaths to calm her body, which had started to tremble. She had not caused this carnage. This was not her fault. She looked at the man again. She noticed the linoleum underneath him and thought it must have been a Sears special because so many farm homes had the same flooring. If you looked closely, there were red and black dots that resembled Popeye's girlfriend, Olive Oyl. Cash felt a giggle rise in her chest and stuffed it back down. She quickly scanned the room and leaned forward slightly to peer into the living room. From what she could see, the shooter was not in the kitchen or the living room.

Cash didn't see or hear another person. But she could sense she wasn't alone. She called "Hello!" in what she hoped sounded like a normal, friendly tone. "Hello," as she moved into the living room. No one. There were two doors in the room. She opened one door and revealed a closet that held a different season's coats. A wooden shelf across the width of the closet held sewing supplies and kid board games, including a deck of cards and a cribbage board that sat on top of Candy Land. The second door she opened led upstairs.

As she took one step up the stairs, Cash called out again, "Hello," and started up. Some of the stairs creaked. If someone was up there, they would know how close she was getting. The top of the stairs was surrounded by a railing with balusters. With her head even with the upstairs floor, Cash looked straight ahead through the balusters into the bathroom. She could hear water dripping. No one was in there—unless they were lying flat, out of sight, in the claw-foot bathtub. Grabbing hold of the floorboards and pivoting around, Cash saw two bedrooms along a narrow hallway. In the first bedroom, all she could see was a window with its curtains pulled shut. In the other bedroom, the afternoon sun was shining through the window. She could see under an iron bed frame, its mattress sagging slightly on wire springs. Nothing under that bed but dust bunnies.

Cash pivoted back around and continued walking up the stairs. "I was out plowing and got thirsty. Thought I'd stop in and see if I could get a drink of water. Looks like there's been a pretty bad accident downstairs. I just want to make sure everyone is okay. You okay up here?"

The hardwood floor creaked as she walked toward the first bedroom. Cautiously, she peered around the corner before entering. The tingling sensation at the back of her neck and head intensified to where it felt like fireflies were flitting around inside her skull. All her senses told her that someone, living, was in this room. She did not want to find another body.

"Hello?" more softly this time. The bed was unmade. Sheets and blankets were thrown helter-skelter. A woman's housedress lay on the floor along with a slip and bra. One oak dresser stood, several drawers pulled open, none of them fully shut. The room was quiet. Too quiet. Cash backed out of the room and did a quick survey of the other bedroom. Nothing was out of place. It was a child's room. A girl's room.

Cash went back to the first bedroom and edged inside. She bent down onto her knees and looked under the bed. Back in the farthest corner, under the tall iron bed frame and wire bedsprings that held the mattress, a small body huddled. Big, brown, unblinking eyes looked out at Cash. Terrified, dull eyes. Cash had seen that thousand-yard stare on boys returning from Vietnam.

Cash knelt and spoke quietly. "Hey. I came to get some water. My name is Cash. Can you come out and help me get some water?"

No response.

Cash scanned the downstairs of the house in her mind. Where was the phone? There had to be a phone. All houses had phones these days. Even ones as wore down as this one.

"Are you here alone?"

No movement. Not even a blink. She knew Borgerud and his wife didn't have any kids, so this little girl must be a field hand's child.

"Is there a phone downstairs? I'm going to go downstairs and find the phone. Where's your mom? Your dad?"

Silence.

"Not up to talking, huh?"

The little girl had started to quiver. Cash smelled pee.

"I'm going to go in your bedroom and get the blanket off your bed and bring it for you to wrap up in, okay? You look kinda cold." Cash stood up. She flicked the bottom of her shirt to get some fresh air. In contrast to the child under the bed shivering in cold terror, the summer heat in the upstairs room with all its windows closed made sweat pour down her back. Cash went into the other bedroom and returned with a small, thin summer quilt. She knelt down and pushed it under the bed to the child. "Wrap up. Keep warm. I'm going to go downstairs and call for help. You stay right here. I'll be right back."

Cash backed out of the room, still crouched down. Watching the child. "I'll be right back," she repeated.

Downstairs, she glanced quickly into the kitchen. The body was still there. She found the phone on a blond end table next to a nubby green upholstered sofa in the living room. Wheaton's secretary answered after three rings.

"This is Cash. I need Wheaton."

"Where are you?"

"Um—a farmhouse. Southeastern edge of Bud Borgerud's section. Out here a couple miles north of the big ditch outside of Halstad."

"Can you tell me what you found?"

"Some guy's been shot."

"Oh."

Silence.

"All right. As soon as I get ahold of him, I'll send him right out."

Just as Cash was getting ready to hang up, she heard Wheaton's secretary hollering, "Cash, wait!"

Cash put the phone back up to her ear. "Huh?"

"Are you okay?"

"Yeah. Just tell Wheaton to hurry."

Cash hung up without saying goodbye.

She walked to the doorway into the kitchen and looked

at the man lying on the floor. She had done her fair share of hunting and, judging by where he had fallen and the blood around him, she thought whoever shot him must have been standing right where she was now. She looked at his shoes. Regular shoes. Not farmer shoes. He was well dressed. Pressed dress pants. A light blue shirt with pearl snap buttons on the sleeve cuffs. A cowboy shirt. Avoiding splattered blood as best she could, Cash walked around to get a closer look at the man's face. It was Bud Borgerud.

Cash stood, hands on slender hips. *Well, who is going to pay me now?* was her first thought. She wasn't a police officer or a doctor. He was already dead and she supposed she shouldn't touch anything. Wheaton would get there as soon as he could. She turned from the kitchen and went back upstairs.

She went into the bathroom to shut off the dripping water. If someone had taken a bath, it was hours ago, because the tub was dry although the faucet was dripping. There was a glass with toothbrushes sitting on the ledge above the sink. Cash took out the toothbrushes, rinsed the glass and filled it with cold water.

She entered the bedroom and got down on her knees by the bed. The girl was still huddled in the corner. She hadn't grabbed the blanket. It lay where Cash had pushed it under the bed. "Here's some water if you're thirsty. Mighty hot in here right now." She edged the glass of water under the bed. "I'm going to open the window and let some air in. It's nice outside today."

With the window open, Cash sat on the floor next to

the bed, her back against the wall. As far as she could tell, the girl hadn't moved. The smell of pee permeated the thick summer air.

"You look kinda scared under there. Back when I was a little kid, younger than you—how old are you? Four? Five?" Cash gathered from a small shift the girl made she was guessing in the right age range. She continued. "I ended up spending a couple nights in jail because nobody knew what to do with me. My mom was gone. Didn't know where my dad was. Maybe not even who my dad was. My brother and sister were in the hospital. Never saw them again. Well, my brother I did. He came to visit me sometime this last year. But my sister? Nope. Mind if I take a drink of your water?"

Cash reached under the bed for the glass of water. Took a tiny sip. Just enough to wet her whistle so she could keep talking. Pushed the glass back under the bed. "Wheaton, the sheriff who's coming out to help us, he helped me when I was a kid like you. Been kinda looking out for me ever since. I think you'll like him. I do."

Cash paused and looked at her hands folded in her lap. God she could use a cigarette. Now probably wasn't the time to light up or leave the kid alone. But damn, she needed a smoke. "Mind if I smoke? Yeah?"

Cash took her smokes and matchbook from the front pocket of her T-shirt. The smell of sulfur from the match strike filled the air. She took a deep drag and blew the smoke across the room toward the window. A slight breeze brought the smoke slowly back into the room, where it curled in wide, slowly moving circles on the air currents. Dust motes danced away from the tendrils of smoke. Cash brushed the ashes from the cigarette into the leg of her jeans, leaving gray smudges on her thigh that she smoothed into the denim fabric with her thumb.

When the cigarette was half smoked, Cash said, "When Wheaton gets here, he'll know what to do. Once he figures out what happened downstairs maybe he'll take us into Ada and we can get some ice cream. Sometimes he takes me over to the restaurant in Twin Valley. Gets me blueberry pie with vanilla ice cream. You think you'd like that? Some blueberry pie and ice cream? I'll ask him to take us there."

Cash rambled on. "Wheaton has a dog named Gunner. You don't have to be scared of him. He's a police dog. That dog is jealous of me 'cause I was Wheaton's friend first. He pretends he doesn't like me but he helped me out once. We rescued a little baby that needed rescuing. Kinda like you need rescuing right now."

Cash was smoking her third cigarette and telling the girl under the bed about what classes she was taking in college when she heard a car pull into the gravel driveway. "I'm going to go look out the window over here and just check, make sure it's Wheaton. You stay right where you are, okay?"

Cash couldn't quite see the end of the driveway, so she unhooked the window screen and pushed it out. She stuck her head out far enough to see the front end of the county cop car. She pulled back in and hooked the screen. "Wheaton's here. Do you want to come out and meet him? Or should I go downstairs and talk to him a bit?"

Cash heard a soft rustle from under the bed. When she

bent down to look, the little girl had pulled the blanket over and around her. All Cash could see was her tousled brown hair and big brown eyes. "All right, you stay right there. Don't move—unless you want some of that water or gotta use the bathroom. I'll talk to him and then come back up for you once we got a plan. Back in a bit."

Wheaton stood in the kitchen doorway, filling the space with his football player–sized frame. He had taken off the farmer billhead hat he wore instead of the county cop hat and was rubbing his hand back and forth across his military crew cut. He looked at Cash and shook his head. Ran his hand over his hair one more time. "How did you find this?"

"I was plowing."

"I saw the Ranchero at the other end of the field."

Cash explained how she had watched the car in the driveway run all morning and since after lunch.

Wheaton nodded in the direction of the car. "I just shut it off."

Cash continued to explain how she decided to come check on the situation. Found the guy. Shot. The gun. "And there's a little girl upstairs. Under the bed. Way back in the corner. I've been sitting up there talking to her. Telling her the story of my life. Well, some of it. Left out the hard parts. Waiting for you to get here."

"No mom?"

Cash flashed on the woman's clothes strewn across the one bedroom floor. She shook her head no.

"Dad?"

Again Cash shook her head no.

Wheaton walked to where Cash stood and turned and looked at the dead man. "Look at this," he said. He went to the body and rolled the man over onto his back. "He was shot, standing, looking at the doorway right where you are standing. Whoever shot him stood right there. Did the girl say anything?"

"No, I think she's in shock or something. I thought maybe he'd been shot in the back."

"No. Look at the angle he was lying." Wheaton gestured at the floor and the direction to the door. "Someone rolled him over. And look, the bullets went right out his back. Those are exit wounds. And it is Bud Borgerud." Wheaton rubbed the back of his neck as if to ease the stress. "He's a trustee at the Lutheran church in town. If I remember right, he even helps teach the confirmation class on Thursday nights. His family's been farming the Valley since his grandpa arrived from Norway. Why the hell would someone kill him?"

Cash shrugged. She lit a cigarette. Black flies had started to come in the open kitchen doorway and buzz around the dead man's blood.

"What time did you first see the car out here?"

"Seven-thirty? Maybe a little before."

"So early morning. Seems like you would have heard something or seen something if this happened while you were plowing. You see any other cars around?"

Cash shook her head no. "Tire tracks of at least one other car in and out but no way to tell when those were made."

"I gotta ring Doc Felix—"

Cash grimaced. Doc Felix was a sorry excuse for a doctor in her opinion. He didn't like Indians and he treated women, in general, worse. But he was the county doc.

"—and get him to come out here and get the body. Take him into Ada. Can you get the girl to come down here?"

"I'll try."

Cash turned and went back upstairs. In the bedroom, she knelt and looked under the bed. The girl was still huddled in the corner but she didn't look as frozen with fright as she had earlier. She had wrapped the blanket tighter around her and she blinked when staring back at Cash.

"Whyn't cha come out from under there and we'll go into Ada with my friend Wheaton until we can find your mom or dad. Come on. Things are safe now. Come on." She reached her hand under the bed.

The girl inched toward her. When she was within Cash's reach, she said very quietly, "I peed."

"S'alright. We can go in your room and get you changed. I woulda probably peed my pants too."

The hand the girl put in Cash's hand was ice cold. Cash gently tugged her out from under the bed, the blanket still wrapped around her. Cash picked her up, blanket and all, and went into the other bedroom. She set the girl down on the bed. The springs creaked loudly. The muffled sound of Wheaton talking on the phone rose up from downstairs.

Cash rummaged through the dresser drawers. "Here's some panties. Socks. You want socks? Pants. And a clean shirt. Should I help you get dressed?"

The girl stared at her. Then glanced at the door.

Cash nodded. "I'm going to grab a few more clothes so you can change later, too. And some jammies. You'll probably need some jammies? I'll stand right outside the door here, with the door open, and you tell me when to turn around." Cash moved to the doorway.

The bedsprings creaked again. Clothes made a soft whoosh as they landed on the floor by the bed. Another large creak and the soft thud of small feet landing on the floor told Cash she had gotten off the bed. "I'm going to turn around now."

The little girl, dark skin suntanned darker, stood by the bed. Her brown hair was a tousled mess. The buttons on her white cotton shirt with yellow ducks on it were one off. Dark-blue slacks, white socks and dirty Keds tennis shoes, laces neatly tied, finished the look. Her eyes remained huge saucers of fear.

"Whatever happened before I got here is over. Things are good now. I'm going to carry you downstairs." Cash bent down and scooped her up. She grabbed the small quilt back off the bed and threw it over the girl. When she reached the bottom of the stairs, Wheaton was standing by the end table with the phone on it, looking out the window. He turned and looked at them.

Cash waited until the girl had a chance to look at Wheaton before pulling the blanket up over the girl's head, which Cash then cradled with her hand. "My friend Wheaton is here but we'll talk to him once we get outside. Gunner must be in the car. Do you want to meet Gunner?" And they walked through the bloodied, body-laden kitchen and outside into the fresh, humid air of a Red River Valley summer.

The sun was shining. Soft white moths floated through the air. A swarm of gnats hovered in midair. Birds in the tree stand next to the house talked to each other. Nearby, Gunner was circling a worn, wood-slatted corncrib filled with dried corn cobs. Cash whistled and the dog's ears perked as he looked in her direction. "Come here, Gunner," Cash called as she went to Wheaton's cop car and opened the back door. She backed in and sat down on the seat, feet on the ground outside the car, still holding the girl. Then she lifted the blanket off the girl's head.

Gunner trotted over. Looked at Cash as if to say, *What are you doing here?* Cash could have sworn the dog's eyes softened when he looked at the girl.

"And that's Gunner."

The girl reached her hand out. One finger touched Gunner's black nose. She slowly withdrew it. Gunner didn't move. "Wheaton found him running down one of these roads out here. Tied in a gunnysack. So, I guess he wasn't really running, more like hobbling along. What's your name?"

"Shawnee." Barely a whisper.

"Gunner, meet Shawnee. Shawnee, meet Gunner."

The girl reached her finger out to touch Gunner's nose again.

They sat quietly, waiting for Wheaton to finish inside the house. When he came out, he walked to the patrol car and leaned his forearm on the open door.

"This is Shawnee. Shawnee, this is my friend Wheaton."

The girl ignored them both. She had moved her small hand to Gunner's head.

"Can you step out here for a sec?"

Cash slid the girl off her lap. Motioned for Gunner to get in the back seat, where he immediately laid his head on Shawnee's leg.

Cash joined Wheaton and leaned on the trunk of the car. They faced the road leading into the farmstead. Closer to the river, farmers had planted alfalfa or clover. Looked like someone had a few acres of potatoes. The air smelled of sunshine and growing plants. They both turned and watched a pickup truck drive down a gravel road a mile over.

Wheaton broke the silence. "Nils Petterson rents this place from Borgerud. It's the old homestead. He works for Borgerud. His wife's name is Arlis."

"Shawnee has to be their daughter then."

"I would guess so. She say anything about what happened?"

Cash shook her head no.

"Let's head back into town. Get her checked out by the doctor." Seeing Cash's look of disgust, he quickly added, "Not Felix. Dr. Larsen, the new guy that just opened a clinic on Main. Just to make sure she's okay. I'll find out where her dad is working, if he is working, and try to find out where her mom is. I want you to stay with her and see if she talks about what happened. I'll take you back to your Ranchero and she can ride with you to the clinic in town, not the hospital. I already called Dr. Larsen. He's waiting for you. I'll wait here for Felix."

WHEATON DROPPED THEM OFF AT the other end of the field. Cash transferred Shawnee from the cop car to the Ranchero. She talked to Shawnee as she drove; she pointed out wheat fields and cows; apple trees in farmyards and the make and model of each car they passed. Halfway to town, the little girl fell asleep. Curled up on the car seat, her blanket pulled tight around her.

Cash remembered being Shawnee's size and age and all the rides in the social worker's car, riding from foster home to foster home. She remembered staring out the car window, fields zipping past, dread sitting in the pit of her stomach. And then the crunch of gravel as the car pulled into a driveway and her social worker saying, "Your new home, Renee." With a sigh, the social worker would always add, "I hope this one works out better for you than the last. You try to behave now. No more fighting and sassing back."

As a child, Cash had her own plan of action. She walked into each new home, each new school, and carefully assessed the situation. Which adult was the meanest? Which adult did you avoid eye contact with? And which kid at school did she pick the first fight with to avoid months of torment? She had found that if she struck first and gave the class bully the fight of his or her life, the chances of everyone leaving her alone for the rest of her stay in that school were secure. Cash was glad that Shawnee had both a mom and dad. One of them would surely come get her.

Shawnee woke as soon as Cash pulled into a parking spot in front of the clinic, disoriented. Tears welled in her eyes.

"Hey, hey, there, there. It's okay. We're at the doctor's. He's gonna give you a quick look over. I'll stay with you. And our friend Wheaton is trying to track down your mom and dad." Cash carried her into the clinic where the smell of alcohol and other medicinal disinfectants assailed their senses. The room was warm in the late afternoon heat and an old lady, her cane across her lap, sat reading a *Reader's Digest* magazine. Cash sat down, still holding Shawnee on her lap. The orange, fake-vinyl chair with steel legs farted with their weight. Shawnee gave a tiny smile at the sound. Cash held her and waited until the nurse, dressed in a starched white uniform, called them into a back office.

The doctor did a cursory exam of the little girl. Listened to her heart and lungs, checked her ears, eyes and nose. Told her to open her mouth and used a wide wooden tongue depressor to look in her throat. He tapped her knee with a rubber-tipped hammer and watched her small foot kick toward him. The doctor asked if she hurt anywhere. Shawnee just stared back at the doctor. She didn't say one word through the entire exam.

"Seems fine to me" was his medical opinion at the end of the half-hour exam. "She might be having a little bit of shock given what Wheaton told me. See if you can get her to eat something. Drink some water."

Cash held the girl's hand and walked her out of the clinic. Put her back in the Ranchero and drove past the county jail. Wheaton's car wasn't parked out front. She drove by the hospital. He wasn't parked there. She drove back to the jail. She took Shawnee into the station where Wheaton's secretary gave them both some chocolate chip cookies from the bottom desk drawer. They sat on the wooden bench across from Wheaton's desk and waited for him to return. His secretary handed them each a green bottle of 7 Up and kept a steady supply of chocolate chip cookies headed their way.

By the time Wheaton arrived, Cash was jittery from the sugar. The little girl needed to use the restroom and Cash went with her. She caught sight of herself in the mirror. Field dust was caked in rings around her neck and onto the shoulders of her T-shirt. Cash splashed water on her neck. Muddy water ran into the sink and left a dirt stain on the cloth roll towel, which she rolled twice to hide inside the metal dispenser. She lifted Shawnee up to wash and dry her hands and then joined Wheaton, ready for some real food.

Rather than take the usual drive to the Twin Valley café, Wheaton walked them to the hotel diner in downtown Ada and fed them both hot roast beef sandwiches. He eyed the little girl carefully as she ate half her sandwich and all her mashed potatoes. As he talked to Cash, the girl chewed more slowly, carefully listening while trying not to look like she was.

"I called around. Asked around. Had to go over to Borgerud's. Talk to his wife. She took it hard. She thinks Shawnee's dad is working their fields near Grand Forks, North Dakota for the week. Her dad was coming home on the weekend. Once they talk to him, I'm sure he'll be here sometime tonight. Miss Dackson still keeps her room here at the hotel. She's gonna keep an eye on our little girl until her dad gets back."

"Miss Dackson the county social worker?" Cash's voice cracked.

"Yep."

"She's still alive?"

Cash went quiet so as not to dredge up any old memories. Instead, she focused on Shawnee. "Miss Dackson will take care of you. She'll let you watch TV down in the hotel lobby until bedtime. And tell her you want hot chocolate before you go to sleep. She's not the best social worker in the world but she's the only one for this county."

Wheaton gave Cash a hard look. Cash shrugged and said to Shawnee, "I'll come back tomorrow and check on you."

The girl looked scared, but Wheaton assured her they were working hard to find her dad. Cash noted that the assurance didn't seem to help Shawnee relax.

"You want your mom, huh?" The little girl nodded once as she stuffed another forkful of mashed potatoes into her mouth.

When Miss Dackson joined them in the hotel café, she slid into the booth next to Wheaton. Her dyed-blond, permed hair did nothing to hide her age. "Hi, Renee. Good to see you." She tsked her tongue against her teeth. "I hear you are doing well in college. We would have never guessed you would do so well given how much trouble you gave us all over the years." She tsked again before she sipped some water. Her voice changed to a singsong, talk-to-little-children tone. "Hello, Shawnee. Looks like you will be spending the night with me. We have a beautiful room upstairs overlooking Main Street. After we get you a bath and into your jammies we can come back down to the lobby so you can watch TV before bedtime if you like."

Cash handed the paper bag of Shawnee's clothes over the table to the social worker. She felt Shawnee lean a little closer to her. Cash instinctively sensed Shawnee's fear of being abandoned. Cash looked directly into her eyes. "I'll come by tomorrow, Shawnee. Maybe your dad or mom will be here by then."

To the adults, she said, "I'm going to head back to Fargo. I'll come out early in the morning and finish plowing the field. Hope I still get paid."

Cash slid out of the booth. At the doorway, she looked back and saw two grown-ups and a very small child, her feet not reaching the floor, her chin barely past the tabletop. It reminded her of the cartoons where a large weight was dropped on one end of the teeter-totter and the character on the other end went flying into the air. She hoped Shawnee would have a soft landing.

Orange, soft pink and purple colored the western sky on the drive back to Fargo. A white shadow moon rose on the eastern horizon. There were dirt clumps on the highway, dropped by farm machinery that had left the fields in favor of halogen-lit farmyards. Machinery that would be refueled and sent back out at sunrise for another day's work, provided that no belts needed replacing and all engine parts were properly oiled.

Like every other night of the summer, Cash went to her

apartment, took a quick bath and changed out of her field clothes into a cleaner shirt and jeans, and headed to the Casbah. She noticed that she felt sorrow to the very marrow of her bones. A night of drinking beer and shooting pool tamped down the feeling.

When she did sleep that night, back in her apartment, she dreamt of a wood-paneled station wagon circling the block around the Casbah. When she bent down to look in the car window, she saw one of her foster mothers and the woman's husband. In the back seat was Miss Dackson, who beckoned her to get in the car. Cash woke shaking and dripping with sweat. She quickly turned on the overhead light, lit a cigarette and drained the warm bottle of beer that was sitting on the floor by the bed.

The stale beer helped wash away the recurring nightmare she'd had ever since she left the last foster home. In the nightmare, the family would drive around until they found her. She always woke up before they could get her into the car. This was the first time Miss Dackson had appeared with them. Thank god it was just a nightmare. Cash finished her cigarette and lay back, flipping her pillow to the cool side. She scrunched it up under her head and neck. She fell asleep with the light still on.

Cash woke the next morning just as the sun rose in the east. Field work didn't wait for birth or death. It didn't occur to her not to finish the plow job she had started the day before. On her drive to Borgerud's field the sky changed from dusty blue tinged with soft pink and orange to summer blue. Once again scattered wispy white clouds drifted across the upper atmosphere. She parked her Ranchero in the empty farmyard. Borgerud's car no longer sat in the driveway. Someone must have driven it away. Tire tracks in the dusty gravel indicated more than one car had driven in and out. She supposed one of the vehicles had been Doc Felix's, who would have picked up the body. A chill ran down her back as she imagined the dead man, Borgerud, lying on a cold metal slab being examined by Doc Felix.

Previous unpleasant run-ins with Doc Felix had compelled her to make Wheaton promise to never, ever, even if she was dead, leave her in the care of the creepy doc. He was a racist who roamed the basement of the county hospital morgue supposedly caring for the dead. Once, in Cash's presence, he smirked and uncovered a naked woman's body on his steel table. Another time he had tried to corner Cash to cop a feel. Cash shivered at the flash of memory. She shook off the feeling and walked to the tractor sitting in the nearby field.

By noon, the field was plowed. She stopped the tractor at the end of the field near the farmhouse. She used her forearm to wipe the sweat from her brow. She surveyed her work. The straight furrows of black dirt were neatly turned over for whatever crop Borgerud had planned to plant.

Cash looked up and down the gravel road. No cars in sight. No dust rising behind vehicles on roads a mile away. The farmyard she stood in was empty. It was probably the first home of the Borgeruds' immigrant ancestors, who would have claimed a 160-acre homestead hoping to make it rich in this valley of deep topsoil. The northeast corner of the dilapidated barn roof sagged halfway down the aged structure. Wooden-slat corncribs stood half empty. The corn still in them, dried and withered, indicated it had been there more than a few summers and winters since it was harvested.

Cash looked up and down the roadway again. Looked at the roads farthest away. Nothing moved. While the farmhouse stood in plain sight, it was evident it stood by itself on the prairie.

She walked up to the house, pushed the screen door open and re-entered the scene from yesterday. No body lay on the kitchen floor. A thin cotton kitchen towel with an embroidered bluebird flying across one corner and the word Tuesday sewn on it was draped across the back of a kitchen chair. Cash could see it had been used in an attempt to wipe up the mess on the floor. A black fly walked lazily over the blood smear that stretched across the linoleum. "Damn Doc Felix," Cash said. She turned on the faucet and held the towel under cold running water. Pink liquid ran down the drain. She rinsed the towel again and again until the water was only tinged with pink.

Cash opened the cabinet door under the kitchen sink, found an old rag, got it wet and wiped up the rest of the blood from the floor. She took both the towel and rag outside and hung them to dry on the clothesline in the yard. Two robins hopped in the grass pecking at bugs or looking for worms.

Cash went back into the house. It felt empty. She walked up the stairs that creaked with her weight and went into the bedroom where she had found Shawnee. The housedress was still lying on the floor along with the slip and bra. She picked up the dress and held it up to herself. The home-made dress fit a woman about her size. Five feet. Around a hundred pounds, give or take a few pounds. She laid the dress gently on the bed. Put the slip and bra on the bed also. She pulled open the dresser drawers. One drawer held women's undergarments. Another drawer slacks and shirts. One drawer held men's belongings. It looked more like a storage room than a room anyone really used. From what Cash could tell, nothing had been moved or changed since the day before.

The other bedroom was untouched also. Even though it was a bright sunny day outside, the room was cool and shaded. Cash reached up and pulled the string to turn on the overhead light. Shawnee's clothes were in dresser drawers. A few dresses hung in a doorless closet along with a couple men's shirts. The bed, minus the quilt Cash had grabbed on her first day in the house to wrap Shawnee in, was neatly made with the sheets and another thin blanket tightly tucked under the mattress. There was a layer of dust on the side table, whereas the dresser in the other room had recently been dusted.

Cash went back into the first bedroom. The bedsprings creaked under her weight as she sat down. She put her hand on the lightweight cotton dress, caressed the soft pink flowers on the material. She stared out the bedroom window, where a sparrow hopped on a tree branch. Her hand tingled as she continued to run it smoothly over the dress. The sparrow became a slight woman, walking along a paved road. The woman looked back over her shoulder. Her brow furrowed. Concern clouded her eyes. She wore jeans, a cotton blouse and tennis shoes. She kept walking down the road, getting smaller in the distance, and every few steps she would glance back at Cash. With her last glance, Cash felt more than heard her say, "I'll be back for her." And then, once again, a small brown sparrow hopped along the tree branch.

Cash pushed herself off the bed, went into the other room and rummaged through the drawer that held the little girl's clothes, grabbed a few more pants, shirts and undies. Back downstairs, in a corner of the living room, she found a worn, well-loved doll sitting in a child-size rocking chair. She grabbed the doll and drove the twenty-some miles into Ada.

It looked to be a lazy day in the small town of Ada. Only a few cars were parked in front of the Five and Dime on

Main Street. The county courthouse, which also housed the
jail, sat a few blocks off Main. After parking the Ranchero
next to Wheaton's cruiser, she walked up the well-worn
granite steps into the county sheriff's office. Wheaton's
secretary looked up as Cash entered. Without taking her
fingers off the typewriter, she said, "He's out northeast of
town helping a farmer chase some cows off the road and
back into the fenced pasture. I think those juvenile delin-
quent Simonson brothers cut the fence last night and chased
the whole herd out. They belong down in Red Wing reform
school." She tsked her tongue. "Drive on out that way, you'll
find him. Just look out for the cowpies on the roadway." She
gave a short laugh before the sound of clacking typewriter
keys filled the room again.

Cash nodded, a silent signal that said yes, she would
avoid the cowpies and she would head out of town to the
northeast. Her half scowl had already relayed her opinion
of sending folks to the state reform school. Like so many
conversations among the small town and rural folks, much
of Cash's communication was nonverbal.

Three miles out of town, Cash saw Wheaton's cruiser
coming toward her on the road. She stuck her arm out the
rolled-down window and signaled for him to pull over.

"Got the cows back in the pasture?" she asked after
she pulled the Ranchero next to the cruiser. Both she and
Wheaton rested their arms on their car door window ledge.
He looked to the east, she to the west. In the distance she
could see a pickup truck sitting half in the ditch, the driver's-
side wheels hugging the edge of the roadway. A couple men,

most likely the farmer who owned the cows and one of his sons, were repairing the cut fence.

Wheaton looked back in his side-view mirror. Shook his head in frustration. "On my way to the Simonson farm." He jerked his thumb back to the two men working on the fence. "One of their cows is missing. See if they are butchering at Simonson's, or see if a Black Angus is mixed in with their Guernsey milk cows. Want to ride with?"

Cash looked down the road. The men were throwing tools and a loop of barbed wire into the bed of their pickup. "Nah. I stopped by Borgerud's and grabbed some more clothes for Shawnee. And a doll. Thought I'd give them to you to drop off for her."

"You can take them to the hotel. Have the front desk call up for Miss Dackson. If she's not there just leave them at the front desk."

"Her dad didn't show up?" Cash asked, though she already knew the answer. The empty farmhouse had told her that. But she hoped Wheaton might have some news about the dad's whereabouts.

"Nope. The deputy I sent up to Grand Forks couldn't find him. The other guys working for Borgerud said he never showed up for work this week." Wheaton stared down the road in front of him. "I don't know what to think, Cash. We dusted the gun for prints and sent the fingerprint cards down to the Cities to see if we get a hit on who fired the rifle; but you know how that goes. Could be weeks before we get something back."

Cash looked down the road in the opposite direction.

Wheaton tapped his thumb rhythmically on his steering wheel, still staring straight ahead. "You think the dad shot Borgerud? Took off with Shawnee's mother and left their girl behind?" Gunner, his dog, lifted his head and stared at Cash until she squinted at him, then he laid his head back down as if he didn't see her.

"Wouldn't make any sense, Wheaton. Indians don't just leave their kids. They would have taken her with if they could. How do we know they were even together? Maybe the dad shot Borgerud and got scared and ran. Maybe the mom shot him? Hell, Shawnee hasn't said anything either?" Cash stared down the road for a good minute before softly saying, "I think she saw the whole thing."

Wheaton nodded. Thumb still tapping out a silent rhythm on the steering wheel. "Well, I have to head over to Simonson's. Deal with a modern-day cattle rustler if that's the case here. Give the clothes to Miss Dackson. Maybe see if the girl is talking yet or not?"

"All right."

Both drivers put their vehicles in gear and headed off in opposite directions.

Back in Ada, Cash went to the hotel and asked the desk clerk for Dackson's room number. The man, who resembled Jack Sprat from the children's nursery rhyme, pushed his wire-rim glasses up on his nose, then, with extraordinarily long fingers, rifled through papers on the desk. Cash guessed him to be mid-forties even though his voice sounded like he was in his eighties when he said, "Room 204. Right up the stairs on the left."

As Cash headed to the stairwell, he called after her. "Sorry, miss, I just remembered. They just walked over to the steak house. Said they were going to grab a bite to eat."

Cash tucked the doll under her arm and set the paper bag of clothes on the front desk. "Can you keep these here till they get back? I'll let Miss Dackson know I left them."

"Ya betcha," the clerk answered and placed the bag at his feet. "It'll be safe and sound, right down here."

Cash walked out into the soft spring air. The Valley summer heat and humidity hadn't hit the area yet. Her jean jacket worn over a T-shirt kept the slight chill at bay. She carried the doll by one arm. A few cars were sprinkled along the street, parked head in at an angle toward the Ben Franklin store on the block. More cars were parked farther down the street in front of the town's only café, steak house, grab-a-cup-of-coffee-in-the-morning restaurant, a sheet of paper in its window proclaiming FINE DINING. A sign over the doorway dimly flashed THE ADA CAFÉ in pale orange neon.

Cash squinted as she entered the dimly lit café. The front windows weren't large enough to fill the room with the outside sunshine, and the dark, wood-paneled interior soaked up the yellow light from the ceiling fixtures. She saw Shawnee sitting in a corner booth, perched on the edge of the leather seat, short legs dangling. A hamburger in a bun was halfway to her mouth. Her eyes widened as Cash approached. She took a small bite and chewed slowly. Slid over to make room for Cash on the booth seat.

Cash noticed Miss Dackson's cotton blouse with a round collar, buttoned all the way to her neck, was tucked into a navy-blue skirt with a thin leather belt circling her waist. *Typical social work wear* ran through Cash's mind.

Out loud, Cash said, "Stopped by your house, Shawnee. Saw your doll and thought you might be lonely for her." Cash set the doll on the seat between them.

"Hello, Cash," said Miss Dackson, trying to hide her surprise at Cash showing up in the café. "How are you today?"

"Can I get you a menu?" the waitress asked as she poured coffee into the white ceramic coffee cup she placed in front of Cash. "Special today is hot roast beef sandwich and cherry pie."

Cash shook her head no. "This is good," she said, reaching for the cup.

"What brings you here?" asked Miss Dackson.

"I had to finish plowing the field out at Borgerud's. Left some more clothes for Shawnee at the hotel. Desk clerk said you were here so thought she might want her doll."

In a lowered voice, trying to pretend as if Shawnee couldn't hear her, Miss Dackson said, "They couldn't find her dad." She sent a pitiful glance in Shawnee's direction while shaking her head in mock frustration.

Cash felt like kicking her under the table. Instead, she sipped her coffee before she asked Shawnee, "Any idea where your mom and dad are?"

Shawnee gave her a blank stare. Moved some french fries around on her plate.

"Still a bit too much to talk about, huh? I get that way.

Can't stand all the grown-up chitchat." To Miss Dackson, she said, "What's gonna happen to her? The two of you gonna stay at the hotel?"

"For now. Wheaton said to give it a few more days, see if one or both of her parents turn up. Wheaton said it looked like only Mr. Borgerud was hurt. Said it didn't look like either of her parents were shot. All we can do is pray that we don't find one or the other of them dea—"

This time Cash did kick the social worker's leg. Shawnee tensed up on the seat beside her. Miss Dackson reached down and rubbed her shin. The young girl's eyes, wide with fear, looked at Cash with unspoken questions in them.

Cash spoke directly to Shawnee. "I'm sure your mom is just fine. If you have any idea of where she might be, any idea that would help me find her, or help me bring you to her, maybe you could tell me that?"

Shawnee's eyes welled with tears. Big drops rolled down her cheeks and soaked into the front of her thin cotton blouse.

"Hey, hey. It's okay if you don't know. I'll find her." Cash used a paper napkin from the metal holder on the table to wipe the girl's tears.

"I wouldn't make her promises you can't keep. You should know the hard reality these children have to live with." Miss Dackson popped a french fry into her mouth.

Cash gave her a cold stare, then spoke to Shawnee. "I see Miss Dackson got you a strawberry malt. You like strawberry? She used to buy me a chocolate malt when I stayed with her. You want another drink?" Cash lifted the malt glass down off the table, at a level where Shawnee could sip from the straw without tipping the glass over and spilling the thick ice cream drink all over herself.

When Shawnee stopped drinking, Cash set the glass back on the table, slid out of the booth and stood looking back and forth between the social worker and the young girl. "I better get back to work," she said to Shawnee. To Miss Dackson, she said, "Remember to pick up the rest of her clothes at the front desk."

Miss Dackson nodded, hand still on her shin. "I know Wheaton thinks a lot of you, thinks you've grown into a fine young woman. I see no one managed to tame you yet."

Cash spun on her heels and walked out of the café.

CASH DROVE BY THE POLICE station. Wheaton's cruiser sat out front, so she pulled into a parking spot and went in. Wheaton was behind his big oak desk filling out paperwork. He glanced up. "Found the cow. No one tells you the exciting side of this work when you get the job. Pulling people out of ditches in the dead of winter. Hauling cows back to their owners. Stopping teenagers from stealing gas out of farmers' fuel tanks."

"Having little girls sleep on the hard benches of your jail, waiting for their mothers to sober up."

"Only one." Wheaton signed a paper with a flourish.

Their conversation reminded Cash of the young man Geno from Red Lake. "Is Geno coming back for the summer?" she asked. During one potato picking season, she had helped find the murderer of Geno's father. After the rest of his siblings ended up in foster care, the young kid had hitchhiked to Ada looking for Cash to avoid foster care himself. He had ended up in Wheaton's care, and Wheaton discovered he had a real talent in art. He took Geno by train to Santa Fe to the Indian art school.

"Maybe. He did good at the art school. I told him if he gets a job for the summer, wants to hang around down there, he might want to stay. He's already been accepted for next year."

Cash sat down on the wooden bench across from Wheaton's desk and started a staring contest with Gunner.

Wheaton continued without looking up from the paperwork. "He'll probably come up at some point. He's always asking about his brothers and sisters."

The dog flared its nostrils. Cash flared hers back at him. The dog snarled.

"What are you doing, Gunner?" Wheaton jerked his head up. His stern look at the dog interrupted the standoff. "Leave my dog alone, Cash. I don't know what you have against him."

Cash crossed her arms across her chest. Thought, *Abandoned me for a dog. And a homeless kid from Red Lake.* Out loud, she said, "Dog don't like me."

And you probably got a girlfriend too you're not telling me about, her inside-her-head voice continued.

"Gunner likes everyone." Wheaton looked down and absent-mindedly scratched the dog behind his ears. Since he had rescued the throwaway dog the two were inseparable, except for the time when Wheaton left the dog with a neighbor while he took Geno to enroll in school.

While Wheaton and Geno were getting Geno enrolled, Gunner had helped Cash rescue a baby from a malevolent pastor and his wife. However, as soon as Wheaton returned, Gunner went right back to snarling at Cash as if he'd never helped her at all. Cash caught the dog's eye and curled her upper lip. Gunner made a soft, deep guttural sound from his throat.

"Quiet, boy." Wheaton hadn't looked up from scratching the dog's head, so he missed the interchange between the dog and Cash.

"No one seems to know where Shawnee's mother and father are. Her mother's from White Earth. That's all anyone seems to know. Borgerud's wife said she thinks she remembers the mother talking about Strawberry Lake. The kid's dad is from up by Naytahwaush."

"That what she said when you talked to her, huh?" Cash asked. "Sometimes when a crew of us are working in the field, she brings out a lunch. Always a plate of sandwiches that remind me of the Lutheran Ladies Aid meetings. She'd be kinda flirty with the men. Never said boo to me."

Wheaton raised his eyebrows. "I don't usually gossip, but I do recall, years back, when Jean—Mrs. Borgerud—was in high school. She was homecoming queen. Captain of the cheerleading squad. Her daddy spoiled her rotten. Gave her some little sports car when she turned sixteen. Rumor has it she got sent to the Cities for about six months, end of her junior year, before her senior year."

"So?"

Wheaton used his big, farmer-sized hands to make a

rounded motion over his stomach. Cash's eyes widened. She had heard about girls being "sent away" for "female issues" but knew of more girls who "had to" get married, which seemed to be the most Christian option.

"She and Bud don't have any kids. That's a big farm with no heirs. Wonder how she'll handle it." He spoke more to himself than Cash now. "Either way, back to the couple who were renting, Mrs. Borgerud says the family got a cut in rent for the dad working the fields for them. Didn't sound like she approved, but doubt she disapproved enough to kill her husband for it."

"Never know what these church ladies are capable of," Cash said softly as she put her elbows on her knees, chin in her hands, and stared at the dog again. Gunner was bored with the game and dropped his head on his paws and closed his eyes. "Loser," Cash said under her breath.

"What?" Wheaton's head jerked up to look at her just as the black rotary phone on his desk rang. "Hello, Norman County." He stood up quickly as he listened. His brow furrowed. His free hand touched his gun, then his handcuffs. "On my way." He dropped the phone down into the cradle. "Gotta go. Bank in Twin Valley just got robbed. Tell the secretary when she gets back from lunch where I went."

"I'll come too."

Wheaton was already by the door. "Nah. Too dangerous. Said they were armed. See what you can figure out about that little girl's parents." And he and his orphan dog were gone.

Cash stuck her hands in her jeans pockets and stared

after him. Since Wheaton had asked her to "help him out once in a while," she had been shot at, tied up and threatened by two guys who'd killed another guy; been locked in a basement root cellar by a murderous pastor, then attacked by that pastor's slightly-off-center wife who seemed to be three people in one body; and that was after being drugged by her college professor who left her with a group of men down in the Cities who were pimping out young women. She hollered after him. "Hell yeah, Wheaton, a simple bank robbery might be too dangerous for me!"

"Oh, yeah, and I ended up killing the pastor," she muttered as she scrawled a note for Wheaton's secretary that read *Out for the afternoon—Twin Valley*.

"God, I could use a drink," she said to a crow that strutted on the jailhouse lawn. "Guess I'll try to find where this girl's parents disappeared to instead." She slammed the door of her Ranchero extra hard. "Something safe!" she yelled to a sparrow that flitted by. She lit up a cigarette, rolled the car window down. She blew smoke into the warm air, listened to other birds talk to each other through the treetops. Thought about the sparrow she had seen at the farmstead that had turned into a woman who said she would be back. Cash blew smoke toward the wisps of white cloud floating across the pale blue sky. With half the cigarette smoked, she turned the key in the ignition, reversed out of the parking lot and headed to Borgerud's farm.

When she arrived at the homestead, she saw Borgerud's wife hanging laundry. White sheets held in place by wooden clothespins stretched down the clothesline. The woman stopped hanging the sheet she was holding and let it slip from her hand. One end was pinned to the line, the other fell into the green grass. As Cash approached her, she stooped, picked up the corner of the sheet, shook some loose grass off that clung to its dampness.

After she pinned the sheet corner to the line, the woman turned to stare at Cash. She had a thin Scandinavian nose and blue eyes. "You're that girl that works the fields around here, aren't you?" Her tone was flat. She brushed loose strands of blond hair off her forehead. White tennis shoes on her feet. While the women in Fargo had taken to wearing pants like the women on TV, Borgerud's wife, who was tall and slender, wore a cotton housedress that touched her knees, like most modest farm women in the Valley. No miniskirt on her like the skinny models in the magazines wore as the latest fashion fad. Cash glanced at the family sedan sitting in the driveway. Not the sports car of the woman's wild and hidden youth.

Cash nodded in response to Jean's question.

"And word has it you help the county sheriff."

"Time to time."

The woman ran her hand down the sheet she had just hung, as if to erase the wrinkles on it. "You found my husband."

A statement not a question. Cash nodded again.

The woman stared at a car that drove down the county road. She watched the small cloud of gravel dust dissipate before it reached her laundry.

"Mrs. Borgerud . . ."

"Jean, folks call me Jean. Did you come to get paid? I saw you finished plowing the field by the old homestead."

Cash shook her head no. "But if you can pay me, I'd appreciate it."

As Jean turned to walk toward the house, Cash said, "I was wondering more what you can tell me about the little girl's parents. Where they might be."

Jean continued toward the house across the neatly cut lawn. Cash followed. Over her shoulder, Jean said, "The funeral's in two days. His family will be coming from Rugby, over in North Dakota. Almost up to Canada. Thought I'd wash the sheets, freshen 'em up, for them to sleep on. Both of his brothers and their wives. Imagine I'll just have their kids sleep on the living room floor. Only have the two spare bedrooms. Watch the screen door so it doesn't slam shut on you. Let me write you a check." She pointed at the dining room table, indicating that Cash should sit down. She walked off down a hallway that led off the kitchen.

On the table were three casseroles. Cash lifted the cloth covering the nearest dish. It was scalloped potatoes with cubes of ham. The other was some kind of tuna hotdish. The third wasn't a casserole at all but a Jell-O salad. Cash's stomach growled. Jean returned with a business-size checkbook ledger in hand. She sat on a chair opposite Cash. She stared at the food on the table.

"That Jell-O's going to melt," Jean said as she pushed away from the table, grabbed the dish and put it in the fridge. When she returned, she sat down, heavy, on the kitchen chair and opened the checkbook. "Where was I? I don't know your real name," she said, pen in hand poised over the check.

"Just make it out to Cash Blackbear. I'll cash it at the bar in Halstad. They know me. Wheaton said you knew the little girl's mom?"

Jean's face paled and her hand holding the pen shook. "My Bud shot. Dead. And how can both her parents be gone?" She looked at Cash. A blue-eyed stare. "I cried, don't have any more tears to cry. Guess we all say that huh? When someone dies. Then the tears rush up on you. I started bawling running the sheets through the washing machine. Thinking Bud's never gonna sleep in bed with me again. You know, we never had any kids of our own. One of Bud's biggest heartaches. No one to farm with. Pass the farm on to." Pen midair, she stared out her kitchen window. "I'll have to find someone to manage the farm. We have fields all up and down the Valley. It's going to take me a while to get over the shock of him being gone." Shook her head and kept staring into space. "I'll have to hire someone to help me manage it."

"I know a lot about farming. Been at it one way or the other since I was eleven." Cash was surprised to hear herself speak.

Jean stared at her. Cash watched the woman's eyes shift from blue to navy when Jean asked, "Aren't you Indian?"

Cash felt a flash of anger. She felt her face tighten, the muscles of her eyes squint and she knew she was giving Jean a look that could kill.

Jean didn't blink. Her voice hardened. "Besides," and she looked Cash up and down, "most women are too soft or dumb. It takes a man to run a farm like this. A man like my Bud." Jean dropped her eyes to the pen in her hand. Looked down at the unwritten check. "Cash Blackbear. What does he generally pay you?"

Cash's voice matched Jean's. "Same as he does the men. Look back through the ledger."

Jean flipped through the small square check receipts. "Huh." She scribbled numbers onto the check. Signed her name in tight cursive. Tore the check carefully from the register and held it in Cash's direction. "We should be square."

Cash folded the check in half and stuck it into her shirt pocket. "Do you know where Arlis is from? Nils? Where they would have gone?"

"I already told Wheaton. I remember Bud telling me she was from Strawberry Lake. Nils's home was farther north. We gave them a discount on the rent in exchange for work and having someone live in the house. Keeps the local teens from using it to drink in." She covered her face with her hands, elbows on the table. "What am I going to do now?" she asked between wash-water worn fingers.

"Do you know if either of them had family over there?"

"Nils's dad is Norwegian. Lutheran. I don't know about Arlis. Got the impression she was more . . ." From behind her hands she searched for a word. "Don't wanna say heathen, but never saw her in church."

Cash's stomach growled again. She put her hand over it and pressed. "Do you have any idea who killed your husband? Why?"

Jean groaned, like a scream held back, her knuckles turned white over her face. Unexpectedly, she slapped her hands on the table. Cash jerked at the sound. Jean's blue eyes shot daggers at Cash as she uttered a guttural, "No!"

Cash felt her pulse race from the sudden change in demeanor. Her own voice rose an octave to ask, "Arlis? Nils?"

"No, no." Jean, as if the outburst had drained her, once again stared out the kitchen window. With a flat voice she said, "We were giving them a break. A good start in life. Why would they shoot him?"

"Any reason you can think of for anyone to want to hurt Bud? Anyone angry at him? Jealous?"

Jean just shook her head no.

Cash pressed on. "Why would they leave their daughter? Wheaton talked to some of your other workers and they thought Nils was working up by Grand Forks. But he never showed for work. Any idea where he is?"

"I don't know. Arlis spoiled that kid if you ask me. Ignored her own husband." Jean absent-mindedly turned a good-sized diamond engagement ring and gold wedding band around and around on her left ring finger before she again buried her face in her hands. Her blond hair fell forward. She slid her fingers toward her temples, away from her eyes. "I wish I knew. I wish I knew. Are you going to try find them? Maybe Arlis saw what happened and got scared and ran. Maybe the girl saw something. Did she say anything?"

"She's not talking."

"Not talking?" Jean brought her hands away from her

face, brushed her hair back as it fell forward again. "Like she's a mute or just not talking?"

"Maybe in shock is what the social worker thinks."

Jean pushed away from the table. Moved the casseroles to the kitchen counter. "I need to finish the laundry before his family gets here. Take his suit to the funeral home in Ada before tonight. I told Wheaton, I have no idea who would shoot Bud. Doubt it was Nils, although who knows? People around here talk, get petty about who has more acres, who got new farm machinery this spring, who has more people working for them. But my Bud was a churchgoing man, a family man, didn't do anything to get killed over. You gotta believe me." She turned from the counter to face Cash, wringing her hands.

It was Cash's turn to push away from the table. "I'll let you get to what you need to take care of. Thanks." She patted her shirt pocket where she'd stuck the paycheck. "I'll run over to White Earth and see if anyone over there has seen Nils or Arlis."

"Wish I had more to tell you."

Cash nodded. "I'll see myself out." And even though she was still smarting over the "Aren't you an Indian?" comment, or maybe because she still was, she made sure the screen door didn't slam behind her as she let herself out. From the Ranchero, she saw Jean looking over the kitchen curtain, watching her leave. In spite of the woman looking down on her, Cash still felt sorry for her as she pulled out of the driveway.

Cash circled back to the small town of Halstad on the

banks of the Red River to the Drive-Inn on Highway 75. A group of teenage girls dressed in halter tops and cutoff jeans sat in the back of a pickup truck, laughing, throwing french fries at each other. A young farmer sat behind the steering wheel, one muscled, suntanned arm resting on the open window ledge. He was older than the teen girls but not by much. His shock of blond hair, with a slight curl, hung over his forehead. Cash ordered a hamburger and fries to go from the waitress who had walked out to the Ranchero.

The driver called out to the waitress as she turned to go inside to place the order. "Alice, did cha hear the latest about Halstad's very own soap opera?" He motioned for her to come closer to his open window. The girls in the back stood up and leaned into the conversation. The guy lowered his voice, and all Cash could hear was a low murmur and the young girls in back gasping while they dramatically covered their mouths with their hands.

Alice shook her head and walked away. Over her shoulder, she said, "I don't think so. You'll owe me for those burgers and fries."

He responded, "I'm telling you, our own little *Peyton Place*." The girls sat down quickly as if hiding but didn't lower the sound of their giggles. When the kid saw Cash looking at him, he gave a two-finger farmer wave and turned to his passenger. A clear sign of "you're not included in this conversation."

As Cash waited for her food, she racked her brain for any knowledge she might have of *Peyton Place*. All she could recall was that in her last foster home, the wife shooed everyone out of the carpeted living room at eight-thirty each night with the admonishment, "Go do your homework." Then she would grab a beer, sit in an ugly brown recliner and turn on *Peyton Place*. Cash learned from other kids at school that the show was about the sexual activity of adults in some small town somewhere that led to shady business deals and murder. At least that's what she could remember.

Just then, Alice reappeared with her meal on a metal tray she latched to the Ranchero's doorframe. "Let me pay you right away," Cash said. "You can take the tray, I'll just take the food. What's the big secret over there?" She nodded in the direction of the pickup full of teens.

Alice shook her head. "He says he knows some woman, prominent woman, to quote him, who is cheating on her husband with someone way younger. Said if I let him order for free he'd tell me her name. Can't believe everything you hear, 'specially from that guy." She shook her head again.

Cash thanked her, paid and watched her walk away. Took two bites of the hamburger before putting it on the seat beside her. She took another look at the carload of kids. The guy saw her looking and winked his blue eye at her. Cash threw him a look of disgust, backed out of the parking lot and headed east to see what she could find out about Nils and Arlis.

CASH DROVE EAST ACROSS THE flat Valley plain. As the early spring brought the promise of summer and fall harvest, farmers were out plowing, harrowing or planting in the warm air. The smell of fresh manure being spread as fertilizer somewhere in the Valley assaulted her nose. She scanned the horizon but couldn't tell where the smell was coming from. In her rearview mirror was the Halstad water tower. Ahead, she could see the Ada water tower, a short round stub on the far horizon. She turned south in Ada on Highway 9 to connect with Highway 10 going east. The land changed from flat prairie to soft rolling hills around the small town of Hawley. She continued on to DL, as folks called the summer lake town of Detroit Lakes. She stopped at a gas station and paid for two large jugs of water, then headed north on 59.

She passed more farmers plowing fields, planting crops. With their black, beady eyes in small round heads, red-winged blackbirds tracked Holstein cows chewing cud in pastures surrounded by the barbed wire the birds sat on. Cash trusted her inner compass to find the gravel roads that took her farther into lake country, into the backwoods of the tamarack forest.

Cash thought of Geno. While he was living at Wheaton's and before he went to art school, she had enlisted Geno to muddle through trying to find who had killed a woman from the White Earth reservation. A woman whose body had washed into the town of Ada during the spring flood.

Geno had taken Cash to visit Jonesy, an old Indian woman who knew something about otherworldly types of things. Geno was born and raised on the Red Lake reservation and knew where to find the Elder. Cash soon discovered that Jonesy, without being told, also knew something about Cash's abilities to sense things other folks couldn't always sense or even understand. What Cash sometimes thought of as her sixth sense.

Cash shook her head to rid herself of the chill that crossed her body as she remembered the dark spirit that had hovered over the graveyard in the small church out on the prairie. Maybe she was lucky her senses seemed to be dimming, she thought. She lit another cigarette and turned on another gravel road, and then onto a dirt road that took her into the muddy driveway of her friend Jonesy.

Jonesy, wearing men's jeans and a red flannel shirt, sleeves rolled up to her elbows, was swinging a long-handled ax overhead in the yard out front. A two-foot log split in half as she brought the ax down with a resounding smack. "I thought I better get the fire going in the stove, get some tea going," she said without making eye contact as Cash stepped out of the Ranchero. "Got some rabbit stew I can heat up too. Thought you'd be by today." She brushed thin wisps of salt and pepper hair off her face. Tucked the longest ends behind her ears. Her long black braid, threaded with gray, hung down her back. She leaned the ax against the cutting block, filled her arms with newly split logs, tilted her head toward the wooden shack that was her home and headed toward it.

Cash filled her arms with more chopped wood and followed Jonesy into the house, which was basically a one-room log cabin. Along one wall a makeshift kitchen consisted of salvaged cupboards and a wood stove. A large, old-fashioned metal milk can held water next to a counter where a washbasin sat. Nearby was a wood kitchen table already set with two bowls, two coffee cups and silverware. On the opposite wall was a single bed with boxes visible underneath. Plants, hung for drying, lined another wall. An assortment of leather and cloth bags hung next to them. Jonesy's clothes were hung on nails or draped over a very old stuffed chair pushed into a corner near the bed.

Cash dropped the wood into a cardboard box next to the stove that held other logs. Broken-off bits of tree bark and wood splinters littered the floor. Jonsey got the fire going in the wood stove while Cash went back out to the Ranchero, brought in the two jugs of water and set them by the metal milk can.

"Miigwech, my girl. Saved me a trip into town. Sit." Jonesy nodded toward the table. Cash sat and sipped tea while Jonesy heated up the rabbit stew. When it was steaming, she placed two bowls on the table.

Cash lifted a piece of meat from the bowl and blew on it. Her stomach gave a slight growl. "I didn't even know I was hungry. This sure beats a tuna sandwich," she said as she prepared to bring the spoonful to her mouth. The rabbit meat was tender and Cash's chest filled with satisfaction as she chewed.

"Where's the boy?"

"Geno's still down at school. He'll be home before the summer ends." Cash's bowl was already half empty. "How'd you know I was coming out to visit?"

"Them crows been flying around all morning chattering away." Jonesy picked a small bone from the stew and chewed on it.

"Wheaton sent me over to find this girl's mom and dad. Nils Petterson, his wife is Arlis. Don't know her last name. They're from around here."

Jonesy's "Hmmm?" asked Cash to give her more information.

"I was plowing this field and I found the owner shot in the house this little girl, Shawnee, was living in with her parents. Borgerud was dead on the kitchen floor and both parents are gone. Girl's not talking at all."

"That little girl's seen enough hurt for one lifetime." Jonesy put the bone down on the linoleum tablecloth and sipped some broth. She looked at Cash, then stared into the space to Cash's right.

Cash felt the air around her head tighten. Her sight went fuzzy on the edges. She slowly ate more rabbit meat.

"Wheaton sure counts on you a lot don't he." It was more a statement than a question.

Cash nodded. "Yeah, he's off chasing bank robbers today. Said it was too dangerous for a girl. Sent me over here on a search mission."

"The girl's mom isn't ready to be found. Her dad . . ." Jonesy shrugged and took another piece of meat from her bowl. "Wheaton needs you more than he thinks he does."

The air around Cash's head cleared, the tightness lifted.

"I'd go find him if I were you." Jonesy pushed back from the table. Filled both their bowls again. "Help me finish off this soup first. Put some meat on your bones."

Jonesy waved Cash off when she tried to help wash the bowls after they finished eating. "Go on. You got work to do. I'll walk you out." Jonesy moved them both outdoors, to the Ranchero. "I wouldn't worry about the girl's mom right now. Keep the girl safe. And Wheaton too. Go on now." She turned and walked back to her shack.

Cash did a three-way turn to get the Ranchero headed out the driveway. Lit up a cigarette. A glance in her rearview mirror showed Jonesy standing in her doorway watching her leave.

As she drove out of the tamarack, she thought about what Jonesy had said. "Her mom isn't ready to be found." From past experience, Cash knew that Jonesy intuited things that so-called "normal" folks missed. She understood that it would be a waste of her time to try find Arlis today and told Cash as much. Cash took a deep drag of her cigarette. There were also the unspoken comments between Jonesy's sentences, the shrug about Shawnee's dad. Cash exhaled the smoke out the window. "Guess I may as well head back to Fargo," she said to the pine trees lining the road. Another part of her brain said, *But swing by Twin Valley to see if Wheaton caught the bank robbers.* At the edge of the tamarack forest, Cash turned north then west on the gravel county roads that would take her to the small town of Twin Valley, on the edge of the Red River Valley.

She slowed as she rounded a curve that took her into the town. She drove down Main, slowed even more as she passed the solid brick bank building. A sign hung in the bank door that said CLOSED. She drove by the café where Wheaton always brought her to get a cup of coffee and a slice of blueberry pie. Geno, before he left to go to school, had convinced her that Wheaton had a girlfriend who was a waitress at the café. Cash still didn't believe it. To her knowledge, Wheaton the county cop had no friends, let alone a girlfriend. She had never seen him so much as smile at or flirt with a woman. He was the Law and people treated him with respect and distance, like a pastor or something. But Wheaton's cruiser wasn't out front. Cash continued slowly to the edge of town, headed toward Ada, where she did a U-turn and drove back to the café.

She parked between an old beat-up Chevy and a Ford that had its back door wired shut. Some folks in the Valley drove their cars into the ground, those they used for hauling tractor parts and baling twine. Farm vehicles. Then they piled the family into last year's model, which was washed and waxed on Saturday afternoon for the drive to church on Sunday morning. The newer car would sit in the driveway all week, while the older vehicle was driven even further into the ground.

Cash ran the flat of her hand over the Chevy fender as she walked past it to get to the café. Rather than slide into a booth, she stepped to the cash register and waited for the waitress to finish pouring coffee for two old farmers, both wearing bib coveralls and cotton shirts with the sleeves rolled up to their elbows. Cash guessed they were the owners of the two farm vehicles out front.

"What can I do for you, Cash?" the waitress asked. She rang a bill of sale and put a two-dollar bill into the till.

Cash wondered how the waitress knew her name. She didn't remember being introduced to her. "Wheaton been in?"

"No. Saw his cruiser over by the bank earlier, but he headed west."

Cash, who had been staring out the window, turned her head and looked at the waitress. She was a pretty woman, with brown hair ratted up and flipped on the ends. She was wearing a white shirt, black skirt and pale pink lipstick. Cash thought, *She was probably a cheerleader back in high school.* She couldn't tell the woman's age, other than she was older than Cash and younger than Wheaton. Maybe this was the waitress Geno was talking about.

"If he stops in, should I tell him you were looking for him?"

"Nah. I'll just stop in Ada."

Cash turned and left. She drove by the Twin Valley bank again. She shook off the feeling that something just wasn't right. She usually trusted her instincts, but things had felt off since the whole shebang with the crazy pastor who wanted to kill her and bury her in the graveyard next to his church.

Cash shook off another round of shivers as she recalled how his wife Lillian chased her from the parsonage to the graveyard, while Cash ran with the baby they had kidnapped in her arms. Lillian was now housed at the state mental hospital, undergoing treatment so she could eventually stand trial. Cash shook her head again, cranked up the radio to a country singer who crooned about his whiskey drinking days, and focused on looking for Wheaton. She lit a cigarette and rolled down the window. She let the wind clear her mind as well as the smoke out of the Ranchero.

She drove past the jail in Ada. No cruiser. Parked at the corner stop sign in the soft shade of an elm tree. She drummed her fingers on the steering wheel. No Wheaton. No Arlis. No Nils. She shifted gears on the Ranchero as well as her own mind and drove to the hotel. *May as well check in on Shawnee.*

She answered Jack Sprat the desk clerk's question before he asked it. "Going up to see Miss Dackson." She threw the words over her shoulder as she walked by the front desk without breaking stride.

Up the well-worn but thickly carpeted stairs, she knocked on the oak door whose brass numbers read 204.

Miss Dackson answered the door without opening it fully or inviting Cash in. She wore her usual social worker uniform of dark skirt, button-down blouse, nylons and short white heels. Cash remembered a foster mother saying, "White shoes after Memorial Day." Cash briefly wondered if it was the same outfit Dackson had worn to drive Cash from foster home to foster home back in the day.

"Wondering if I could talk to Shawnee?"

Miss Dackson, without opening the door any farther, looked back over her shoulder. Turned back at Cash and said, "Um, she's been moved to a foster home."

Cash narrowed her brown eyes to slits. "Where?"

"I don't think I can divulge that information. She's a ward of the state until one of her parents shows back up." Cash could hear the disdain in the woman's voice, as if she were sure Shawnee's parents weren't going to come looking for her.

Cash bit her lower lip to avoid saying something stupid. She stared at the flowered wallpaper on the hotel walls long enough that Miss Dackson shifted her weight from one foot to the other and closed the door another eight inches.

"I need to talk to her. Wheaton asked me to handle this case while he's working on the bank robbery over in Twin Valley. I think you should just give me the name of the family you placed her with."

"You always were a pig-headed little one, weren't you? No wonder you kept getting moved around. Always too big for your britches." The door closed another inch.

Cash bit her lip harder and nervously touched the pocket where her pack of cigarettes was. "It doesn't make sense to waste time just so you can have Wheaton tell you the exact same thing. Where is she?"

"Borgerud's." Another two inches.

"Borgerud's." Cash couldn't keep the surprise out of her voice. "What the hell is she doing there?"

By now, Miss Dackson was speaking through a crack in the doorway. "Mrs. Borgerud is depressed after losing her husband. She said taking the child in was the least she could do and maybe they could cheer each other up."

Cash stared in disbelief. *Cheer each other up, my ass.* She turned on her heels and thumped down the hotel stairs. She heard Miss Dackson shut the door and quickly slide the chain on the lock.

"Stupid bitch!"

Jack Sprat got busy ruffling papers as Cash stormed by.

Cash fumbled her cigarettes out of her T-shirt pocket, lit up, threw the match on the ground and hopped into the Ranchero. Metal hit metal when she slammed the car door. Tires spewed dirt as she backed out of the parking spot. A mother yanked her child's arm to pull her out of the way as Cash floored the pickup and rounded the street corner, sending more dust and dirt up into the air as she ignored the speed limit on her way out of town.

Cash had hated the social worker since she herself was a child. Back then, Miss Dackson had control over her life and never listened to Cash, instead kowtowing to the well-to-do farmers who professed to be good Christians wanting to foster "poor Indian children." *Bullshit to all of them*, Cash fumed. She pounded the steering wheel, rolled down the window and screamed "Damn!" into the Valley air, over and over.

When the Borgerud farm was in sight, she lit another cigarette. Breathed smoke deep into her lungs. Willed herself to calm down. By the time she threw the Ranchero into park in the farmyard and stepped down from the pickup, she felt steely calm. The winter inside her bones contradicted the warm spring air, the small white butterflies floating over green grass and the short cherry tree in bloom.

She knocked on the screen door and heard Mrs. Borgerud's footsteps approach. With the sun dropping to the western horizon, light didn't reach into the front porch area. It made the woman a shadow on the other side of the door.

"Yes?"

"I need to talk to Shawnee."

"Um. I believe she's getting ready for bed."

"I need to speak to her."

"You can't keep disturbing me. She's resting and I still have things I need to get done for the funeral. She hasn't said a word since she got here. Silent injun I guess."

Cash clenched and unclenched her fists as they hung at her hips. Took a deep breath. "Wheaton asked me to find out where her parents are and how your husband got shot," Cash repeated. "I need to speak to Shawnee." She heard soft footsteps approach the door behind Mrs. Borgerud.

"Hey, girl." Jean turned and sharply addressed the child. "I told you to go lay down. Now get back . . ."

Before she could finish her sentence, Cash pulled the screen door open and pushed herself past the woman and into the house.

"Hey, Shawnee, I stopped by to talk to you. Come on outside, we can sit out at the picnic table." She put her arm across Shawnee's shoulders and led her past Mrs. Borgerud, whose body radiated rage.

A wooden picnic table sat under an apple tree with blossoms that would be bursting with fruit come fall. Cash sat Shawnee down on the side of the table still warmed by the sun hovering over the western horizon, which also meant they were facing the house where Mrs. Borgerud still stood in the doorway, watching them. Anger was clearly visible on her face, even through the screen of the door.

"How you doing?"

Shawnee looked up at her. Tears filled her dark-brown eyes without dropping, held in check by her long black lashes. Cash watched her small, skinny chest heave with each deep breath.

"It must be scary getting moved to a place with someone you don't know. It happened to me a bunch of times when I was your age. You gotta be tough. I'm looking for your mom and dad."

A tear fell down the girl's left cheek.

"As soon as I find them, you'll get to go home. I promise you. If it's the last thing I do, okay?"

Another tear fell.

"I drove over to White Earth today. You ever been there?"

A small nod.

Cash put that information into her brain. The girl knew where White Earth was.

Cash stared at the farmhouse. Jean had left the doorway, or at least backed out of sight. Cash figured she was standing off to the side, trying to hear what she and Shawnee might be talking about. Even though Cash was naturally soft-spoken, she lowered her voice even more. "Told my friend Jonesy I was looking for your mom. She didn't think I'd find your mom today. Jonesy just seems to know things. So, I came back here, see if you remember anything you want to tell me."

The girl looked up at Cash. The water safely held back in her eyes again. She swung her legs back and forth under the wooden bench.

"Could I bribe you to talk? Promise to bring you an ice cream cone?"

The tiniest of smiles reached Shawnee's lips, but she shook her head no.

"If you know something that can help me find your mom, your dad, then I could help get you out of here."

The girl hung her head and swung her legs faster. Picked at a hangnail on her thumb until a dot of red blood appeared, which she promptly licked off. She looked up at Cash with dull eyes. The tears had been displaced by despair or hopelessness; Cash couldn't tell which.

"It's okay. I'll figure it out. Meanwhile, you're gonna have to stay here. All I can tell you from my own experience is don't let it get to you. The one thing I do know is that your mom is coming back for you. Just might take a while. Meanwhile, eat the old lady's veggies and try not to pee the bed."

Again, the tiniest smile appeared at the right corner of Shawnee's lips.

"I gotta go. But I'll be back to check on you. If she does anything to hurt you, all you gotta do is tell me and I'll handle it." Cash stood up and reached her hand out to Shawnee.

Shawnee put her small hand in Cash's and let herself be led back to the farmhouse. Her steps dragged the closer they got but Cash kept walking them forward. At the door, Mrs. Borgerud stepped forward, a grimace of dislike on her face, and held the door open for Shawnee to enter.

"Get in there and lay down. Bedtime."

Cash let go of Shawnee's hand and gave her a soft push forward between her shoulder blades. "I'll be back." Shawnee entered the house without looking back.

"You don't need to be checking up on us. Hanging around here. If she says anything I'll call Wheaton and let him know." Mrs. Borgerud pulled the screen door shut with one hand, using the other to block the doorframe as if to prevent Cash from storming the house.

"Wheaton is working on the Twin Valley bank robbery." *Wherever the hell he is.* "I'll be back tomorrow to check on her." Cash turned sharply and went back to the Ranchero.

Mrs. Borgerud stood at the doorway until Cash pulled out of the driveway.

Cash drove into Ada and swung by the jail. Still no cruiser. *Where the hell are you Wheaton?*

Frustrated, Cash decided to call it a day and head back into Fargo. She drove south on Highway 75. On the out-skirts of Moorhead, she swung by Al's house, her sometimes main squeeze. Cash was still trying to figure him out. He was a Vietnam vet who owned his own little place with an attached garage where he ran a small business working on cars and the occasional farm tractor. He was a settled kind of guy which made Cash, who considered herself seriously unsettled, nervous. Mostly, she tried to avoid him but he had a way of showing up and coaxing her into going out to eat or joining him to shoot a game of pool against Shyla and her boyfriend Terry. Maybe she wasn't trying to figure him out so much as she was trying to figure herself out.

Al's pickup was parked in his driveway. Cash kept driving, through downtown Moorhead, across the bridge and into Fargo straight to the Casbah. It was earlier for her than usual but what the heck. She had run into nothing but dead ends all day and damn, still no sign of Wheaton. She needed a drink and the sound of pool balls dropping into the pocket. She pulled into an empty parking spot outside the bar, grabbed her fringed-leather cue stick case out from behind her car seat, slung it over her shoulder and walked through the swinging screen door.

Ole Johnson and his brother Carl were already sitting at the twelve-foot-long mahogany bar. Ol' Man Willie was drinking himself back to his childhood in his corner booth. The lights were dim. The mood said night, even though the sun outside wouldn't set for another hour and a half.

When Shorty Nelson, the bartender, who was as much a fixture in the bar as the flashing Hamm's Beer Bear sign and the sawdust on the floor, looked over and saw Cash enter. He held up a longneck, to which she nodded yes. He popped the top and slid it across the bar. She slid two dollar bills toward him and said, "Dollar in quarters."

Change in one hand and beer in the other, she put a quarter on the pool table, leaned against the wall and finished her beer while she waited her turn to play.

Jim, an old flame, was across the bar. He lifted his cue stick in her direction. An indication he wanted to play partners with her, but she did her best to ignore him. Jim had been her pool partner and frequent bed partner until one day she saw him in a local restaurant—with his wife and little daughters. She had always known he was married but the *idea* of him being a married man didn't sink in until that sight. "Not playing that game anymore," is what she said to him as he sidled up close to her.

"C'mon, Cash, I need me some Cash," he wheedled, groping her around her waist as he planted a sloppy kiss on her neck.

She pushed him off. "Go home to your wife, Jim." She ran the table to sink the eight ball just as Shorty called out, "Last call," to which she raised two fingers signaling she wanted two more longnecks.

Shorty shook his head no as he set one longneck on the bar. Cash leaned on her cue stick and stared at him. He shook his head again.

"Your shot, Cash. Stripes," said the guy who had just put quarters into the table. Cash took her shot, sunk the twelve and fourteen before missing on the eleven. She killed the beer she had and walked up to the bar to get the one sitting there.

Emboldened from winning and drinking all night, she said, "You're not my dad, Shorty," as she took the beer and nodded toward the pool table. "He'll pay as soon as he loses."

"You gotta cut back, Cash. You don't want to end up like Ol' Man Willie there."

"Thought a bartender's job was to sell beer and mine was to drink it." She drank half the bottle in a series of big gulps before heading back to the pool table to finish off the game.

After sinking the eight ball, she pointed toward the bar and said to the farmer who lost, "You can pay for my beer up there."

She broke down her cue stick, put it in its case and left for home.

The ringing phone woke her up. She stumbled out of bed and unplugged the cord in the kitchen to shut out the noise. She threw water on her face, brushed the fuzz off her teeth, got dressed, and downed an aspirin with half a cup of coffee before she plugged the phone back into the wall jack on her way out the door. Outside, she sat in her Ranchero; the newly risen sun had warmed the inside of the cab. Cash felt late for something. She smoked her cigarette and blew the smoke out the window as she sorted facts in her brain, figuring out what day it was and whether she was supposed to be plowing a field or putting in seed corn for Borgerud?

Cash thought back to Shorty not serving her two beers at closing. She had trouble sleeping ever since she accidently killed the pastor over by Twin Valley. When she threw the knife at him, she had hoped to just stop him, give herself a way out, not watch him bleed to death there on the kitchen floor. She used to drink to just drink, have fun, hang out; now she knew she was drinking to keep the nightmares at bay. To blur the edges of the world around her. She also knew she had no desire to quit. She turned the key in the ignition.

Cash had planned to work for Mr. Borgerud all season but since he was killed, and his wife and she had a sincere, mutual dislike for each other, Cash decided she had best find another farmer to work for. Something to get her through until wheat harvest when farmers were always looking for grain truck drivers. Same with beet hauling season.

But first, she decided to check in with Wheaton. She was done being mad at him for not inviting her along to catch the bank robbers. Well, mostly done being mad. She figured whatever he was busy doing yesterday, he should be done with by now and back at his desk or in his patrol car. She wanted to talk to him, to see if there was anything they could do to get Shawnee a better place to stay. See if he had learned anything more about Borgerud's murder. See how the bank robbery got handled.

When she parked in front of the jail, she sat for a moment, her hand on the gear shift, and looked around for Wheaton's cruiser. Nowhere in sight. She climbed out of the Ranchero and looked up and down the empty street. No tan cruiser with lights on top. She ran up the granite steps that led to the jail.

Wheaton's secretary stood up rapidly as Cash entered. She wore her Midwest ladies uniform, a shirt-style dress with a narrow belt around her chunky waist. Long strands of dark-brown hair escaped her French twist, which was usually neatly pinned on the back of her head. She brushed back the loose strands nervously with one hand. "I've been calling you all morning! Where's Wheaton? I haven't seen him since yesterday when he went to Twin Valley on that bank robbery business. Now he didn't come in this morning." The tone of her voice scolded Cash. "Why don't you ever answer your phone? I know Wheaton has some secret way to reach you. I see him call. Hang up. Call." She put both hands on her hips, elbows akimbo. Her voice trembled, on the verge of tears. "He's never late. He never disappears."

"What?" Cash turned on her heels. "I'll run by his house."

"I already did. He's not there."

The secretary sat down with a thud. Cash turned back around. Brown eyes filled with dread locked with brown eyes filled with dread.

"I called the FBI in Minneapolis. They handle bank

robberies. Federal crime you know. They haven't heard from him either. Said they'd send some folks up this way later today." She looked away from Cash, at the phone on the desk, moved some papers around. "I'm worried."

"I'll drive over to Twin Valley. Try and retrace his steps." Cash started to walk away until the secretary's next words stopped her.

"And Borgerud's wife called. Told us to stay away from her and that little girl."

"Huh. Like that's gonna happen."

Cash ran out to her Ranchero. She drove east out of Ada, right into the morning sun. She pulled the visor down over the windshield and scanned the fields in either direction as she drove. Maybe Wheaton had run off the road, rolled over in a ditch; disaster scenarios ran through her mind as she chain-smoked. Farmers were out in the fields. Clouds of dust followed them in the wake of plows dug into the earth pulled by John Deere or Massey Ferguson tractors. One farmer navigated an old, nondescript tractor that pulled a manure spreader, filling the air with the smell of cow dung. Cash rolled up her window for a mile or two. With this many farmers out in their fields, if Wheaton had run off the road, surely one of them would have seen him.

The Twin Valley bank clerks—one who looked like he just graduated high school with his black suit jacket riding high over boney wrists, and a woman showing the first signs of wrinkles at the corners of her eyes and love handles on her hips—informed Cash that two men and a woman had robbed the bank and headed southwest out of town in an old Rambler, light blue in color.

"Same thing we told the sheriff when he came barreling in here yesterday," the female clerk said. "Barely got the information out to him and he was off after them. You saying you haven't seen him?"

"Never made it back to Ada."

"It was two young men, didn't look like hoodlums at all. Dressed like 'going to town'. Tall, skinny guy and a shorter one. Both wore handkerchiefs over their mouths. After we handed over the money they ran out and jumped in the car. Driven by a young woman. All I could tell was she was wearing a yellow dress, yellow blouse maybe."

The recently-graduated-from-high-school clerk chimed in. "We just handed over the money and watched them drive away." He pointed in the general direction of Fargo–Moorhead. "Then we called the sheriff."

"You say they headed southwest?"

Both clerks nodded.

"If Wheaton shows up back here can you call the jail in Ada, or tell him to call? Secretary's worried."

Both clerks nodded. Cash went out to her Ranchero. The streets of Twin Valley were nearly empty. Three cars outside the café. One lone car outside the beer joint. Cash brushed some loose strands of hair off her face. Lit a cigarette one-handed, bending the match and striking it in a move learned a couple years ago from a vet home on leave. She blew cigarette smoke into the air and drove west out of town.

About two miles out, she pulled over on the shoulder of the road and surveyed the vast prairie that lay before her. Not a hill in sight.

Cash looked again at fields spread out on either side of the road. They were either plowed and ready for planting or already planted. Somewhere within each square mile sat a house. Early farmers had quickly learned that thirty-below winter winds blew straight across the flat land. They built their sod homes or log cabins in the middle of a stand of trees that would function as a wind barrier. Now, many decades later, the structures had become two-story wooden homes for rapidly multiplying families, or newer ranch-style homes that sat snug to the ground.

As the first settlers gained wealth, they bought up the land of poorer farmers, or the land of those who left to the never-ending skies of Montana or the shipyards of Seattle. Other farmers moved to Anchorage through a government program, eager to settle the new state of Alaska. They abandoned their homes, whose timbers rotted with the seasons and sat, crookedly, at the end of quarter-mile-long driveways, overgrown with ditch grass, waiting for the next strong winter or summer windstorm to bring them down. Cash saw all this as she scanned the flat land, eyes sliding from north to south and back again, her gaze about a foot off the ground. Looking for any sign of Wheaton.

She saw black field dust to the northwest, someone harrowing a tract of land; a few miles to her right, a John Deere tractor pulled a plow down a gravel road, throwing up a gray cloud. Red-winged blackbirds flew from stiff weed shaft to stiff weed shaft ahead of her. On her left, in the direction of Fargo–Moorhead, were at least five miles of flat fields broken by small clumps of trees, signifying those abandoned homesteads.

Cash squinted, shutting out the telephone wires running between tall wooden poles spaced about every three hundred feet. She willed herself to see the land before the settlers, before the farms, before the pine-tree-circled prairie churches and graveyards. In her mind's eye tall grass moved in gentle waves to the tree line of the Red River on the western horizon; to the south and the Wild Rice River tree line cutting across the land, meandering to the Red.

Cash sensed more than felt a brush of air across her neck and shoulders as she looked southwest. Again, she scanned the horizon but didn't see anything out of the ordinary. But she had learned to trust the subtle messages often given to her. She got back into the Ranchero, drove to the mile corner and turned left to continue her zigzag journey on the back country roads.

She drove slowly, watching the landscape. Cash figured that if she had robbed the Twin Valley bank she would head straight west to the North Dakota border, or even north toward the Canadian border, a quick drive of less than two hours. However, the tingle of air on her neck got stronger the more she drove southwest. If she kept going, a zigzag beeline would eventually take her into Fargo–Moorhead.

While she watched the fields, ditches and farmyards for

any sign of Wheaton's cruiser, she thought about Shawnee. Wondered how she was coping with Mrs. Borgerud. Cash shook her head and lit a cigarette, blew the smoke out the window. She still couldn't believe Miss Dackson had let the woman take the child. And where were the girl's parents? Cash figured Arlis was hiding out somewhere over at White Earth, but where was the dad? He couldn't have just disappeared, although it had been known to happen. Cash flashed on Jonesy's offhand shrug. Folks were rumored to have run off with the carnies every time a county fair happened. Or you heard the gossip of "so-and-so went up to Alaska to work the pipeline." Or "he got drafted." And then you would never hear of them again.

Cash was lost in cigarette smoke and deep thoughts when out of the corner of her eye she caught a low-to-the-ground form running across a plowed field. It was headed her way. She slowed even more. Gunner. She braked to a stop in the middle of the road and jumped out.

The dog ran directly to her, circled the Ranchero, then circled Cash. His tongue dangled from his mouth with every labored breath. Cash dropped to her knee. "Where you been Gunner? Where's Wheaton?" At the mention of Wheaton's name, the dog ran circles around the Ranchero once again.

"Hey. Hey. Slow down." Cash grabbed the dog as it tried to run by her. "Sit." She commanded. The dog at least stood still, though it didn't obey the command. Cash reached into the truck and pulled out her thermos that held day-old coffee. Filled the cap full and placed it on the ground. The dog lapped it up, then took off around the truck again.

Cash surveyed the land in the direction the dog had run from. About three miles over were two clumps of trees. Judging from what she knew about farmland, they were probably eighty acres apart. One stand of trees was larger than the other, which meant it was most likely a farmstead where a family lived. The smaller stand of trees would be the old homestead with a falling-down house, maybe an old barn, certainly an old-style slat corncrib.

"You gonna ride or run?" Cash looked at Gunner. He jumped into the Ranchero and sat on his haunches.

Cash headed for the tree stands. Gunner stared straight forward out the window. When she passed the yard with the newer farmhouse, she noticed the neatly tended grass lawn and a vegetable garden with the season's first Bibb lettuce peeking out of the ground; rhubarb that had already gone to seed; and an asparagus patch with spindly ferns heralding the end of that vegetable's season.

As Cash neared the smaller grove of trees, Gunner stood up on the seat. Cash slowed to watch for the driveway in. There it was. Overgrown with ditch grass like she expected but flattened in two strips, which indicated someone had recently driven in or out. Gunner pressed his nose to the glass in front of him. Dog snot smeared her windshield.

Cash spotted the rear end of Wheaton's cruiser before she even turned into the old farmstead. She had been right about the tree stand being an old homestead. The cruiser was angled headfirst into a stand of lilac bushes next to a graying house with shattered windows and a door hanging on by the bottom hinge. Her heart sank. She searched the lilac bush, the surrounding brush and the windows with shards of glass, hoping to see Wheaton walk out the broken doorway. Nothing moved. Only Gunner's labored panting broke the heavy air. Her hands on the steering wheel started to sweat and shake. As soon as she braked and opened the car door, Gunner jumped over her and out the truck. He sat by the rear bumper of the cruiser, staring at her.

"Wheaton," she called out.

"Aramhuph!" emanated from the trunk.

Cash ran to the front door of the car, opened it, and flipped the latch to pop the trunk open.

Gunner jumped up with front paws on the back fender. Cash stared at Wheaton who blinked furiously as the bright sun hit his eyes. A dirty blue handkerchief covered his mouth. Cash untied it and grabbed him by the elbow, pulled until she got him to a sitting position. His legs dangled over the back fender.

Wheaton continued to blink and gasp for air. His wrinkled shirt and pants stank of sweat. His hands were handcuffed behind his back. Cash ran back to the Ranchero and returned with the stale thermos of coffee. She held it up for Wheaton to drink. After big gulps, he rasped, "I think they threw the keys over in that direction." He pointed his head toward the trees.

Cash broke a long branch off the lilac bush and used it to sweep the grass and weeds as she walked back and forth between the car and the tree line. It seemed to take forever before she caught a glint of sun on metal. Car keys, jail keys and handcuff key all on one big ring.

As soon as Wheaton was free, he said, "I'm gonna step around the house and see a man about a horse."

Cash sat heavily on the fender of the open trunk. Her hands had stopped shaking. Her heart rate had slowed. A red rage built in her solar plexus. Wheaton came around the corner of the house, right hand flattening the fly over his zipper. Cash jerked up, hands on hips. "What the hell happened?"

Wheaton stopped up short. "What do you mean?"

"How'd you end up in the fucking trunk?"

"I . . ."

"You what? Blinked?" Cash's voice raised another notch.

"Cash . . ."

"Don't *Cash* me. What the fuck happened here? You're the goddamn sheriff." She kicked the tire of the cruiser. Slammed the trunk shut. Threw the keys at Wheaton.

"I thought the girl was a hostage. A clerk from the bank."

"What?!"

"She looked normal. Wore a Sunday, go-to-church yellow dress. White shoes."

"She was the getaway driver!" Cash screamed.

She yanked open the driver's door of the Ranchero and was climbing in when Wheaton said, "Hang on a minute, would you?" He waved a big hand toward the cruiser. "I think they siphoned my gas."

"Jesus Christ."

Cash stormed back toward the house. Walked around in the knee-high grass. Saw an old shed on the opposite side, pulled the lopsided wooden door open, almost ripping it off in her rage, and found an ancient, stiff garden hose and an old hand saw. She cut a three-foot length of hose and threw it to Wheaton, who had followed her. He grabbed a rusty gas can sitting on the dirt floor and they both walked silently back to the two vehicles. Cash took off the Ranchero's gas cap and ignored Wheaton as he sucked gas into his mouth, spit it on the ground, and then successfully siphoned some gas into the can.

"Follow me into town?" Wheaton said.

Cash chain-smoked her way into the town of Ada, following Wheaton, riding almost bumper to bumper on his taillights. In the solitude of the Ranchero, she yelled a stream of swear words at the man in the cruiser ahead of her.

When he pulled into the Standard gas station on the edge of Ada, she slowed and hollered out the car window, "I'll fucking kill you myself if you ever fucking die on me." Then she gunned the motor and spun out of town.

She didn't remember crawling into bed after leaving the Casbah that night. When she rolled over in the middle of the night and hit a body next to her, she sat up and found herself staring at Married Jim.

"Get the fuck out."

She pushed him off the mattress before flopping back into a dead sleep.

Cash sat on the oak bench in the county jail. She avoided eye contact with Wheaton and spoke to him through his secretary. "Does he know why and how Shawnee was placed with that old bag, Mrs. Borgerud?"

Wheaton looked directly at her and answered. "It's a county social service issue. I didn't have any say over it. Mrs. Borgerud asked to care for the child, from what I understand. Said she was trying to do the Christian thing and all since it happened on their farm."

"Christian thing my ass. She probably just wants someone to weed her garden for free. Or wash her undies," she said, still not looking at Wheaton. "Did he ever tell you how he ended up in the trunk?"

The secretary raised her eyebrows and looked sideways at Wheaton before she turned and started filing papers in the metal cabinet behind them.

Wheaton set his coffee cup down on the desk in front of him. "I told you; I saw them pulled over by that old farmstead. Told the boys to get outta the car. A girl was sitting in the driver's seat. She looked scared. Dressed all nice. Thought she was the bank teller. Held hostage. As soon as the boys stepped out and I had my back to her, she stepped out of the car and put the gun to my ribs."

"And Gunner sat there like a dumbass?" The dog, who

was lying on the floor next to the desk, lifted his head. Cash glared at him until he put his head back on his paws.

"I told him to stay in the car."

"That was real smart." Cash directed her words at the top of the filing cabinet on the opposite side of the room.

"Next thing I knew I was handcuffed and in the trunk of the cruiser. I could hear them talking. First, they talked about taking the cruiser, but Gunner wouldn't let them get in and then he jumped out before one of them could shut the car door. I could hear him snarl every time they came near the trunk. Finally, they decided it was too obvious to drive around in a cop car. That's when they siphoned the gas and took off. Pretty sure they were headed toward Fargo. One of them mentioned Williston over in North Dakota. Told the FBI they might be headed there."

He tried to catch Cash's eyes as he spoke but she stared at the wall over his left shoulder. Spoke to his secretary again. "I didn't find Arlis. Mrs. Borgerud tried to stop me from talking to Shawnee. At least she didn't throw me in the trunk of her car." She paused and looked directly at Wheaton until he looked away. "How in the hell did a woman whose husband was just killed get a child placed with her anyways?"

"I told you; not my jurisdiction. Social Services deals with placement, not me. She's in grief. Maybe Miss Dackson thought they would cheer each other up. Nothing criminal about that."

"Wanna bet?"

"Cash." Wheaton sighed. Pushed away from his desk.

"I'm gonna go try talk to Shawnee again. I'll tell Mrs. Oh-My-Poor-Husband's-Dead-and-I-Inherited-a-Few-Thousand-Acres to give you a call if she tries to stop me."

"The funeral's today. They'll be at the church over in Halstad." Wheaton tried again to catch her eye. "When you went over to White Earth, did anyone say anything about Nils? Where he is?"

"Jonesy said I should try find him."

"She say why or where Nils might be?"

"Nah." Cash lit a cigarette. Smoked. Dropped the ash on her pants leg. Brushed it into the fabric. "I got the feeling she thought he needs to be found." Cash gave a short laugh. "Or maybe she was talking about you." After a quick glance at Wheaton, who looked embarrassed, she continued, "She did say Arlis isn't ready to be found." She stood up. "Guess I'll swing by the church."

"You don't need to do that. I'll drop by and offer my condolences from the department."

"You get all the fun." Cash smushed her cigarette butt in the ashtray on his desk and left the jail.

She drove aimlessly through the side streets of Ada. The sky was bright blue. A soft breeze tussled the blond hair of babies and toddlers who sat on quilts while their moms planted lettuce and tomatoes in postage stamp–size gardens, unable to leave their farm heritage completely behind. It all looked so damn peaceful. Cash was too aware of how mothers slapped babies' hands with wooden spatulas, pulled and twisted ears of a child that wouldn't listen. How children of all ages could get locked in bedrooms for days for acting too big for their britches. She shuddered to think of Shawnee in the Borgerud home. She swung out of town and headed in the direction of the farm. May as well check it out while everyone was at the funeral.

The Borgerud farmyard was empty of cars. Tire tracks indicated vehicles had gone in and out of the gravel driveway. Cash pulled the Ranchero behind the barn, out of sight of anyone driving by. She walked the short distance to the house, hollered "Hello" through the screen door. No one answered, so she walked in. Plates of what everyone referred to as funeral sandwiches sat on the dining room table covered with plastic wrap: lunch meat sandwiches on white bread, cut on the diagonal, lettuce going limp. A couple plates of homemade cookies, also covered in plastic wrap, sat next to pickle dishes filled with cinnamon sweet wedding ring pickles, dyed bright green, and bread and butter cauliflower and carrot pickles. Cash opened the fridge. Plates of deviled eggs, large pitchers of lemonade and iced tea, and a big bowl of potato salad next to three smaller bowls of Jell-O salad. She opened the oven. Sure enough, there sat a pink baked ham stuck with cloves; circles of yellow pineapple adorned the top. Decorative. The Protestant Mourners Feast.

Cash left the dining area and walked down a hallway. Past a guest bedroom with suitcases on a chair next to the bureau. Next, another guest room. A dress was thrown on the bed. Someone had changed their mind about what to wear last minute. A bathroom. Another bedroom. Ah, a pair of small scruffy tennis shoes sat under the bed. The paper bag that Cash had left in the hotel with spare clothes for Shawnee was on the floor at the end of the twin bed. From where she stood, Cash could see it still contained Shawnee's clothes. The oak dresser that matched the twin bed in the room boasted a ballerina and an angel knickknack on a white doily.

Cash walked into the room and opened the closet. Men's going-to-church clothes. A pair of shoes like Bud Borgerud had on when he died. She opened the dresser drawers. Men's underwear and work clothes. What the hell? She looked carefully around the room. On the bedside table was a coloring book with a box of eight primary color crayons. She flipped through the coloring book. Out fell a plain white envelope. Shawnee had drawn a house in a grove of trees. Outside the house—it didn't take a genius to figure out the picture—stood a dad, a little girl and a mom. The mom was the tallest figure with a smile. The dad looked happy also. The sun was scribbled over with black crayon as was the little girl's mouth. *Damn*, thought Cash. She put everything back neatly on the bedside table.

She went to the last bedroom at the end of the hall. It was a woman's room. Clearly Mrs. Borgerud's. High heels neatly lined up against a short wall next to the closet, which was filled with housedresses, church dresses, and some fancier shiny dresses that one would probably wear to a dance at the VFW in town. A long bureau with a mirror held makeup, a hairbrush, Avon perfume bottles. The drawers held women's undergarments, miscellaneous papers, clothing meant for yardwork, shorts, cotton pullover blouses, and finally, pajamas in the bottom drawer. But other than a wedding picture on top of a taller bureau on the opposite wall, nothing else in the room indicated it was shared. *Huh, so Mr. and Mrs. Borgerud slept in separate rooms. Or at least got dressed in separate rooms.*

Cash sat on the edge of the bed. Picked at the tufts of the chenille bedspread. Willed her mind to pick up any sense of the woman who slept here. Nothing. Cash, frustrated with herself, stood up and left the room.

Back to the room Shawnee slept in. She sat on the twin bed with the pink ruffled bedspread that matched the pink curtains. Both the bedspread and the curtains had creases, the kind that remain after folded materials are removed from their package. Cash assumed they were put up for Shawnee. After Mr. Borgerud was killed? It seemed like all his clothes were in this room, but it was decorated for a girl child. Again, Cash willed herself to pick up any feelings that might be floating in the air of the room. Sadness overwhelmed her chest. Constricted her throat. She tried to determine if she was connecting with Shawnee or the dead man. No idea. She shook her head again and left the room.

A quick walk through the house revealed nothing but a typical farmhouse. A Sony television in the living room. All the furniture freshly dusted and polished. Cash hoped none of the work had been foisted off on Shawnee. Couch, recliner chair. Church folding chairs, metal, set around the walls for visitors after the funeral. Worn work boots by the back door. Work jackets hung on nails pounded into a board. Just for the hell of it, Cash let the screen door slam behind her as she exited.

As she walked across the yard to where her pickup was stashed, she saw a line of cars a good two miles away, a trail of Fords and Chevys kicking up road dust. Cash quickened her pace and reached the back side of the barn before any of the cars entered the driveway. Damn, she must have spent longer in the house than she realized. Rather than get into the Ranchero and risk being seen as she drove away, she sat on the back bumper and contemplated her next move. Parked, the vehicle was out of sight from the house. She doubted funeral goers were going to tour the farmyard. She reached in the car window and grabbed her thermos. Glad she had filled it up from the coffee pot at the jail. It wasn't hot anymore, but it quenched her thirst.

She sat in the grass with her back to the wall on the corner where she could peek around and see the cars pull into the yard. Cars parked diagonally, nose in toward the house. Those at the tail end of the procession parked on the county road. Cash swatted at mosquitos and summer flies. The visitors' voices carried across the farmyard, indecipherable from the distance. Cash chewed on a blade of grass. Watched wisps of white cloud pass overhead. Listened to the birds call each other through the trees of the windbreak. Heard a small animal scurry through the grass. She peeked around the corner occasionally. Men, suit jackets and ties off, stood in the yard smoking. Younger kids, but not Shawnee, ran around the house in a game of tag.

Cash sat and waited for an opportune time to leave. With

her back against the barn, the sun warmed her till she was lost in a daydream, thinking back to when her brother had showed up at her door late one night, home on leave from Vietnam. She hadn't seen him since she was three, when her mom had rolled the car in the ditch and Wheaton had taken Cash and her mom to the jail, and her brother and sister were taken to the hospital. Her whole family had disappeared overnight. And then one night sixteen years later, a sharp knock woke her from her sleep. The veteran standing outside her door had asked around and someone had pointed him in the direction of Cash's apartment in Fargo. He camped out on her kitchen floor, played solitaire and smoked dope nonstop. Then he helped her rescue some girls that were being sold into "white slavery" down in the Cities. Then he had re-upped. Said he couldn't take it in the "real world." She missed him. Every so often a letter with government-issue red, white and blue edges would arrive in the mail. His favorite closing line was *Only the good die young.* Cash, not aware of what her hands were doing, rolled blades of grass into even thinner strands and absent-mindedly tied them in knots.

Laughter coming from the tree line directly to her left snapped her out of her reverie. A young man was walking toward her. It took her a second to recognize him as the guy from the Drive-Inn, the one who had talked about *Peyton Place.* He was dressed in black suit pants and a white shirt, tie askew. He had his arm around the waist of an innocent-looking teen. The girl looked up at him in adoration, giggling, her hair neatly ratted up and back combed into a hair-sprayed flip. She was in a pale-blue summer dress, a thin belt at her waist.

Both stopped abruptly when they saw her sitting in the grass. The girl's hand flew to her mouth and she blushed. The guy stared at Cash, then smirked and nodded in recognition. "Drive-Inn." With a swagger, added, "See no evil. Hear no evil. Speak no evil." Cash nodded. He grinned as he pulled the girl in closer to his hip and kept walking.

The two separated as they rounded the corner of the barn into the sight line of anyone looking that direction from the house. Cash didn't need to guess what they were doing in the woods while the adults were mourning and eating sandwiches and Jell-O in the house. She was also pretty confident neither one of them was going to say anything about her.

"Damn." She stood up. Stood in sight of the house. Scanned the yard, house, driveway. Filled with cars. The county road still lined with vehicles. No one seemed to notice her. So, she got into her Ranchero and drove out from behind the barn, moving slowly behind the cars parked by the house, past the kids playing, the men smoking and talking, and the teenagers in a gaggle around the picnic table in the yard. Knut, a man who she occasionally drove grain truck for, saw her, gave a farmer's wave, like seeing her there was not out of the ordinary in the least.

It wasn't until Cash had passed the cars lined up on the county road that she stepped on the gas and got the hell out of there. She imagined Jean Borgerud's look of disdain if she had caught Cash in her house. The woman had made it clear she didn't like Indians. It made Cash all the more worried about Shawnee.

It was getting on to the middle of the afternoon. Without much thought about it, she drove to the Borgerud farmstead, where the farmer had died.

In just a few short days, the place had become desolate. Maybe it just felt that way because she knew what had occurred there. A kitchen window, without a screen, was open, and the café curtains moved slowly with the spring breeze. There wasn't even a lock on the door. She walked right in.

The kitchen table held a stack of empty beer cans. Local kids had already found a new drinking spot. Murder didn't seem to deter them. Or maybe that was part of the attraction. A way to scare the girls into farm-muscled arms.

Cash walked up wooden stairs that creaked with each step. Eye level with the landing, she scanned the floor before going farther. No one visible, thank god. Rumpled sheets and bedspreads thrown to the floor in the bedroom where she had found Shawnee indicated beer-drinking couples had made their way upstairs. She put the bedding back together. The other bedroom was equally used, but this one had Hamm's Beer cans on the nightstand. She tidied that room up also. Carried the empties back downstairs. Rummaged through the kitchen and found the garbage can under the sink. She emptied ashtrays and put the beer cans in the trash.

She looked at the linoleum floor. No sign that a man had died right there. A fat black fly walked across the door of the bottom kitchen cabinet. Its wings glistened iridescent in the soft sunlight that filtered in through the windows. As she watched the fly move across the wood, Cash spotted blood splatter on the bottom of the kitchen cabinet. She found an old dishrag, got it wet and washed and rewashed the cabinet until the water from the rag, when rinsed out, didn't run pink. She closed the kitchen window and left the house.

Walked the perimeter. Walked out to the barn, pulled open a wood-slat door that creaked more than the house stairs, peered into the dark, dank space. The air inside the barn was cooler than outside. Dirt floor. Straw thrown around. Smelled of cow shit and old mice. It was clear that it had ceased being a working barn years ago and now held rusting farm equipment that might raise a fair penny at an antique auction if kids didn't steal it first.

Cash pushed the door shut and, with her back to the barn, surveyed the house, the Ranchero sitting in the driveway, a stand of chokecherry trees and the old corncrib. Blue sky, white wisps of cloud. Silence that can only be heard in farm country. She recalled Gunner circling the crib the day she'd found Bud dead on the floor. A faint buzz caught her attention and she focused her gaze in that direction. The slightest of breezes brought the smell of decay. Cash widened her nostrils and sniffed the air. Bile rose in her throat. She quickly plugged her nose. Whatever animal had crawled into or under the corncrib was dead now.

Cash walked through the tall grass between the barn and corncrib. A raccoon maybe, a feral cat that didn't make it. The stench intensified the closer she got and fueled her curiosity. By the time she was within four feet of the structure she had pinched her nose shut harder and was breathing deeply through her mouth. The buzzing was louder. Thousands of black flies swarmed around the base of the corncrib.

Has to be a raccoon or cat. She watched the flies move along what was left of a creature. She walked back to the closest chokecherry tree, broke a four-foot-long branch off with newly formed leaves. She pinched her nose again and walked back to the mass of flies. Gently brushed them away. Maggots crawled along a human arm.

Cash dropped the branch and ran back to the chokecherry stand. She breathed fresh air. Gave herself a pep talk. "Go on. Get back there. Whoever it is, it's dead. Get back there." Plugged her nose, returned gingerly, picked up the dropped branch and shooed flies off the arm. *What the hell.*

As she peered at the arm, she could see that the rest of the body was stuffed under the corncrib. Maybe a raccoon had pulled the arm out. Damn, maybe Gunner had pulled the arm out before she called him to the car to meet Shawnee. Cash gagged as she got a visual image of the arm in Gunner's mouth. She backed away again. At the chokecherry stand she turned, fought down the urge to throw up while leaning against a narrow tree trunk, then ran to the house.

She forgot she was mad at Wheaton for almost getting himself killed. The telephone in the house was still connected. She hoped he was back from the funeral as she dialed the jail. "Hey, is Wheaton back yet?" she said, when his secretary answered on the second ring.

The secretary must have handed the phone right to him, because his voice followed. "Yes?"

"There's another body out here at Borgerud's. Dead."

"Who?"

"I don't know. Been dead a while. An arm with maggots. I can't tell if it's male or female. Arlis or Nils? Or some other poor soul."

"Stay there. I'll be right out." He hung up the phone.

Cash stared at the handset. She was usually the one who hung up on him. She sat on the overstuffed, worn couch. Ran her hand over the nubby fabric. And stared into space.

Years ago, in one foster home or another, she had learned to leave her body. Fly over treetops, across wheat fields. She loved the feeling of freedom that came with soaring through the air. Gliding over the land. The travels allowed her to escape the everyday struggle of one more sarcastic put-down, one more beating. One more violation of her body.

As she waited for Wheaton, she willed herself to head west, soar above the trees that lined the Red River. Swoop down until she skimmed the murky water. A voice called her back to the farmhouse. In the kitchen doorway stood a man, a cigarette hanging from the corner of his mouth, thin tendril of smoke circling his head in the still air. He had black hair, combed back, one strand hanging down his forehead, Elvis-style. He gave her a lopsided grin and said, "Only the good die young." And evaporated into thin air.

Cash jerked back into her body. She closed her eyes and slowly opened them. Looked at the doorway. No one was there. Only the smell of cigarette smoke lingered and she wasn't smoking. The man wasn't her brother, even if it was a phrase he often wrote. When she reached in her pocket to get a cigarette her hands were shaking. Just as she lit up, she heard a car pull into the driveway, tires on gravel.

"Cash. Where are you?" Wheaton hollered.

She moved to the front door. "Here," she hollered back. "You gotta come see this."

Wheaton followed her in the direction of the corncrib with Gunner at his heels. Cash hung back by the choke-cherry trees and pointed in the general direction of where the body was.

Wheaton plugged his nose the closer he got. "Goddamn." Even Gunner sat and didn't venture nearer.

Wheaton came back shaking his head. "What were you doing out here?"

"Nothing. I was at Borgerud's after the funeral and drove over here. Just to see if I missed anything the last time I was here."

"Can't tell who it is."

"Nope. I went and looked in the barn, caught a whiff of something. Remembered Gunner running around the corncrib the day we found Borgerud. Walked over and saw that mess." She shivered as a chill ran up her back. Folded her arms across her midsection, held herself in.

Wheaton blew air out his lungs. "Phone still work in there?"

Cash nodded.

"I'll call Doc Felix and tell him to come out here. Get the body."

He stuffed his hands in his back pockets. Stared at the paper-thin white clouds moving across the sky. "I'm glad you found me." Then he hurried across the overgrown lawn, into the house. Cash stayed where she was, smoking. She watched a small dust cloud rise in the air a few miles over. It moved slowly so Cash surmised it was a piece of farm machinery, not a car. She moved to meet Wheaton as he came out of the house.

"Doc Felix is on his way. Told him to bring some help. Up to you whether you want to wait here or not."

"As much as I hate the guy, I think I'll hang around. Curious to see if we can tell who it is."

Wheaton nodded agreement. "You looked through the house?"

"Yeah, nothing different. Better tell old lady Borgerud to get a lock on the door. Kids been in there drinking and fornicating."

Wheaton threw her a look. "Fornicating?"

"I'm going to college. Learning big words." She blew smoke rings into the air. She wasn't completely done being mad at him.

After that, they waited in silence. Wheaton sat in his car with both front doors open to get a cross breeze. Head on the headrest. Eyes closed. Cash sat on the wooden steps of the house and smoked a few more cigarettes.

Doc Felix arrived in an unnecessary cloud of dust as he maneuvered the county hearse down the road like he was driving in a speedway race. He didn't bother to wait for the dust to settle as he stepped out of the vehicle. Two young orderlies, dressed in hospital white, got out of the car after him.

"Where's the stiff?" Doc Felix hollered across the yard to Wheaton. "And how are you, Squaw Cochise? You seem to have a knack for tracking dead bodies. Some ancient inborn trait?" He pretended to be looking at tracks on the ground, then raised the flat of his hand over his eyes and looked around.

Cash gave him the finger.

Wheaton walked over to him. "Quit," he said sharply. Then, "Follow me."

The four men walked to the corncrib.

Cash couldn't hear what the men were saying, then she heard, "Goddamn," and the sound of one of the men retching. She stayed seated and watched as one of them returned, got what looked like a white plastic sheet out of the hearse. She heard more swearing, more retching. Then the two orderlies, one of them pale green in the face, carried the body to the hearse. Doc Felix scurried ahead and opened the back hatch for them to slide it into the long car.

Again, she could only hear the tone of their voices from where she sat. Doc Felix sounded whiny and sarcastic. Wheaton's voice was sharp and firm. The two young orderlies walked to the edge of the nearby road ditch and smoked cigarettes. One guy would inhale and then blow the smoke out his nose as if to erase the smell that still lingered there.

When they finally left, Wheaton came and sat down on the step next to her. "Young Indian man. Might be Nils." He shook his head. "What the hell happened here?"

Cash shrugged.

"You didn't get a lead on his wife, Arlis?"

Cash shook her head no.

Wheaton was silent. Stared across the flat land. "The girl's too young to bring in to try identify him. And he's all chewed up. Not a sight to show a kid."

"Did he have a billfold on 'im?"

"We didn't check. Those orderlies were barely holding it together as it was. Doc will look him over once he's downstairs in the morgue at the hospital. You coming?"

"I ain't going down there. Doc Felix is bad enough with all his Squaw Cochise bullshit and I don't think I can handle the smell any better than that one guy could."

"Follow me anyways and you can wait in the hallway. I can let you know what, if anything, they find."

CASH SAT ON A WOODEN bench in the basement of the county hospital staring at her tennis shoes, thinking, *For someone who doesn't go to church I sure sit on enough wooden pews.* Then her mind moved to contemplating buying a new pair of tennies. Cold, antiseptic air followed Wheaton when he came out of the morgue where Doc Felix worked performing autopsies on the deceased. As far as Cash knew, he never saw any breathing patients—thank god.

"No billfold." Wheaton, who stood a bit over six feet, looked down at her.

Cash felt childlike small with him towering over her, so she stood up. At five-two, it didn't do much to equalize their height. She breathed deep and swelled her rib cage out. Made her feel bigger at least. "You think it's Nils, though?"

"Yeah. You said his family is over by Naytahwaush?"

"Yeah, but I didn't go up there, remember."

Wheaton sat down on the bench. Cash sat back down.

A door shut on the floor above them. They heard the wheels of a cart or wheelchair move across the ceiling overhead. Metal on metal sounds came from Doc Felix's workroom.

"I hate to do it, but I think the quickest way to make a positive ID on this guy is to ask Mrs. Borgerud to come in and see if she recognizes him. Nils worked for them. She must have seen him at some point around the farm." He rubbed his hand over his cheek. Brushed his crew cut back. "Will you ride out there with me? I'll see if she'll come in. It'll be a rough one. Day of her husband's funeral and all. But I'd rather get it done today."

Cash listened to him talk himself into the decision. "Let's go." She stood up.

He pushed on his knees and, like an old man, lifted himself up. "Don't want to do this. But the sooner we know, the better."

"How did he die? Didn't crawl under that mess of dried corn on his own I don't think. How long has he been there?"

"Hard to tell. It's been warm this past week. Maybe a bit longer than Borgerud? Maybe around the same time? You sure you didn't see anything else suspicious that morning?"

"Nah." Cash bit at a hangnail. "Just the car running. Didn't see anyone else. Whoever shot Bud was gone before

I got there. But not too long before. This guy had to be dead longer, right?"

"Think so. Doc can't tell right off if he was shot or stabbed. Said he'll know more once he gets a good look. Let me go tell him we'll be right back."

Cash moved away from the morgue door to the marble steps leading out of the basement. When Wheaton came back out they walked up and out to the hospital parking lot.

"Why don't you follow me," he said. "The little girl can ride with you, not in the cruiser. She knows you."

The Borgerud yard had a few stragglers still parked near the house. Cash guessed at least a couple of them were the in-laws of Mrs. "Call Me Jean" who she had mentioned were staying for the funeral.

"You coming in?" Wheaton asked.

"I wasn't going to."

"Come on."

For the second time that day, unknown to Wheaton or Jean, Cash climbed out of the Ranchero and approached the farmhouse screen door of the Borgerud home. The sounds of dishes being washed, dried and put away mingled with the funeral-soft voices of the women who were helping clean up. Cash looked around the yard. No teens gathered. No men left smoking in the driveway. Wheaton knocked.

"Oh! Yes?" Jean peered out the screen.

"Mind if I come in? Or better yet, can you step out here for a minute?"

"Uh." Jean looked behind her as if to check with someone

or get permission. "Sure thing," she finally said, pushing the screen door open. Cash and Wheaton had to step back so she could get out the door.

"Who is it?" someone called from the kitchen.

"Wheaton," Jean called back. "I'll just be a minute."

Wheaton took his hat off. "First, I'd like to offer my condolences again, and sorry to bother you on this day when I'm sure you have enough to handle."

"Thank you." A distraught look crossed Jean's face. "It's been a hard day. My relatives are still here. We're cleaning up right now. So much food left over." She avoided looking at Cash.

"I hate to do this today, and I wish I had a gentler way to break this to you, but we found a body under the corncrib at the other homestead."

Jean turned white and slumped to sit on the top step.

Wheaton called through the screen door, "Can someone bring us a glass of water?"

A woman appeared shortly, glass in hand. Wheaton took it from her and indicated with a head nod that she was to go back inside. He handed the glass to Jean, who took a couple big gulps. "You okay?"

Jean nodded but didn't stand up. The color still drained from her face. "Who?"

"That's why we're here. We don't know who. But you know the men who worked for your farmland so we were hoping you could come take a look, make an identification."

"My guests." She gulped more water. Moisture had

formed on the outside of the glass in the warmer air outside. She wiped the wetness from her hands on the skirt of her dress, leaving five long streaks of damp that dried quickly in the heat.

"I'm sure they'll be fine helping out. Finishing up on their own. I'll drive you in and right back."

Cash noticed Shawnee hadn't been mentioned.

Wheaton continued. "The young girl can ride with Cash. She can ride with Cash. No sense scaring her by having her ride in a cop car."

"Shawnee?" Jean's color was returning. "She can stay here with my husband's relatives." She stood. On the top step, she was eye level with Wheaton and looked directly at him, still avoiding Cash.

"I want to bring her with," Wheaton stated firmly. "Cash, can you go in and get her?"

"No!" Jean turned and hollered back into the house, moving her body in front of the door handle. "Gladys, bring the girl out here."

Shawnee came out, corralled by two women. Her dress, two sizes too big, matched the size of heartache in her eyes. Cash recognized the shame on the little girl's face. She remembered foster mother after foster mother who would buy her church clothes to "grow into" while any old hand-me-down worked for every day. The go-to-church clothes were always kept behind when it came time to move Cash to another home.

When she held out her hand to Shawnee, the silent girl grabbed it and squeezed. Pinched lips and squinted eyes from the three women followed them to the Ranchero. A disgruntled Jean climbed into Wheaton's cruiser and threw a dirty look at Cash out the window.

Shawnee stared out the passenger window on the way to the hospital. Cash asked her about her mom, her dad, her favorite toy. All talk was greeted with silence. Cash gave up and turned on her country western station and lit a cigarette for the rest of the ride into town. In the hospital basement, Cash motioned for Shawnee to hop up on a bench in the hallway. Unable to reach the floor to plant her feet, Shawnee swung her legs nervously as they waited for Jean and Wheaton to come out of the morgue.

"Aiiiii." A sharp scream emanated from behind the closed door. Shawnee jumped and grabbed Cash's arm when Jean came out, leaning on Wheaton with black mascara-stained tears streaming down her pale face. He had one hand under her elbow, another under her other arm. He half carried her out into the hallway.

"Nooo!" Jean screamed when she saw Shawnee and Cash. Shawnee leaned into Cash, buried her face against her chest. Jean hollered "Nooo" again before it turned into a high-pitched scream. She pulled Wheaton toward the stairs and they both stumbled up. Wheaton didn't loosen his grip.

Doc Felix poked his head out the mortuary door. He opened his mouth but before he could get any words out, Cash snarled, "You better just shut the fuck up." She hoisted Shawnee up onto her right hip and carried her upstairs and out into the bright sunlight.

Wheaton and Jean were sitting in the cruiser with

both front doors open to let air move through. As soon as Wheaton saw Cash and Shawnee, he got out of the car and met them halfway.

"Whyn't you take this little girl to the café and get her a burger and fries? And a strawberry malt." He handed Cash a ten-dollar bill. "We'll be by in a bit."

Cash raised her eyebrows.

"Doesn't make sense to talk right now." His hand on her free shoulder moved her toward the Ranchero. "See you soon."

At the café, Cash watched Shawnee eat her burger like the girl hadn't eaten in a week. She still didn't talk. Had answered Cash's questions about what to order with small nods and shakes of her head. The girl, finished with her hamburger, dipped a french fry into ketchup. "When's the last time you ate?" Cash asked.

Shawnee looked at her, looked at the fry and popped it into her mouth. Her cheeks bulged with food. Cash remembered other foster kids who ate like that. Stuffed as much food into their mouths as possible, trying to eat everything at once because who knew when there would be food again. She had also heard some kids ate to fill the loneliness inside themselves. Cash herself rarely ate. She couldn't recall when she had decided that food was a waste of time and energy. There had been so many struggles in various homes over what to eat, when to eat, how to eat, what she could or couldn't eat, that at some point she just decided to forgo all the drama.

"You know, Shawnee, this BLT is the best thing I've eaten

in a month. You like the fries, huh?" Cash took a bite of the sandwich she had ordered.

The little girl nodded, dipped another fry in ketchup and popped it in her mouth with the other half-chewed fries.

At that moment, Wheaton entered the café. Jean was nowhere in sight. He sat down heavily in the booth across from Cash. The waitress appeared with a white ceramic coffee mug in one hand and a steaming glass carafe of coffee in the other. "Cream and sugar?" she asked. "Need a menu?"

Wheaton shook his head no to the menu and said, "Cream and sugar." To Cash he said, "Can't say much," as he leaned his head slightly in Shawnee's direction. Cash knew immediately it was Nils Petterson who had been stuffed under the corncrib as feed for the raccoons and barn rats. She pushed her plate with the remainder of her sandwich toward the edge of the table. Wiped her face with a paper napkin.

"And Jean?" she asked.

"Took her back to the farm. Shawnee will spend a night or two here in town with Miss Dackson again." At Cash and Shawnee's surprised looks, he quickly added, "Just till Mrs. Borgerud's company leaves. She said they were only going to stay a few more days. Help her sort through her husband's things. Finalize some of the estate dealings. He had a will so with no other heirs everything goes to her."

Shawnee hung her head. Her dark hair hid her face. Cash pulled her in close. "What's the matter?"

Shawnee just shook her head no.

"It'll only be a couple days," Wheaton said.

"Do you want to stay with Miss Dackson?"

Shawnee shook her head no.

"Go back to Borgerud's?"

She furiously shook her head no. Cash could feel the little girl trembling.

Wheaton looked frazzled. He drank some coffee. Ran his hands over his buzz cut. Took another drink. "We don't have other options, Shawnee. I'm sorry."

"I'll make another run over to White Earth. See if I can find your mom. How's that?" Cash spoke to the top of Shawnee's head. She felt warm tears drop onto and slide off the arm she held around the little girl. Cash glared at Wheaton.

He looked contrite. "If I could do something else, Cash, you know I would."

Both turned as the café door opened. Miss Dackson walked in. A white patent leather purse carried on one arm matched her white pumps. Her hair was tightly curled and she smelled of hairspray. Cash guessed she might have just come from the beauty parlor down the street.

"Hi, Shawnee. I understand you're going to spend a couple nights with me again," the social worker said, without acknowledging Cash or Wheaton.

The false cheerfulness in her voice grated on Cash's ears. Shawnee scooted closer into Cash's side. Wheaton rubbed his hands over his buzz cut again. Cash gently untangled Shawnee from the safety of her arms. Brushed the girl's hair away from her face and cupped her cheeks in her hands. "I'm gonna go back to White Earth and find your mom. This isn't going to last forever. I promise."

Cash backed out of the booth and stood aside so Miss Dackson could reach in and take the girl by the arm and lead her out of the café. Cash slid back into the booth and took a drink of the strawberry malt Shawnee hadn't finished. It was lukewarm. Cash washed the sweetness from her mouth with a gulp of water from a plastic glass.

"You maybe shouldn't promise things you don't know that you can deliver."

"What are you talking about?"

Wheaton looked around the café. No one was in there except for them and the waitress, who sat at the end of the counter flipping through the small jukebox in front of her. He lowered his voice anyway. "Jean said she thinks it was Shawnee's mom who killed her husband, Bud. And probably Nils too. Said they were behind on rent and that Nils and Bud had argued before about how much work Nils had to do for him in trade."

"That doesn't make any sense. Why would Arlis kill her husband and Bud because they argued? Seems like they were the ones mad at each other."

"Jean also said she's heard rumors about Nils and different women. Said she heard he had a girlfriend up in Crookston. And maybe one over in Bagley too. Jean said maybe Arlis reached her breaking point with him and all the other women. Maybe Bud walked in on a fight between Nils and Arlis. That's what Jean thinks maybe happened."

Cash flashed on the young kid in the pickup truck at the Drive-Inn. *Our own little* Peyton Place. "So they both got killed the same morning? And you believe her?"

"I don't know what to believe. If we can find Arlis, then maybe we'll get some answers. Meanwhile, Jean asked for a couple days to get over Bud. The shock of seeing Nils really upset her again. She doesn't want to have Shawnee in the house while she talks about it with her other relatives. Wants to spare the girl any more hurt right now."

"Such a big heart." Cash munched a french fry. "So who is going to tell Shawnee about her dad?"

"I talked with Miss Dackson about that."

"You can't have her tell her." Cash stood, ready to chase after the woman and child.

Wheaton reached out and held her back. "No one's telling her yet. Hell, for all we know, she saw him get killed. Miss Dackson talked to a psychologist up in Crookston. He said that sometimes when the trauma is too big for a kid, they go silent. They can't talk. He told Miss Dackson we should try find her mother, and this kind of news, *if* she didn't witness the crime, would best be told to her by her mom."

Cash slid back into the booth. They both sipped their drinks. Wheaton his coffee. Cash the strawberry malt followed by plain water.

"So who killed Bud?"

"She thinks Arlis did. Why else would she disappear?"

"She got scared?"

"Maybe he knew Arlis killed Nils."

"Maybe—maybe isn't facts."

More sipping of tepid drinks.

"Don't you have any feeling, any intuitive sense of what happened here?" asked Wheaton.

Cash didn't know how to tell him the feelings he was referring to were either not arriving or were so murky and clouded that they were useless to them.

Cash slurped the last of the malt and pushed the tall glass to the middle of the table. Her hair framed and hid her face like Shawnee's had earlier. When she looked up, there was a deep emptiness in her eyes. Normally they were brown, but there was so much sadness in them they looked black.

Cash fiddled with the discarded paper wrapping of the straw from the spent malt. "You know, Wheaton, something's different since that whole incident with the pastor. Maybe if I hadn't killed him—I didn't mean to, but I did. Maybe god, or whoever is out there in charge of these things, took my gift away. That's what Jonesy calls the knowing things. A gift. Maybe it got taken back like all the good toys that get left at a foster home."

"You know that's not how it works, Cash. Jonesy must have told you that, too."

"Then how come I didn't sense Nils there when Gunner was sniffing around that first day? Why did it take me so long to go and check the house the day Bud was killed? Maybe if I had checked it out sooner he'd still be alive. How do we know how long he lived after he was shot? Maybe if I had got there earlier." With nothing left in the malt glass to sip, she gulped the rest of the water from the glass.

Wheaton caught the attention of the waitress, ordered himself a slice of pie and got them both a fresh hot coffee. He cupped the mug with both hands like he needed the warmth to keep him going, even though it was springtime warm outside. "You didn't mean for that to happen. That whole situation was a lot for anyone to handle. And besides, that's not how the universe works."

"Every time I got something good, it was taken away." Her hair once again framed her face, hiding her. "Not saying the pastor was good. But what you and Jonesy call my gift. Or whatever it is."

"That was then. This is now. And that's not how life works. Not how it's supposed to work. Some of those homes you were in were as crazy as that pastor and his wife. And that was a difficult situation to deal with. You handled it the best you could. Kept the baby alive, and yourself. You did the right thing, Cash. I understand that you feel guilty. I'm not saying it's the same but I went through hell in Korea, in the war over there. Many times I was in a kill-or-be-killed situation. I'm sitting here breathing, alive to tell about it. Although I never talk about it. Don't want to. Still get nightmares sometimes."

Cash lifted her head and looked at him.

"Yeah, nightmares." He sipped his coffee. Looked at her over the rim of his cup. "I'll probably have nightmares now about a girl in a yellow dress stuffing me in the trunk of my cruiser."

Cash covered her mouth with her hand to stifle back a laugh. "You scared me to death."

"You? How do you think I felt? I'm glad you used your senses and found me."

"Most of that was just common sense. Thinking like, where were they headed, how would they get there. I might not have found you if it hadn't been for the mutt." Cash blinked rapidly and took too big a drink of too hot coffee, all to push away the fear she felt at the thought of Wheaton gone.

"Mutt? What do you have against Gunner, anyways? That's a good dog right there."

Cash avoided the question. "I did get a sense that Shawnee's mother walked away and that she plans to come back for her. I can drive over to White Earth tomorrow and try again. Kinda late to head that way now. I don't want Shawnee with that woman. Seems kinda twisted to me that Mrs. Borgerud even asked to take care of her. I just never buy the good deeds all these upstanding citizens say they're doing."

"All those foster homes influenced your feelings about people around here. Jean's good people, from what I've seen. Turned her life around after a bit of wild living as a kid. Married Bud. Settled down. Active in the church and town." Wheaton took a forkful of pie.

"If I have a feeling, it's that I don't like or trust that woman." Cash slid out of the booth. She placed the ten Wheaton had given her earlier on the table. "I haven't paid yet. I'll stop by tomorrow after I get back. Let you know if I found her or not."

Wheaton tried to put the ten back in her hand. "If you do find her, it'll help a lot if you bring her in so I can talk to her."

"Yep, sure thing." She put the ten back on the table.

Cash walked to the hotel. The same clerk who had been

on duty before was there again. The look on his face begged her not to give him any trouble. She nodded calmly as she walked by. Instead of heading up the oak staircase to Miss Dackson's room, Cash plopped into a large, overstuffed chair in the hotel lobby. It faced a fireplace that took up half the wall. Curlicues and maple leaves rose up on either side of the ornate, hand-carved oak mantel. The shelf that ran the length of the wall held a large vase of tulips, daffodils and some other flower Cash didn't recognize. Old-fashioned gasoline lanterns graced each end of the mantel. Cash had a vague memory that in her mother's home, where she lived until she was three, their house had been lit by lanterns like that. No electrical wires ran to that tar paper shack.

She ran her hand down the worn arms of the wool chair. It too felt familiar. In fact, it might even be the same chair, that when she was a child and had stayed in the social worker's rented hotel room between families, maybe it was the chair she had climbed into. Back then the chair was as big as a couch to the small girl she was. This chair, in this hotel lobby, made her homesick in a way she hadn't felt in forever.

This feeling of being a child, the feeling of a home, stilled her being in a way she hadn't felt since the trauma with the pastor and his wife. She lit a cigarette. Dropped the match into the brass ashtray standing at the side of the chair. Blew the smoke into the air over her head. Stared at the fireplace, empty of wood. Willed herself to empty herself of feeling. To ignore the man behind the desk in the lobby surreptitiously staring at her. She willed her mind to travel up the staircase and into the hotel room. Miss Dackson sat at a small wood desk, writing in what looked like a school notebook. A neatly made twin bed was behind the chair she sat on. Shawnee was curled under a cotton blanket on a twin bed on the opposite wall. Her black hair spilled across the pillow under her head. Overwhelming sadness enveloped the space around her.

Cash continued to smoke the cigarette even though she no longer felt she was in her physical body. She willed herself to travel out the hotel window, to float just under the white wisps of cloud that drifted across the clear blue sky. Out to the Borgerud farmstead, where she hovered over the house where she had found Bud. She couldn't get close to the corncrib, or it wouldn't let her, so she continued to float above the house. A space opened in the roof where she could look down through the upstairs bedroom floor, down to the kitchen floor.

The her, the Cash who was floating in air, flipped into darkness, into nighttime. Stars filled the sky above her and a crescent moon hung near the end of the Milky Way. When she flipped back to looking down into the house, a man and woman were arguing. Cash couldn't tell who the couple were. It didn't seem like they were the girl's parents. She tried to glimpse their faces but they were shadow people. Cash tried to look around the upstairs, tried to find Shawnee. She wasn't there.

"Hey. Watch what you're doing." The desk clerk's sharp voice jerked Cash back into her body. "You dropped ashes on the chair."

Cash looked down. A half-inch-long cigarette ash had fallen on the chair arm. The cigarette had died out between her two fingers. She dropped the filter into her hand then swept the ash on top of that and put it all into the ashtray. She used her index finger to brush off the gray ash that clung to her palm. "Sorry," she said, still half in, half out of the meditative state she had been pulled out of.

"If you're not going to get a room, or go up and visit the kid and social worker, you're going to have to leave. The lobby is for guests." Exasperated hands on hips.

Cash stared at him. He finally dropped his hands and looked away, after he came to the realization he was no match for her. She stood up and left the hotel.

Like she'd told Wheaton, it was too late to drive to make the trip over to White Earth. The sun slid to the western horizon as Cash drove back into Fargo down Highway 75, the road that ran parallel to the river. She kept the Ranchero at the legal speed limit. Gave a farmer's wave to folks headed north while she went south. Noted which fields were plowed, which planted. The car window was rolled down and she caught the acrid smell of a chemical fertilizer. The image from the hotel of the man and woman arguing would flash in her peripheral vision every so often. Instead of putting any attention on the images, she focused instead on the smell of the trees and damp clay of the Red River. Once she hit the edges of town, the scent of newly mowed grass filled the air. She pulled into the parking spot in front of her apartment before noticing a familiar pickup parked in the spot next to hers.

Al, her new sometimes pool partner and her sometimes bed partner, was sitting on the bottom step. She had met him when a friend of a friend introduced them so he could oar a boat, with her in it, to Ada during the spring flood. Wheaton wanted her help to find the identity of a woman who had washed into town. It was Al who had held her, gave her space, fed her, let her sleep in his bed, after she had killed the pastor.

Al stood as she stopped the Ranchero, his hands hooked into front pockets. She avoided eye contact as she parked but noticed he was wearing clean jeans and what looked like a neatly pressed, pale-blue plaid shirt that made his dark skin seem even darker. As a backyard mechanic most of the time, his clothes were grease stained, with a rip here or there. He'd cleaned up to come sit on her steps. Cash felt a twinge of embarrassment as she was aware he had tried a couple times to call her phone, and now here he was, sitting outside her apartment. She had a habit of unplugging it from the wall or, if it was plugged in, ignoring all calls unless it was the three rings-hang up-two rings-hang up-three rings code she and Wheaton had worked out.

"Hope you don't mind me dropping by." He gave her a crooked smile.

"How long you been sitting here?" Cash realized she sounded rude. She kept one hand on the car door as if she might hop back in and take off.

"Not that long. Figured I'd wait till dark. They're having a tournament over at The Flame. Thought you and me could partner up. Take home the big bucks."

"Don't suppose Shyla and Terry are gonna be there?" They were the couple Al and she usually shot with. Shyla was the closest thing to a competitor Cash had found in the Fargo–Moorhead area. Cash glanced into the front seat of the Ranchero. She couldn't just jump back in and take off and Al stood blocking the stairs up to her apartment.

"Nah. Neither one of them is much for bars."

"I gotta change," she finally muttered, and moved toward him.

He stepped aside. "I'll just wait out here."

When Cash reached the top of the stairs, she glanced back down. Al was seated on the bottom step, looking at the buildings across the street. She shook her head. She always said stupid stuff when he was around. She hadn't done any field work all day. If he wasn't sitting downstairs, she would have walked on over to the Casbah wearing what she had on. Now because she said she needed to change she had to at least find a different shirt to put on.

Downstairs again, Cash told Al she'd drive to The Flame. She was surprised when he climbed into the seat beside her. She had expected him to drive his own vehicle across town. Cash answered Al's questions about her day with clipped yesses and nos. After that, they rode in silence with country singers Patsy Cline and Charley Pride serenading them from the car radio.

At The Flame, Al ordered a pitcher of beer, signed them up on the bracket sheet. The Flame seemed darker than most bars, if that was possible. Almost naked women pole danced in the spotlight on a tiny stage next to the bar, their bleached blond or ebony black hair ratted into big beehives. Each billiard table had an ornate long lamp hanging over it so the pool players could see to shoot. One of the reasons she liked to shoot for money at The Flame was because the male pool players' attention was often pulled away from the game to gawk at the dancers as they gyrated for dollars. She watched Al out of the corner of her eye. He didn't seem to get distracted by the women. He stayed in the zone while taking his shots and watched the table and other players between turns.

One team was exceptionally good. Cash had never seen them before. She played enough around town that she had played the best of the best more than once. You win some, you lose some was almost her philosophy. That team's tall, skinny, farmer-type guy with sharp elbows could bank anything. His partner had a square mustache over plump lips that he pursed before every shot. He would softly tap the cue ball to hit the stripe he was aiming for, sink it, and then everyone watched the cue ball move silently, slowly across the table until, with perfect English, it was lined up exactly on spot for the next shot. Both had their own expensive pool sticks. Skinny guy's had pearl inlay on the handle. Mustache had a shooting stick and a breaking stick in a custom-made leather case. Cash took an instant dislike to the two of them. Not because it was clear from the first game they were the team Al and Cash would have to play at the top of the winner's bracket. Something about their arrogant air and mocking eyes gave her the creeps.

Most people's games got sloppier as the night wore on,

more beer was consumed and the dancers seductively lost more of what little clothes they wore. That team, even though they were drinking, seemed to acquire keener, sharper eyes as the games progressed. Al and Cash won their own games easily, moving up each time on the bracket sheet.

Al saw Cash watching the other team. "Nothing to worry about," he whispered, his breath tickling the hair near her ear before he ran the table against the team they were currently playing. Cash shivered. Goosebumps rose on her arms. She walked to the bar and checked the brackets. After they won this game, there would be two more games if both they and the other team kept winning. Then they would play each other.

As she looked back at the tables, Al lifted his cue, indicating it was her turn to shoot. As she walked back, she saw a lone woman sitting in a booth. Beer in a glass sat on the table before her. She was absent-mindedly wiping the condensation off the glass. She took a sip. She looked out of place to Cash. She was wearing dress pants and a light-colored blouse with a rounded collar. Her hair was neatly combed. Cash looked around the bar.

Wives and girlfriends of other men shooting in the tournament sat together in booths drinking beer poured from pitchers; or they stood, their drinks on a narrow ledge that ran along the length of the wall. They wore skin-tight jeans and halter tops that showed their cleavage. When their partner missed a shot they called out, "Damn!" or "Get back in the zone." The men would grab a kiss between shots for "good luck." Feeling up the women they would later fantasize was the stripper on stage. The girl in the booth did not belong here.

Cash took her shot, cleared four solids off the table and left the cue ball softly touching the eight ball so the other team would need to bank around it to even get to one of the stripes. Defense strategy. Al gave her a lopsided grin.

"I gotta make a phone call," she said as she leaned her cue against the wall where he stood. "Be right back." Al raised his eyebrows in surprise considering her aversion to phones.

Cash ignored the look and his "What?" and walked to the back of the bar. Past the door to the strippers' back room, where they exited and entered to the stage. Past the wooden door labeled WOMEN. The smell of the urinal cakes assaulted her senses as she passed the men's restroom. Near the back exit a black and silver pay phone hung on the wall. She picked up the handset and listened to the phone's inner workings as she dialed zero.

"Operator. How may I place your call?"

"Collect to David Wheaton in Ada, Minnesota. From Cash Blackbear." She looked down the hallway into the bar area. Al was watching her.

Five rings later, Cash heard a tired "Hello?"

"Collect call from a Cash Blackbear. Will you accept the charges?"

"Yes. Cash?!"

She could hear a TV in the background and in her mind's eye she saw Wheaton nervously shift the handset of his phone from one ear to the other. It sounded like he set a glass or cup on the counter. More phone sounds as the operator connected them.

"Cash?" he said again once they were connected. "What's wrong? You okay?" His usually calm voice barely hid his fear.

"I'm fine. I'm shooting pool here at The Flame in Fargo. There's a skinny guy and a shorter guy shooting pool. Never saw 'em before. And a very prim girl sitting in a booth drinking by herself." She lowered her voice and faced the exit door, although it was highly unlikely anyone past the bathrooms could hear her over the noise of the stripper music and billiard balls dropping. "Would you recognize the bank robbers if you saw them?"

"Damn right I would."

"I don't know if I'm right, you know how my mind's been messed up lately, but maybe you want to drive over and see if it's them." She looked toward the pool tables. When Al saw her look in that direction he held up her cue stick to indicate it was her turn to shoot. She faced the exit door again. Twisted the metal cord around her wrist. Untwisted it. "Wait, they might recognize you. Maybe you should call the Fargo cops."

"I will. On my way."

"My turn to shoot." And she hung up.

She walked back to the pool tables. Al handed over her cue stick. "They lost. We got stripes." His eyes asked questions she didn't answer.

She walked slowly around the pool table. Lined up the cue stick on the white cue ball. Looked at different possible shots from different angles. It would take Wheaton a good half hour to get from Ada to Fargo. The longer she could prolong the games between now and when he got there the better. She played slow. Played defensively.

"What's going on?" Al asked as he stood by her. Each with a beer in hand, both with the butt of their cue sticks planted on the floor.

She just shook her head no. Took a sip of beer. Gave a slight nod to pay attention to the guy bent over the table attempting a jump shot. Snap! The cue ball flew off the table, hit the wall three feet from where they stood and bounced to the floor. Skinny guy picked it up as it rolled toward him and handed it back to the guy, who mumbled, "Thanks."

Cash ignored Al's questioning looks. She fell back on years of habit and practice as she ran six balls on the table. She muttered "Damn" under her breath as the cue ball didn't go where she wanted. Left without a sure drop, she nicked her stripe and left the cue ball sitting on the rail. Al shook his head. When she went back to the wall rail to take a drink, he asked, "You sure you're okay?"

She nodded. Out of the corner of her eye, she saw Skinny sink the eight ball. He and his friend Mustache paid no attention to the dancers. They barely drank their beer. Neither looked at the woman sitting in the booth. In fact, it appeared they intentionally, studiously, ignored her.

Cash watched Al watch her. She saw him, like so many other soldiers she had seen come back from the war, start scanning the bar. Starting at the front door, eyes slid across the farmers and small-town businessmen seated at the bar nearest the dancers, across the people shooting pool and those standing against the wall or leaning on their cue sticks, waiting their turn to shoot. He looked down the bathroom hallway, then reversed the process.

She watched him slide his eyes back to Skinny and Mustache. He caught her eye. Intuitively he must have sensed they were the source of Cash's discomfort. He didn't linger but kept his eyes moving. Cash followed his eyes. He looked back at the bar. One bartender was on the phone. He too was scanning the bar. He made the briefest eye contact with Al and Cash. Then his eyes spent a fraction of a second longer on the two men who hadn't lost a game. The bartender turned his back to the crowd where he could watch the patrons in the mirror behind the liquor bottles. The two men being watched had won every game in the bracket. One more and they would be playing Cash and Al.

The other teams were still going back and forth, dropping one ball at a time. The combination of women gyrating ten feet away and the possibility of winning was messing with their focus. Cash appreciated the delay. Skinny and Mustache were playing to win. It was clear they weren't going anyplace until they had a chance at the big money.

Just as Al cut the eight ball into the side pocket to win the game for them, four Fargo police, in full uniform, gun on one hip and handcuffs on the other, entered by the front door. The air in the room crackled with electricity. The blond dancer, down to her gold sequined bikini, gyrated slower. Husbands who were out on their wives, businessmen who didn't want their names in the paper, pool shooters who might have had a joint or downers in their pocket—everyone determinedly ignored the cops talking to the bartender.

It had been known to happen in the past, that The Flame was raided by the cops because the dancers sometimes engaged in extracurricular activity when more than a dollar was tucked in their G-string. Regulars knew to keep their heads down and not call attention to themselves if the cops showed up. Cash guessed that those were the thoughts running through most people's minds as the bartender and cops huddled at the farthest end of the bar.

Not wanting to call attention to themselves, everyone in the room moved in slow motion. The air in the room became muffled. Cash, who leaned over the table to hit the one ball into a corner pocket, saw Skinny and Mustache make eye contact for the briefest second. Mustache, without looking in that direction, unfurled his pointer finger from around his cue and pointed toward the booths. Skinny acknowledged it by a slight tip of his glass of beer.

Cash stood up after taking her shot and walked to the other end of the pool table, where she could see into the booths. Girlfriends and wives, who—even though they were drinking in a strip joint—smirked at the women on stage. Farm girls with cow shit still on the bottom of their shoes thought they were better than the women dancing. Cash saw one woman wink at her boyfriend or husband. The lone woman, who acknowledged no one and who no one else acknowledged, had slid to the outer edge of the booth. Her square purse sat on the table. She was ready to move.

In her peripheral vision, Cash saw Skinny and Mustache

unscrew their cue sticks and put them in black leather cases. As unobtrusively as possible, they started to move toward the front door, hugging the bar rail on the wall farthest from the cops. As they moved, two cops moved toward the pool tables. Two cops moved toward the front door. The woman slid out of the booth and moved soundlessly in the direction of the bathrooms. She had been invisible all night. No one paid her any mind, aside from Cash. They were all focused on the cops. Cash moved quickly after the woman. From a distance she heard Al say, "Cash."

As if it were all happening in another dimension, behind her she heard scuffling and yells. Her only focus was the pale blouse of the woman walking away from the chaos, purse over her left arm. White cigarette smoke swirled in the air as they moved in the direction of the hallway. The woman passed the stage door, the women's room, the men's room, and reached with her extended arm for the exit door. Cash, hoping to stop her before she could get outside to the alley, kicked her square in her lower back. The woman had already turned the doorknob and the kick sent her flying onto the gravel in the alley.

The smell of stale beer, piss and old cigarette smoke assaulted Cash as she rushed to jump the woman on the ground. A strong arm reached across and stopped her. Wheaton reached down and picked the slight woman up, twisting her arm behind her back as he did so. When the woman saw Wheaton, she said, "You," and spit in his direction. Instinctively, Cash slapped the woman across the face as hard as she could.

"Stop, Cash," Wheaton admonished as he pulled the woman's other arm behind her and clicked on handcuffs.

The woman glared at Cash. "Squaw," she hissed.

Before Cash could slap her again, Wheaton pushed the woman out of Cash's reach. "Let's take her inside. Open the door."

Cash did as requested. She reached back and grabbed the purse off the ground. Put it over her left arm. She couldn't resist furtively putting her foot onto the door ledge so the woman stumbled as Wheaton walked her inside.

Inside, the bar was lit up like the midway at a fairground. It was brighter than when the bartenders called "Closing time" and hit the ceiling lights. Lights were turned on that Cash didn't know existed in a bar. All the cops were at the front of the joint, with Skinny and Mustache in handcuffs.

Pool shooters stood against the far wall, arms draped over their women who had exited their booths. All eyes on the scene by the door. Half-naked dancers had emerged, glittery robes covering skimpy bikini-wear. Three stood in a clump near the stage door. Two sat on the stage, legs crossed over knees showing a lot of thigh promise. Disinterested farmers and businessmen sat on barstools turned to the front doorway. Thoughts of forbidden sex forgotten. The pool tournament forgotten.

"These your guys?" one of the men in uniform asked Wheaton when he walked the woman toward them.

Wheaton nodded. "This one, too." He handed off the woman to one of the officers.

"We'll take 'em in. I'll call the Cities and get the FBI up here. These three are looking at some federal time. If you can fill out a statement on what occurred the other side of Ada, that'll save us some time. Won't need to run down to Ada tomorrow."

Wheaton looked back at Cash, who was standing four feet behind him. "You okay? I'll go with them." He looked at his watch. "Another hour or so it'll be closing time here. Want to meet at that restaurant south of town? I'll get you an early breakfast."

Cash pushed down the urge to say "Take me with you" and nodded in agreement. She stood frozen in her spot until all the cops and robbers left the building.

As soon as they left, the lights in the bar went down, strippers returned to their respective places backstage or on the pole. Men faced the bar to drink and ogle. Pool players shot practice games while a couple men figured out how to fairly reconfigure the players brackets. A constant buzz of speculation filled the bar. Everyone replaying the night's events. Lots of *I knew something was hinky with them two.* All playing second-hand detective.

Al raised his eyebrows at Cash. She shook her head no, indicating she wasn't ready to talk. "Rack 'em up. Your break." She set the purse on the stool near the rail next to their beers.

They played a quick game while a decision about the tournament was made. It was finally announced that all last games played were scratched and everyone would play from the last series of wins-loses that occurred just before the bust. Cash and Al ended up one game down and easily won the payout.

After breaking down their cues, they walked out to the street. Cash carried the purse over her arm like she owned it and threw it in the Ranchero along with her cue stick. Like a typical guy, Al didn't seem to notice.

They stood outside the bar in the space between two trucks. The flashing neon beer sign hanging over the tavern gave them enough light to see each other's faces, with a red or blue hue depending on the flicker. Cash told Al about the bank robbery in Twin Valley, about finding Wheaton in the trunk of his cruiser.

"What made you think it was them tonight?"

"I don't know. Guess it was the woman sitting alone in the booth. The folks at the bank said the driver of the get-away car didn't look like a bank robber. And Wheaton said that when he pulled up next to them on that country road, he thought she was a hostage. Then she pulled a gun on him. Sitting in the bar tonight, she certainly wasn't a stripper, and what woman goes to a joint like this all by herself to just sit in a booth and drink beer? Those two men went out of their way to avoid looking at her. They were the odd three out here tonight."

"And that was Wheaton?"

"Yeah." She blew smoke rings into the air. "He's looked out for me since I was a kid. I was ready to kill him myself when I found him in the trunk of his cruiser." She blew another smoke ring. "Right now I'm supposed to be helping him find this little girl's mother."

Al raised his eyebrows.

"Long story short, a shot farmer, dead; then I found the little girl's dad rotting under a corncrib on the same farm. And the mother is missing. Little girl saw something but she isn't talking at all. In shock, everyone says. I've been to White Earth once to try find the mom and I gotta go back there tomorrow."

"Did the mom kill them?"

"I don't think so. The dead farmer's wife has Wheaton convinced the mom killed them both. I think the mother's scared and running." She dropped her cigarette butt and ground it out with the heel of her shoe.

They stood quietly next to each other, not quite touching, leaning on the bed of her Ranchero. Watched a few cars pass on the street. Heard laughter down the block as a drunk couple walked to their car.

Al finally broke the silence. "You gonna come by?"

"Nah, Wheaton wants me to meet him at Shari's. I should head that way. You'll have to catch a ride home with one of the folks going your way."

"Just dumping me, huh? Stop by tomorrow after you get back from White Earth."

"We'll see." She moved to get into her Ranchero.

Al reached out and pulled her into his arms. His shirt smelled of bar smoke. He kissed the top of her head and flicked the braid that hung down her back. "I've missed you."

Cash looked up and, without making eye contact, kissed him, then pushed away and said, "Gotta go."

As she backed away from the curb, she looked over out the passenger window. Al was standing where she had left him, watching her leave.

AT THE ALL-NIGHT DINER, WHEATON GAVE Cash an update on the robbers over the "late-night trucker's special": two eggs, hashbrowns, bacon and steak. "The guy with the mustache is the girl's brother. And she and the tall guy are shacking up, to use their words. They wouldn't say where the money is. You didn't happen to see a purse in the alley when we grabbed her?"

Cash, mouth full of egg, made direct eye contact with the sheriff and tilted her head in a noncommittal way. She didn't say yes or no. Just chewed her food.

"Cops were going over to the Dew Drop Inn Motel when I left. See if the money is there. I'll have to talk to the FBI at some point. They'll be charged with the robbery and kidnapping." Wheaton moved his eggs around on his plate without taking a forkful.

"Prison time." Cash picked up a piece of crispy bacon and bit off an end. "Where they from?"

"Bumfuck, Egypt."

"Huh?"

"Sorry. Antler, North Dakota. We had to look it up on the map. Almost to Montana. Sits on this side of the Canadian border. Guess they thought they could come this way and rob the wealthy, give to the poor. Some Bonnie and Clyde reenactment. Probably still living in sod houses out that way."

Cash had never heard him sound so bitter. Hell, she would have pounded the piss out of the woman herself in the back alley if he hadn't stopped her. She finished her bacon and dipped her toast into the egg yolk.

Wheaton added, "Glad you called. Like I've always said, trust that feeling of yours."

Cash repeated what she'd told Al. "Wasn't no feeling, something was just off about the three of them. Especially the girl sitting in the strip joint all alone. And her not being a stripper." Cash switched subjects, wanting to make Wheaton feel better. "I'll try to find Arlis tomorrow. Or at least see if I can find out where she is. That little girl needs her mom, not some do-good dead farmer's wife. Probably won't get going until later in the morning. Might actually sleep in for a change."

"Don't speak ill of the dead, Cash."

"I'm not. His wife, not him."

"She just lost her husband. Grief will do funny things to you. If you find Arlis, bring her into Ada. Hopefully we can straighten out what happened to Bud and Nils."

Cash nodded even though she had no intention of turning the woman in until she found out for herself what Arlis's story was.

Wheaton, finished with his trucker's breakfast, stood, put a dollar on the table for a tip, held out a twenty to Cash. "For gas. Figure I better start paying you something for all the work you do for me. I requested some money from the county budget for next year. Give you a little something for all the field work you miss."

Cash stuffed the bill in her jeans pocket. Mumbled,

"Thanks." Thought to herself, *Money's good but don't count on me giving up field work.*

RAIN FELL ACROSS THE PRAIRIE. Cash drove under a pale-blue sky, the tar roadway damp, rays of sun peeping through fast-moving clouds. She was following a dark, blueish-gray storm cloud rapidly heading east. A sheet of rain fell from northern horizon to southern horizon about five miles in front of her, the storm headed in the same direction she was going. Cash always marveled at how on the prairie, one could see the rain as it fell in the distance.

In the winter, one could watch a snowstorm move in, watch its cold, white flakes envelop the world. She remembered a time when she was out plowing in the hottest of the summer months. A hot, muggy day. Sun beating down. Three miles over, on the other side of the Wild Rice creek, a white funnel cloud dipped out of a gray cloud, kicked up field dirt and moved northwest. The sun never stopped shining on the field she was working. Nothing could change her love of the land she had known and worked her whole life.

She left the Valley and entered the White Earth reservation. Drove around lakes and into the tamarack forest. The Ranchero spun through mud as Cash made her way to Jonesy's place in the woods. As usual, Jonesy had a pot of tea going and some venison stew ready to share with Cash when she arrived. "It's almost like you knew I was coming," Cash said as she sat down on a wooden chair that had seen better days.

"Hmmph." Jonesy put a steaming bowl in front her. "What brings you back?"

Cash told her about the bank robbers and the arrests at the pool tournament. "And I'm still looking for the little girl's mom. Arlis. Found her dad under the corncrib on the Borgerud farm."

Judging from Jonesy's noncommittal reply and expression, Cash guessed the old woman had known this when Cash first visited. "Why didn't you tell me I wasn't going to find him alive?"

"Don't know everything. All I saw was nothingness when I tried to get a feel for where he was." Jonesy smashed a potato from the stew and put it on a saltine cracker. Topped it with a piece of venison and popped the whole thing in her mouth. End of that conversation.

They ate in silence until Jonesy asked, "What are you going to do with the purse?"

Cash asked, fork of venison halfway to her mouth, "What purse?" Then it dawned on her. "Oh! I forgot!"

She jumped up from the table, went out to the Ranchero and reached behind the seat where she had thrown the purse and cue stick the night before. She had totally forgotten about it. She hoped Wheaton had, too. She carried it back into Jonesy's, holding it in front of herself with both hands like a valuable package. She set the square pink purse with its stiff, rounded pink handle on the table next to her bowl of stew.

"Open it," said Jonesy, popping another venison cracker sandwich in her mouth.

Cash looked at the purse. Whatever she needed she just stuffed in her pockets. Fake ID driver's license in back pocket on the right. Real ID on the left. Money in the right front jeans pocket. Same place for car key. Cigarettes in the front shirt pocket. Purses were foreign objects in her world.

"Open it."

Cash reached out and flipped the fake gold latch that held the two halves of the purse together. It fell open a few inches. She opened it further. Pulled out a small stack of bills held together with a rubber band. A tube of Avon Pink A Ling lipstick and a pocket mirror. No ID. She didn't pull out the handgun. Instead, she pushed the purse to Jonesy's side of the table.

Jonesy took out the handgun. Cash watched as the older woman turned sideways in her chair so the gun was always pointed away from where they sat. She fiddled with the gun, releasing the cylinder. Tipped the barrel, emptied seven .22 cartridges into her hand. "Right size pistol for a woman to carry." She closed the barrel, put her finger on the trigger and aimed at the opposite wall. She put the gun back into the purse and dumped the .22 shells in after it. "How much money you got there?"

Cash flipped through the bills. Two hundreds. Mostly twenties and some ones. "Maybe three hundred at the most."

"Huh. Not a lot of money for having robbed a bank. Wonder where the rest of it is?"

"Wheaton said they were checking the hotel. I suppose their car, too." She fanned through the money again. "Guess I better give him the purse," she said, while she thought to herself, *I could get a couple good used tires for the truck with this amount of money.*

"When I was a little girl, my gramma told me, be careful what you think. Thoughts are real, they travel out into the world." Jonesy stood up and put her empty bowl in the dish basin on the kitchen counter. "You never know when someone standing right next to you can hear what you're thinking."

Cash looked at Jonesy. Jonesy didn't look back, just rinsed out her bowl and threw some water out the door into the plants that grew in a pot off to the side of the doorway. Cash slid all the money back into the purse. Threw the lipstick and mirror in also. Snapped the purse shut and pushed it away from her.

"I don't think you're going to find Arlis. Probably best to just wait until she finds you." Jonesy reached for Cash's empty bowl. Washed, rinsed and watered the plants again.

Cash left soon after. She stashed the purse behind the car seat again before she drove to the small village of Pine Point. On the drive, she thought about the conversation with Jonesy. Maybe she wouldn't find Arlis. Maybe she'd have to wait for Arlis to find her. But, she figured, in the meantime she could put herself in the vicinity of where they were most likely to connect. Five black-haired kids, riding barefoot in cutoff jeans and T-shirts, raced her down the road on their banana-seat bikes. She honked the horn and stuck her arm out the window to let them know she was turning. They raced on by. She stopped at her friend Bunk's house.

Bunk's mom answered the door. "She went to DL.

130 · MARCIE R. RENDON

Bowling league night." She closed the door, leaving Cash standing on the steps to watch the kids on their bikes. Two of the bigger kids reached out and latched onto either side of the bumper on the rear end of a pickup truck going down the road. The other kids raced to catch up. All were screaming and laughing.

Cash drove back the way she had come but stayed on the main roads instead of driving the back roads through the tamarack. The way was longer but gave her time to think. Wheaton wanted her to find Arlis and bring her in for questioning. Jonesy didn't think Arlis wanted to be found. Cash didn't want to find her and turn her in to Wheaton if it meant Shawnee wasn't going to get to be with her mother. Cash distrusted Jean Borgerud way more than she distrusted Arlis, and she hadn't even met Arlis yet.

As she turned north onto Highway 59, the earlier storm was a thin dark line on the far eastern horizon. Callaway, the first small town on the road, had a population of 209. Nothing was open. Not that in a town of 209 there was anything to be open. Farther up the road, she stopped at the liquor store in Ogema for a pack of cigarettes. "I was looking for Arlis Petterson. Seen her around?" she asked the clerk.

"Can't say as I have," he answered as he handed her the cigarettes and change.

Cash noted that he didn't say he didn't know her.

Cash got gas at the store in the town of White Earth. Asked the cashier behind the counter if she knew where she could find Arlis Petterson. The clerk shook her head no without making eye contact as she counted out change for her. Cash got the feeling that even if she knew Arlis, she wasn't going to give out that information.

Next, Cash stopped at the Red Apple Café in Mahnomen. Slid into a booth. Her friend Debbie was waitressing there. Cash had frequented the café during the period she was tracking down the killer of the woman who had washed in with the spring flood. Debbie had given her information about area churches and kept her fueled with coffee; they had become friends. She was farm-girl pretty. Blond, blue-eyed, with strong legs and arms. Her hair was in a beehive with clips on either side over her ears to hold her hair back, keep it out of diners' plates. She was maybe the only waitress there, no matter what hour of the day, come to think of it.

"Hey! Haven't seen you in ages." Debbie put a cup of coffee on the table in front of Cash. "Where you been?"

"Working."

"Heard they didn't charge you for the incident with the pastor and his crazy wife."

"Nope. Let me go. Self-defense."

"School?"

"Finished out the year. Was hard to concentrate after everything that went down but I passed."

"Still doing field work?"

Cash nodded.

Debbie looked around the empty café, then sat down in the booth across from Cash. Put her chin in her hands as she leaned on her elbows. "Pretty slow today. At least until all the farmhands come in around supper time. Hang around. Find yourself a farmer to marry."

Cash laughed. "I don't think so. They're all hoping for the homecoming queen, not the Indian field worker."

"You still working for the county sheriff?"

"Kinda. He's trying to get me some money from the county commissioners for helping him out. And maybe a work-study thing through the college."

"You should get paid for the work you do. Beats waiting tables, I bet." Debbie gestured around the café. Both women laughed.

"Wheaton has me trying to find this woman, Arlis. She took off after this farmer, Bud Borgerud, was shot. And then I found—" Cash caught herself midsentence. Nils's death wasn't public knowledge yet.

Debbie didn't notice her misstep. "What's the skinny on that? Guy shot as in, like, shot dead? Everyone's talking about the sheriff getting thrown in the trunk by the bank robbers over in Twin Valley, but no one's said anything about a guy murdered."

Cash nodded.

Debbie leaned forward on her elbows. All ears. The biggest news in a town the size of Mahnomen tended to be who got drunk on Friday night and ran in the ditch. News that someone was shot and cops were looking for a woman who was missing could keep the café open a few hours extra for a couple nights. Farmers and their wives would sit and throw the news back and forth across the dining area with different folks vying to be the one with the juiciest pieces of gossip. "First the bank robbed over in Twin Valley and now our own *Helter Skelter* right next door in Norman County."

"Not quite. He was shot. We don't know why. But not a grisly cult murder." Cash flashed on Nils under the corncrib. "Least not that we know of. Borgerud rented his farmhouse out to this woman Arlis and her husband Nils."

"Nils? Wouldn't be Nils Petterson would it?"

"Yeah, that's him."

"He married a girl from around here. Could be Arlis. From over by Strawberry Lake? Heard they had a little girl."

"Yeah, that's her. Girl's not quite school age. She's not talking, not because she can't but more like maybe she's in shock or something. We think her mom headed this way without the little girl for some reason."

"And Nils?"

Cash shrugged in a noncommittal way.

"I can keep an eye out. Keep my ears open. Where's the little girl?"

"In a foster home."

They drank coffee in silence.

Debbie shook her head. "Hard to believe. People getting shot right here. Our boys getting killed in Vietnam. Seems like half my high school class is gone." Tears filled her eyes. She grabbed a paper napkin from the metal container on the table and wiped them away. "I swear to god, I have to stop crying like this."

"What's going on?"

"Oh, my brother got back a couple months ago. The guy is crazy. Sleeps on the floor. A car backfires and he acts like he's back in the jungle. He's staying at the folks' place just out of town here. They're ready to ship him off to the VA down in the Cities or over to Jamestown. Over in North Dakota."

"My brother stayed with me for a while," Cash said. "He slept on the floor too. Stayed stoned most of the time. Or drunk. He re-upped. Said he couldn't take it in the real world. Writes me every few months. Last I heard he's still alive."

"My brother got into a fight with some guy the other night. Stupid pool game at the liquor store in Ogema. Both are vets from what I hear. Some stupid pissing contest over who saw the most action."

Cash had no response. She'd been in her share of bar fights. Never had her nose broken that she knew of. And she knew that the war was doing something to the men who were over there and made it back.

"The guy's last name is Nodin. My parents don't know what to do."

Cash recognized the name Nodin even though she didn't know the guy. She suspected he was the one who killed Lori, left her for dead, and then her body washed up in Ada during the spring flood. She found Lori's people over in North Dakota and her body had been returned to them. But there had been nothing concrete, only drunk gossip, to connect Nodin to her murder. The last she had heard of the elusive Nodin, he was arrested for DUI but the cops had let him go in the morning. She had driven over at Wheaton's suggestion, talked to the Mahnomen police, but apparently the guy was still free and doing damage.

"I've heard of him before. I was at a tire party out at Shell

Lake some months back and my friend Bunk warned me to stay away from him. His brother was all kissy on me but Bunk grabbed me away from him. Everyone there said the Nodin brothers are bad news."

"The one I'm talking about was bad news before he went in the service. He's even worse news now."

The bell over the café door rang as a petite farm wife shepherded two towheaded kids through the door. All three were sunburned.

"Lake season," Debbie said, rising. She was referring to the Valley residents who flocked to the local lakes on the reservation each summer. They stayed in cabins that surrounded the lakes. Some wives and kids whiled away their summer days swimming and floating in black rubber inner tubes; their farmer husbands would arrive on Friday night or early Saturday morning if all the fieldwork was done, or if they had a hired hand to mind the livestock. The men would return to their farms on Sunday night. The small town of Mahnomen was a stopover town on the way to or from the lakes. "Back to work. Good to see you, Cash."

Cash nodded. She finished her coffee and left a dollar under the cup on the table. She waved at Debbie as she left.

Outside the air smelled of damp earth, cut grass and hot pavement. Humidity weighed down the air after the earlier storm. Cash looked to the east. Not a cloud in sight. Nothing brewing to the west except what was going to be a brilliant sunset. She drove toward Twin Valley. Drove past the café in that town. She had to admit to herself she was checking to see if Wheaton's car was parked out front. She still didn't know for certain if he and the waitress there were dating. Four miles out of Twin Valley, she turned around and headed back to Mahnomen and down the road to a corner bar.

She had a beer, played a game of pool against herself. That early in the evening, all the other patrons in the bar were there to drink, not socialize. They were noncommittal when she lied and said she was looking for her cousin Arlis. She drove a few miles down the road to another corner bar. Another beer. Another round of head shaking, no one had seen Arlis. Another game of pool against herself. As the sun dipped in the western horizon she backtracked on the road to Mahnomen and drove down Highway 59 to Ogema.

The Ogema liquor store was the place to be. Sold liquor, hard liquor for takeout and 3.2 beer to drink inside. And it had a pool table. Same clerk was behind the counter as earlier in the day. He slid her beer across the counter toward her. "Still looking for Arlis?"

"Yeah."

"Haven't seen her. What about you, Boots? Seen Arlis around?" he asked a woman sitting at the bar. The woman shook her head no. The two people sitting with her shook their heads no also.

Cash took her beer and put two games' worth of quarters on the pool table. Leaned against the wall and watched a couple guys playing against each other. One was okay, although he'd probably had too much to drink already. The other shooter was barroom good. Probably the kind that got better the more drinks he had. No other people around.

When it was Cash's turn to play, she dropped her quarters, racked the balls so the winner could break.

"Girl's night out?" The guy asked as he broke and three balls dropped. Two stripes and a solid. The belt buckle on his jeans was a solid beaded eagle head. His grin didn't match the sarcasm in his voice or eyes. "I'll give you a head start." He played a solid into the far-right end pocket. His English wasn't that good but he made two more straight-in shots before missing.

Cash slacked off. Some men hated for a woman to be a better pool player than they were. She missed a straight-in shot on purpose and watched his reaction.

"Too bad, girly. Hate to beat a good-lookin' woman."

Cash leaned on her cue and watched him make the rest of his shots until he choked on the eight ball.

He winked. "Givin' you a chance."

Cash nodded. Missed again. On purpose.

The guy made his eight ball and called to the previous player. "Rack 'em up, Jim Beam." And to Cash. "Let me get you a drink." He held up her bottle and hollered to the guy behind the bar. "Another one."

Cash sipped her beer and watched the new guy lose. Her quarters were next. She slid them into the machine and listened to the familiar sound of the balls dropping and rolling to the end of the table. She racked them up and nodded for the winner to break.

"Must be lonely out there tonight. You trying for a second

chance?" His voice implied something other than shooting pool. Tall and slim, he wore the usual well-worn jeans and T-shirt in addition to the beaded belt buckle and a denim vest with round medallions of thunderbirds on each front pocket. His black hair was shoulder length. Ever since AIM, the American Indian Movement, hit the news fighting for Native rights, Indian men and women were growing their hair out. Many wore their short braids wrapped in red cloth to show their solidarity with AIM. This guy's hair wasn't yet long enough to braid.

While she waited for him to chalk his cue stick, she put another round of quarters on the table. This time she gave him a run for his money. But let him drop the eight ball for the win.

"You were sandbagging, huh, girl?" He laughed. "Calvin," he bumped his cue stick to his chest, "owns this table. Hey, Jim Beam, get your girl over here and play partners against us. Finally got a partner who might be able to play." With a wave of his cue stick he indicated Cash. "What's your name, girl?"

Cash looked at him. His eyes were dark, dark brown. The grin and easy moves of his body didn't match the flat darkness of his eyes. "Geraldine." She said the first name that popped into her mind.

"Well, Geraldine, you and me gonna own this table tonight."

After a couple games, Cash was ready to head back to Fargo. She hadn't found Arlis and the other couple were really no match for her or Calvin's playing, although she continued to sandbag.

She watched Calvin sink the eight ball, then unscrewed her cue, held both halves in her hand and said, "Gonna call it a night. Gotta work tomorrow."

"Girl, another three beers and I'll be falling in love. Hang on. Later I can teach you some pocket pool tricks."

Cash glared at him.

"Oooh, hard to get huh. I'm telling you, I'm falling in love."

"Shit man, leave the girl alone," Jim Beam said as he put some quarters in, leaning on the pool table to steady himself. His girlfriend stood with her arm around his waist. Hickeys circled her neck.

At that moment the bar door opened and a new guy walked in. "Holy damn, look what the north wind blew in. Damn, Nodin, thought they'd at least keep you locked up for a few more days."

Oh, Calvin Nodin. Cash flashed on her conversation with Debbie at the Red Apple and Bunk's warning at the spring tire party about the Nodin brothers. She put two and two together.

Calvin laughed. "Call me Houdini. Can't keep a good man down."

"Ain't nothing good about you but your fists. Shit for brains."

"Shush. You'll scare away my new wifey here. Found one who can shoot pool. And drink."

Cash moved away from the pool table, toward the door. Cue stick halves in one hand. Cue case in the other.

Calvin grabbed her arm. "Where you goin', angel? We ain't done here yet. Night's still young. Want you to meet my buddy, Cochise. Cochise, meet my soon-to-be wife, Geraldine." He wrapped his arm around Cash's shoulder. "We were just talking about shackin' up for the night."

Cash ducked down out of his arm and moved again toward the door. Calvin grabbed her waist-length braid and yanked her back toward him. Turned her so she faced him. His eyes were black pinpricks. "I said we ain't done yet."

Cash acquiesced. Slumped her shoulders down. Submission. As he dropped her braid, she took a step back, dropped the cue case and one half of the cue stick to the ground. Without pausing, she grabbed the remaining cue stick with both hands and hit Calvin square across the temple. He dropped, out cold. Cash picked up the other half of her cue stick and case and walked out the door. Behind her she heard whoops and hollers of "Damn, he's out cold." And "Who the fuck was that?"

Cash jumped in her Ranchero. Her hand shook so bad she could barely get the key in the ignition. Her legs shook too as she put in the clutch, slipped the vehicle in gear, stepped on the gas and reversed out of the parking lot. Two miles out of town, with no cars following her that she could see in the rearview mirror, she pulled over, opened the car door, leaned out and puked. The smell of stale beer gave her the dry heaves. She leaned back into the truck and breathed in the cool night air. Willed her breathing to slow down. She rinsed her mouth out with stale coffee from the thermos sitting on the passenger seat. Spit it out onto the pavement. Lit a cigarette. Put the truck back in gear and headed to Fargo.

So that's Nodin. With speculation and gossip as evidence, there was no way to charge him for the murder of Lori. Although after her encounter with him tonight, Cash was now certain he was her killer. Clearly, he was a man on his way to Stillwater, where he'd either be a model prisoner or do half his time in the hole, in segregation. Anyone that angry, that messed up, was a prison sentence waiting to happen. *Damn, I need a beer.* Cash veered around a deer carcass that lay on the shoulder of the roadway.

The fear she felt when Nodin grabbed her braid and pulled her back was new. She was used to being in tough situations and trusted herself to get out of them. But seeing real insanity up close with the pastor and his wife had changed her perception of safety in the world. Not that she had ever really had safety, but she had always trusted herself before. But when she, as a reflex to protect herself, threw the knife at the pastor and it stuck in his neck—when he pulled it out and blood spurted all over—that was a scene that replayed over and over in her mind. That and the image of his crazy wife chasing her down the road, screaming at the top of her lungs, while Cash ran with the baby, getting herself and the child to safety. Now she always slept with the light on in her apartment. She didn't trust her intuition the way she used to. She scanned the area around her before getting into or exiting her car. She drank too much even while she told herself it wasn't a problem.

As she drove south, the Big Dipper hung in the sky behind her. The Milky Way glittered like a snowstorm at the edge of the universe. Cash chain-smoked with the window down, the night breeze blowing through the cab of the Ranchero. She let the wind empty her mind of all thought.

"NO ONE'S SEEN HER." CASH once again sat on the wooden bench in Wheaton's jail. "I checked in Callaway, closest place to Strawberry Lake, where everyone says she's from. Mahnomen, Ogema. No one's seen her. I had a run-in with that guy Nodin in Ogema. Bet money at the pool table he's the one who killed Lori."

Wheaton was busy at his desk. The dog Gunner lazed at his feet. "What kind of run-in?"

"Just an argument at the pool table. He's the kinda guy that just looks for trouble."

"We don't have enough to bring him in on that woman's death."

"Just a matter of time before he does something that gets him caught. Guys like him shouldn't be out walking around. Breathing air the rest of us need."

"Be kind. Can't do anything until he messes up good. By the way, Shawnee went back to Borgerud's."

Cash sighed. "Why? Don't answer."

Wheaton sorted through and signed some papers on his desk. Cash made ugly faces at Gunner.

Wheaton glanced at Cash. "Do you remember seeing a purse in the alley when we nabbed the female?"

"A purse?" Cash kept her eyes on Gunner.

"Twila, that's the woman's name, said she had a purse she dropped in the alley when we grabbed her."

Cash didn't answer. She didn't know why she was avoiding the question. In her mind she saw the small wad of cash, the pink lipstick, the gun. She didn't know why but she shook her head no without making eye contact with Wheaton.

"Probably picked up by one of the tramps that travel along the tracks." He went back to his stack of papers.

Cash stuck her tongue out at Gunner and got up to leave. "Guess I'll go see if I can get a real job. Something that pays more than gas money."

Wheaton put down his pen. "We should know after the next county commissioner meeting whether they approve my request for some money for you. I also talked to the college. You might be able to do an internship here at the county jail through the criminal justice program. They would pay work-study during the school year."

Cash turned back around. "I can quit school?"

Wheaton stood up. "No. Of course not. You'd get college credit for work here. A few hours a week. You finish school. It would be a paid work-study internship."

Cash turned on her heels and left.

She drove aimlessly around the county. Up and down gravel roads. Looking at the fields. Soybeans and sugar beets were popping out of the ground. Migrants, who traveled from the Rio Grande Valley in Texas each spring to sleep in substandard shacks, were out in the sun hoeing beets. They worked from sunup to sundown in family groups. Backbreaking work. Hot sun burning down on you all day. No shade whatsoever out in the middle of a field.

It was a job she had tried once and quit. Early one

morning, as the sky was changing from nighttime black to dawn blue, her foster father had driven her to the farmer's homestead and hired her out for the day. Cash had watched money change hands, money she never saw. As the sun peeked over the eastern horizon, the farmer had loaded everyone up into the back of a grain truck and hauled them out to his field. The other workers, mistaking her in her Nativeness for one of them, had tried talking to her in Spanish, to which she could only reply, "No hablo español."

She had hoed one row of beets and then walked the four miles back to the farmer's house and told him she had a driver's license and to reach out to her when he needed someone in the fall to drive beet truck. Her insurgence had cost her a beating and a summer spent throwing hay bales. But to her mind, it was worth it.

Cash stopped at the bar in Halstad and asked the bartender if he knew of anyone hiring. "Not today. You might want to try over at the farm co-op." As she turned to leave, he added, "I did hear that Mrs. Borgerud was looking for a farm manager. With Bud gone, she needs some help managing all their acreage. They got land all the way from here to the Dakota side of Grand Forks."

Cash just looked at him before she said, "She's not going to hire someone that looks like me."

"Reckon you're right. But whoever she hires will be looking for workers."

Outside, Cash lit a cigarette and looked up and down the street. Nothing was moving in the town. The other bar across the street had one car parked on the side street. The potato house on the block would be busy in the fall but sat empty now. She watched the occasional car drive down Highway 75. Everything seemed to be at a standstill. No real work. No sign of Arlis. Shawnee back at Borgerud's. Couldn't throw Nodin in jail although she did wonder if he was in the hospital. Wheaton either didn't have a girlfriend or was keeping her a secret from Cash.

Cash walked to her Ranchero, but instead of getting in she leaned against its door, still facing the bar across the street, deep in thought. She didn't know why she had lied to Wheaton about the purse. *Okay, I didn't lie*, she told herself. *I just didn't tell him.*

"Got myself in a jam this time," she said out loud, as she turned and got into her truck.

Once again, she drove the back roads of farm country. She found herself at Borgerud's farmstead. Thought of the two dead men she had found. Grass had started to grow in the space between the tire tracks of the driveway. The lawn wasn't mowed. The upstairs curtains were pulled shut and the kitchen curtains were askew. She sat in her truck, window rolled down, and took in the farmyard and surrounding acreage. The field she plowed had been harrowed and was ready for planting. It seemed like ages ago. The corncrib looked like it was ready to fall over. The barn, same.

Slowly, she got out of the Ranchero. Breathed in the afternoon air. Clover was growing somewhere nearby. Not too hot of a day. Not too cool. Birds flitted from branch to branch of the chokecherry trees. A shiny silver hasp, secured with an equally shiny padlock, was screwed into the worn wood doorframe that had paint chips falling off. Anyone with any sincere intention could easily unscrew the hasp or break the wood frame with a crowbar. But in a country culture where folks never bothered to lock their doors, folks would respect the lock on this one.

She walked around the house. Crickets and grasshoppers flew out of the tall grass with each step. At the back of the house, two wooden doors sat at a diagonal against the foundation of the house. A storm cellar.

Before electricity ran in the Valley, folks used their storm cellars for storing root vegetables, canned goods and homemade wine. Even after electricity arrived, the storm cellars were where families ran when funnel clouds appeared on the western horizon. Cash recalled one story of a family whose home was picked up by a tornado with a young boy in it. According to the local story, he woke up naked in a field two miles over. Traumatized but alive.

Flattened grass indicated someone had walked there recently. Always curious, Cash pulled up one of the doors and peered into the unknown. She could make out four stone steps leading into darkness. She threw open the other door. More light streamed down, and she could make out more stone stairs and a dirt floor. Not expecting an answer, she hollered before venturing downward. "Hello?"

At the bottom step, she stood and waited for her eyes to adjust to the darkness. The walls were made with large rocks, no doubt hauled from farms where the early frost melt each spring pushed rocks up out of the frozen ground. The space was cool and smelled of fresh dirt. On a makeshift wooden shelf was a flashlight, a kerosene lantern and canned goods. Cash turned on the flashlight and looked around the space. White cobwebs hung down from and across the ceiling, which were the first floor's wood floor joists. An army cot sat against the opposite wall, with a worn quilt and flat pillow on it.

"What the hell?" Cash asked out loud. The presence of someone else in the space raised the hair on her arms and she ran up the stone stairs into sunlight. Out in the fresh air, she stood bent over, hands on knees, breathing heavily. She stood and looked down into the cellar. No one was there. There was no one in the yard but the grasshoppers. But someone had been sleeping in the root cellar. Hadn't Wheaton checked the cellar the day she found Bud? She tried to remember if he had walked around the house, inspected the property. She couldn't remember. She had been so focused on Shawnee, and she hadn't thought to check the cellar in any of the previous times she'd been out here. Her mind raced. Had Bud's killer been hiding down there? Had Nils's killer been hiding? Why would someone hide in a root cellar to wait to kill someone? She realized she was still holding the flashlight. She would have to go back down and return it to the shelf. Exactly where she had found it.

She took deep breaths to gather the courage to head back down the steps when she heard an engine nearby. She ran around the corner of the house and saw a two-toned car kicking up dust, heading across the pasture behind the barn toward the main road. The car had a good quarter-mile run on her. All she could do was stand and watch it climb the small ditch down the road and take off, spewing road gravel and dust behind it. No way to tell the license plate or who was driving. Cash had a momentary thought of jumping in the Ranchero and chasing it down, but the other vehicle had too good a head start. Instead, she watched it speed away.

When the car was nothing but a speck of dust on the western horizon, she returned the flashlight to the cellar. Closed the doors to the hideaway. She walked through more tall grass to get to the dilapidated barn. A walk around the barn revealed a sliding back door that at one time could be opened to let the cows out to pasture. Tire tracks indicated the car had been parked in the barn and driven across a path in the pasture that was indiscernible from the road and driveway.

A quick inspection of the barn told her nothing other than a car had been parked near the back door. She closed the sliding door, walked to the front of the barn and opened the door there. There were footprints on the floor that indicated someone had walked out of the barn to the house. Cash lined her foot up against one of the prints. It was about the size of her foot.

Mrs. Borgerud? Arlis? Why would either of them be out here? Or one of the migrants who was tired of the run-down shacks the farmers provided? Cash sat on the front steps of the house and pondered the situation. Nothing came to mind. No intuitive inspirations. Finally, she stood, brushed the dirt off the seat of her pants and was about to head into Ada to see what Wheaton thought about it all.

Instead, she reached behind the car seat and pulled the gun out the purse. It fit the palm of her hand. She recalled Jonesy opening the gun chamber. She fumbled a bit at first but then got it open and was able to load three bullets, the same .22s she used in the rifle she kept behind her car seat.

She imagined that at one time a whole row of fence posts had kept cattle out of the yard. Now, a lone wooden post, graying with age, stood by itself. She stretched out her arm and took aim at it. Pulled the trigger. The backfire jerked her hand upward. The next shot she cradled her right hand with her left to steady her aim. She hit the post, more by luck than skill, she figured. As she looked at the splintered post, she briefly wondered who had held the rifle that killed Bud. Was Nils shot? Gunshots that no one heard except, probably, Shawnee? If Cash heard a gunshot out here, early in the morning, she would guess that some kid was out doing rifle practice, shooting at rabbits. Growing up in the Valley, that would be her first thought, not that someone was getting killed. It was too much to think about. She unloaded the gun and put it and the remaining shell back in the purse. She looked at the money but didn't take it out. Put it all back with her rifle and cue stick and headed back to Ada.

WHEATON'S SECRETARY LOOKED UP FROM her typing when Cash entered the jail office. "Wheaton's out on patrol. Or so he said. Think he headed over to Twin Valley again," she said with a wink when Cash asked where he was.

"I'll swing by tomorrow or the next. I gotta find some work. And I need some food."

"I got half a roast beef sandwich left from lunch if you want," the secretary offered.

"Nah, I'll run to the Drive-Inn in Halstad. Get a burger and a malt."

Cash gassed up at the Standard station. The day spent driving had put her tank at less than a quarter full. The attendant checked the air in the tires and told her they were good to go. She headed west again to the Halstad Drive-Inn, where she pulled in next to the same pickup with the same smartass sitting at the wheel. No girls were with him. He flashed a grin when he saw her.

"You following me?" he asked through his open window. "This could be your summer of love. Looks like I'm free tonight."

Cash was sorry she had both windows rolled down. "Find someone your own age, kid."

"I did. Now I'm going for experience."

Just then the waitress appeared at Cash's window. "What can I get cha?" she asked, pencil and check pad at the ready.

"Burger and fries. And a babysitter for the kid next door."

"Ignore him. He chases anything with a skirt on. I would say he's harmless, but he's left a string of broken hearts at the high school. Don't know what girls see in him myself. I'll be right out with your order." She tucked the pencil behind her ear and headed back inside.

"She thinks I'm conceited." The guy said it loud enough for everyone nearby to hear. In a lower voice to Cash he said, "Can't be. I'm perfect."

Cash shook her head and tried to ignore him.

"I got a new job today," he continued. "Going to manage the Borgerud farm."

Cash looked at him in disbelief.

"She needs a man"—he sat up straighter in his truck—"to help her out. I been working my dad's farm for more than half my life. Know what needs to be done and how to do it. Don't need a college degree to farm."

"You," she said. "You're going to be her manager? Are you even out of high school?"

He had changed from flirt to smug confidence. "Bet I'm as old as you, girl. When did you graduate? Heard you left the county and moved to Fargo. I been asking around about you ever since I saw you hiding out at the funeral." He paused and grinned at her. Then went back to smug. "I could hire you on. Saw your name in the checkbook when Jean showed me the scope of the job. And people her husband had hired on before. You're Cash Blackbear, right? Not too many Indian women around here doing field work. Figured it must be you. Heard you people are good workers when you're not drinking." He reverted to flirting. "You and me could be a team. Do some plowing. Catch my drift?"

Cash stared out her windshield. She felt like turning the key in the ignition and leaving without her food. She had heard the thing about drinking a hundred times. Maybe a thousand. Invariably, anyone she worked for asked, did she drink? If so, how much? She had never missed a day of work. There had been times when she showed up with the smell of beer reeking from her pores, but that was no different than many of the men she worked alongside.

She glanced over at the guy. He was mimicking what he'd heard his dad and others say. He had to be her age or younger. Even if he was her same age, he was still younger. Life had treated him well. He had a confidence she herself had never felt. He was sure of his place in the world and had his daddy's money to get him what he wanted. She needed to work. He worked because he could and his daddy's farm would become his. She wanted to keep an eye out for Shawnee. He probably didn't know the little girl existed. She needed to know who shot Mr. Borgerud. Probably all he knew was that Bud's dying gave him a job. She wanted to know who killed Nils. And she needed to figure out who was camped out in the cellar of the old homestead. She turned to face him. "What's your name?"

"Jeff Johanson. I think you drove grain truck for my dad a few times. We have the biggest farm in these parts. Next to Borgerud's."

Cash nodded. She recognized the name if not the guy sitting in the truck next to hers. "What kind of work you need done?"

"Need a couple folks to head up toward Crookston and get the spuds in the ground."

She shook her head. "I only work the fields around here."

"Got a north forty that needs someone to run a disc over it. And another field that's almost ready to bale."

"I can disc. Could swing by tomorrow, just tell me where."

"You know where the old homestead is? Where they

found Bud? Damnedest thing, huh?" He didn't wait for an answer. "It's a couple miles north of there. Just follow the gravel road north from the farm road. I'll have the machinery in the field ready to go, early."

"How did you get the job?" Cash couldn't stop herself from asking.

"I stopped by to offer my condolences again." He used his flirting voice to say it. "Offered help if she needed it. She told me she was looking for a farm manager. Convinced her I was man enough for the job." He flexed the muscles of the arm he had resting on his open car window.

The waitress arrived with Cash's food. "He giving you a hard time? I can get the manager to tell him to leave. He hangs around here all the time. Usually he's got a truck full of jailbait teenyboppers."

Cash shook her head. "Nah. It's all right. Sometimes you gotta just ignore ignorance."

An older model Dodge Dart pulled into the Drive-Inn filled with giggling teenage girls.

"Here come the cheerleaders," the waitress said. "Now he'll leave you alone. Like a rat after cheese."

Cash ate her burger and fries and watched the laughter, flirting, hair flipping and seductive adjusting of halter tops by the girls vying for Jeff's attention. He seemed to have enough to go around. When the waitress came to retrieve the metal tray that rested on her car door, Jeff turned his attention from the girls and said to Cash, "See you in the mornin' then."

She nodded and left.

At least she'd found some paying work, she thought as she headed out. She turned up the radio station and listened to a heartbroke guy sing goodbye to his country darling. The music made her thirsty for a beer. She looked to the west to gauge what time it was. With the sun hours from the horizon she figured she had the rest of the late afternoon and evening before she could realistically show up at the Casbah for a drink and pool.

The first thing she decided to do was drive into Ada and talk to Miss Dackson. See if she had any luck finding Arlis. It was the social worker's job after all to locate a child's parents, if possible.

While the county offices were in the same building as the jail and courtrooms, the social worker, at least during Cash's lifetime, had mostly lived and worked from her hotel room. For the first time, Cash wondered if the county paid for her hotel room so Miss Dackson would have a place to store foster kids between homes. She nodded at the hotel clerk as she entered. He side-eyed her, looked nervous, then quickly rifled through papers like he had important work to tend to.

At the landing at the top of the heavily carpeted stairs she knocked on the thick oak door of room 204. She heard a chair scrape across a hardwood floor and the click of heels walking toward the door. "Cash, what brings you here?" Miss Dackson asked, surprise in her voice, as she opened the door, closed it and removed the chain lock, then reopened the door, but not wide enough for Cash to feel like she was being invited in.

"You know that Wheaton asked me to try and find Shawnee's mother. I've been to towns over at White Earth and folks haven't seen her lately. Have you?"

"Well, no." Miss Dackson leaned against the doorframe. "I mean, I haven't seen her either. I drove over to Strawberry Lake yesterday"—*We must have missed each other on the road*, Cash thought as Dackson continued—"to where it says in the records Arlis last lived before moving over here with Nils. Rest his soul." Miss Dackson made the sign of the cross. "I can't believe some Indians are still living in tar paper shacks. And they wonder why the state is moving kids to nice, Christian homes."

Cash, rather than meet Miss Dackson's eyes, focused her gaze down the hallway as the woman continued. "No one admitted to seeing her at all lately. If they're not lying to protect her. I'm beginning to wonder if she's even alive."

"Of course she's alive."

The certainty in Cash's voice made Miss Dackson stand up straight. "How can you be so sure? Everyone else who was at the farmhouse is dead. Except Shawnee. If they"—she threw her hands up in the air—"killed everyone else, why did they, whoever did it, leave her alive?" She paused to sort through her own thoughts. "I suppose because she's a kid. But if they killed Arlis, where is her body? Shawnee must be in shock because she still isn't talking." She leaned back into the doorframe. "I hope Arlis is alive. I was hoping I'd find her and then we could tell Shawnee about her dad." She paused. "If she doesn't already know. I hope to God she didn't witness her dad or Mr. Borgerud get killed." She crossed herself again.

"She's alive," Cash repeated. She stared down the long hallway of the hotel, which was wallpapered with a dark-green floral print. The oak woodwork was dark as was each door down the hallway. While Cash knew there were windows in each hotel room, the only light in the hallway was a single lightbulb hidden inside a glass globe. It reminded her of a scary movie, she couldn't remember which one, that she had seen on a black-and-white TV screen. She looked back at the social worker. "How's Shawnee? Wheaton asked me to check in on her too, but Mrs. Borgerud isn't making that easy."

Miss Dackson stood straight again. Pursed her lips before saying, "Well, you know, Cash, you're just barely not a kid yourself. I don't know why Wheaton has you doing a grown-up's job. I'm the county social worker. It's my job to look after Shawnee just like I had to look out for you. Abandoned by your mom. Couldn't find your dad. Not that we can leave kids with just their dads anyways. Good Christian homes. Two parents. I have to see that Shawnee's in the best place to be taken care of. Like I said, those Indians over on the reservation are living in tar paper shacks. They could move into government housing, but no, they'd rather live in the woods."

Cash felt her pocket. Her cigarette pack was there. Instead of lighting up, she took a deep breath. Looked back down the hallway before saying, "I'm the one who found her." After a slight pause, she added while giving Miss Dackson a cold stare, "And like we both know, Wheaton asked me to make sure she's okay."

"I suppose it can't hurt. Let me call Mrs. Borgerud and

arrange a visit." She glanced at the slim watch on her right wrist. "You could drop by there now before the supper hour."

Cash nodded. She stood waiting for Miss Dackson to go make the call. Miss Dackson stood waiting for her to leave. Cash had more experience at holding her ground than the social worker.

Finally, "I'll be right back." Miss Dackson turned and closed the door, and Cash, who leaned against the wall in the dark hallway, heard the click of heels heading back across the hotel floor. Through the thick door she heard the murmur of Miss Dackson's voice, then the click of heels back toward the door. Cash stood up as she heard the social worker reach the door.

"If you head out there right now, you can see Shawnee for half an hour."

THREE COUNTRY SONGS AND TWO cigarettes later, Cash pulled into the Borgerud farmstead and saw Shawnee sitting all by herself at the picnic table in the yard. The other thing Cash noticed was Jeff Johanson's pickup truck parked in the driveway. She noted that it was not out by the barn or farm equipment in the yard, but near the house.

"Hey, Shawnee, were you sent out here to wait for me?"

Shawnee looked at her with big brown eyes. She nodded yes. Her right leg started swinging and she sat on her hands, which grasped the picnic table bench as if to hold her in place.

"Are you up to talking yet?"

Shawnee's leg swung faster. Her hands gripped tighter.

"That's okay. You don't have to talk if you don't want to." Cash sat in silence with the young girl. Both looked off into the distance. Watched a barn swallow swoop across the yard. Listened to a woodpecker that neither could see. Watched small white butterflies flit around.

Cash spoke again. "I'm still looking for your mom. I went over to White Earth but no one seems to have seen her. And I went back to where you lived. It seems someone's been sleeping in the storm cellar. Any idea who that would be?"

Shawnee's eye's widened and she shook her head no.

At that moment, Jeff, the new farm manager, walked out of the house. The screen door slammed behind him as he used both hands to tuck his shirt into his blue jeans. Cash had been with enough men to know that the tucking in of the shirt signified that recently the shirt had been off. And most likely other pieces of clothing as well.

Jeff caught her eye. Ran his fingers through his hair to smooth it down. He grinned like a boy caught with his hand in the cookie jar but with no guilt or shame for his behavior. "Hard work being a farm manager," he said over his shoulder as he hopped in his pickup. Out the window he said, "I'll have that disc out in the field for you in the morning," and pulled out of the driveway.

Cash stared after him. Finally, she returned her focus to Shawnee. "Listen, Shawnee, I need to know that you're okay. Does Mrs. Borgerud spank you?"

Shawnee shook her head no.

"Does she put soap in your mouth?"

Another no.

"Give you enough food?"

A tiny "yeah" escaped Shawnee's mouth.

Afraid of shutting her down again, and hoping she would say more, Cash instinctively didn't acknowledge the soft word.

"Make you clean the house?"

No words, just a nod.

"But she's not beating you?"

Another tiny headshake.

"All right." Cash paused, saw the shadow of Mrs. Borgerud behind the closed screen door. "I'm gonna need to go. I'm doing what I can to find your mom. You just hang tight, okay?"

A tiny "okay."

"Go ahead and go back in. I'll stop by in a couple days to check on you again."

From the picnic bench, Cash watched the small girl walk slowly back to the house. At the screen door she turned and gave a small wave before she disappeared inside.

Goddamn men. Damn social workers. Cash ran through the whole list of folks she wanted to damn to hell as she got back into the Ranchero and drove away. Social workers who took kids and put them in "good" homes where kids were made do adult field work or clean entire houses while biological children watched Saturday morning cartoons. Kids beaten for minor infractions of rules that were never fully explained until some foster parent exploded in rage. She damned to hell all the foster mothers and fathers of homes where she herself had lived. She damned to hell all the men who called themselves fathers but forced hands up thighs and slid hands down backs. To hell with them all. *Has Jeff been sleeping with Jean this whole time? For how long? She has to be at least twice his age.* Cash remembered back to when she first saw Jeff at the Drive-Inn. He had said something about *Peyton Place* right there in Halstad. *Was he referring to himself and Mrs. Borgerud? Damn.* Cash hit the steering wheel.

She had been driving aimlessly on back country roads, trying to sort through everything that had happened. Who killed the two men? Where was Arlis? Did she kill them? Did Jeff kill them? She could imagine him sleeping with Jean but killing seemed a little out of his reach. Her mind swam with thoughts about all that had happened, and apparently was happening, since she found Mr. Borgerud's body.

When the rusted-out Ford Fairlane pulled alongside her on the dusty road it took her by surprise. Nodin, hand on steering wheel, leaned across his empty passenger seat. His dark face contorted in rage. "Hey, bitch, pull over. Think you can fuck with me."

Where the hell did he come from? Cash hit the gas. Pulled ahead. *How the hell did he find me way out here?* She rapidly scanned the countryside. Deep in her own thoughts, she had left Norman County and was now in Mahnomen County where she could see the Mahnomen water tower in the distance. No other car on the road. No tractors in the beet and potato fields that went on for miles. Nor a farmhouse in sight. Cash glanced in her rearview mirror. Nodin appeared bigger than she remembered. He leaned forward as his big hands gripped the steering wheel. He sneered, his face contorted in rage. Her first thought was to get back to Ada. She didn't need to be somewhere no one knew her.

At the next crossroad, she took the turn without slowing, spewing gravel. The Ranchero fishtailed and she had to work to keep the truck out of the ditch. She headed back toward safety, toward Ada. Nodin followed. Dust billowed in the air behind both vehicles. Nodin rammed the Ranchero from behind. Cash jerked forward, whiplashed back. She tightened her hands on the steering wheel, fought to keep the Ranchero on the road. She glanced in the rearview mirror. Nodin was trying to pull alongside her.

She pulled into the middle of the road, intent on keeping him behind her. She wouldn't stand a chance if he got ahead of her and blocked the road or drove her off it. The Fairlane had more horsepower than the Ranchero so she knew she couldn't outrun him. He continued to hit the Ranchero from behind. Nodin would slow up, then gun his car forward into hers. The Ranchero jerked forward each time and Cash had all she could do to keep it on the road.

Cash looked frantically back and forth between the rearview mirror and the road ahead. Her heart dropped. A pickup truck was coming toward them. Cash stayed in the middle of the road until the last second, then she moved enough to the right to let the pickup pass. Staring wide-eyed from the pickup was Jeff. As soon as he passed, she pulled back into the middle of the road. All without lifting her foot from the gas. The Ranchero stayed on the road.

In the rearview mirror, she saw Jeff drive past Nodin, turn

into the ditch, and come back at them while he continued to drive in the shallow trench. His truck jounced up and down and he swerved into a stubble corn field just in time to miss a field driveway.

"Shit." Cash thought he was going to help her, but instead he sped past both vehicles, pulled onto the road in front of Cash and kept going.

Nodin rammed the Ranchero again. Over the roar of both engines and the wind rushing through the vehicle, Cash could hear, "Pull over bitch. I'll kill you. Fuckin' whore," followed by a string of more obscenities.

Time stopped. With adrenaline pulsing through her body, Cash continued to grip the steering wheel. Kept her foot pressed on the gas pedal. Her mind was on autopilot trying to keep the maniac behind her while keeping the Ranchero on the road. Crossroads whipped past. When she dared to glance, the speedometer needle was buried on the right side of the dial, jumping, flickering as she kept her foot on the gas. Dirt fields, plowed fields, fields where green was just popping out of the ground went by in a blur. No other vehicles came at her.

She saw the Ada water tower miles ahead across the flat plane of the prairie. If she could make it into town, she might get out of this alive. The Ranchero jerked as once again the Fairlane rammed her from behind.

Cash glanced in the rearview mirror. The wind from his open windows blew Nodin's black hair away from his face. Strands of it flew out the driver's window. His hands gripped the steering wheel. His eyes spewed hatred. He was laughing. Enjoying tormenting her. Enjoying the chase. Confident he would win. A cold shiver ran down Cash's back, made her whole body shake slightly as she kept moving forward. She didn't know what else to do.

In the midst of the chaos and fear, with her attention single-mindedly focused on the road in front of her and the maniac behind, Cash couldn't integrate the high-pitched wail of the siren. It wasn't until she saw the flashing red lights in her rearview mirror that she realized there was a cop car behind Nodin.

She jerked her eyes back in front of her. Half a mile ahead, Jeff was standing in the middle of the road, his pickup parked in the ditch. His arms waved frantically, signaling her to turn onto the crossroad next to him. Cash, against every instinct that told her she was headed for a rollover, did as instructed. She fought the wheel to keep the Ranchero upright as she braked, leaned as if her small body could keep the truck upright, and despite her fear, took the corner at top speed. She braked as soon as possible. The dust behind her was too thick to see what happened to Nodin. When the air cleared, she could see Jeff's pickup about a quarter of a mile behind her. Wheaton's cruiser, lights still flashing, was parked diagonally across the road. He and Jeff were standing in the road, both pointing at Nodin's car, which was resting on its roof a football field's length into the field. When Cash had braked, the pink purse slid forward from under the seat. She kicked it back under with her heel and got out of her truck.

Cash felt dust on her tongue when she gulped for air. She

doubled over to catch her breath. Stood up quickly, afraid that Nodin would crawl out of the wreckage of his car and run across the field with all intents to kill her. Nothing happened. The dust settled. The silence of the country descended on the road and fields around her. A red-winged blackbird landed on the road a few feet away and pecked at a bug or worm on the road. A grasshopper hopped. She could hear the murmur of Jeff and Wheaton's voices as they carried through the air.

Cash looked at the carnage down the road. She watched the two men walk out to Nodin's car. Even from the distance, Cash could see Wheaton had his gun out. She had never seen him remove it from its holster or use it in all the years she had known him. The men approached the overturned car, one on each side, and stooped over to peer inside. Both men stood up and looked around the field. Cash's heart jumped in her chest. Clearly, Nodin wasn't in the car. She scanned the field. Didn't see anyone running toward her or away from her. Then, Jeff pointed in one direction and he and Wheaton headed farther across the field. Another ten feet or so, Wheaton bent down. Cash couldn't make out what he was looking at. Jeff hollered, "Cash!" and waved her over.

Still shaking, Cash walked the distance. It didn't occur to her to get into the Ranchero and drive. Down the gravel road she saw where she had made the sharp turn and gravel had spewed off the road to reveal smooth clay. Another set of tire tracks went straight across the road, skipped the ditch, and flew into the field.

She walked into the ditch. Ditch grass scratched her bare

ankles. Walked across the dirt clods of the plowed field to where Wheaton and Jeff stood. Nodin's body lay crumpled in the dirt facedown. She looked back toward his car. The windshield was shattered with a body-sized hole in the middle of it.

"What the hell did you do to piss him off? Who is that?" Jeff spit out.

Cash looked at Wheaton. "That's Nodin."

"Who the hell is Nodin?" asked Jeff. His face, already white, was drained of color. He no longer looked like the cocky young man who had walked out of Mrs. Borgerud's back screen door just a few hours ago tucking his shirt into his pants and buckling his belt.

"Trouble," was Wheaton's reply. "You okay?" he asked Cash.

"Always," Cash answered, although she had her hands shoved in her jeans pockets to hide the shaking coursing through her whole body.

"Wanna tell me what happened?"

"Wanna get me a hot roast beef sandwich?"

Jeff, his tidy, rural farm life jerked upside down, turned in a circle before looking at them both like they were crazy. "You guys, there's a dead body in the field."

"Son, run back into town and get Doc Felix out here to pick up Nodin and take him to the morgue. See if the Standard station can send a tow truck out to get the car?" Wheaton reached into his back pocket, pulled out his leather billfold, extracted a twenty and held it out to Jeff, who stared at Wheaton's hand. "Here. Take it, for gas. I appreciate you coming to get me. Sorry you had to see this.

I'm going to take her to get something to eat. Find out what happened." He stuffed the twenty into Jeff's hand. "I'll swing by your dad's place when I get back. You're still living at home?"

Jeff nodded. Turned in a circle again, before facing both of them, looking from one calm face to the other. Stuffed the bill into his jeans pocket.

"You okay to drive?" Wheaton asked Cash, "or you gonna ride with me?"

"I'll drive."

Wheaton and Jeff walked back to their vehicles. Cash trudged back across the field, up the ditch and down the road to her pickup. Turned it around and followed Wheaton's cruiser east across the flat plain to the café in Twin Valley. She chain-smoked all the way there.

While sitting in the café waiting for the hot roast beef sandwich, Cash told Wheaton about her run-in with Nodin at the Ogema liquor store. She left out the part where she clocked him with the cue stick. Said one of his friends must have told Nodin about the Ranchero she drove. Only way he would know it was her driving when he spotted her on the back roads.

After the sandwiches were half eaten, Wheaton wiped crumbs off his mouth before speaking. "I was parked at a crossroad east of town, only a quarter of a mile from you. Kids come out this way after school to drag race down these farm roads. No farms for miles so they think they're safe. I saw the cloud of dust you and Nodin were making. I was going to turn on the flashers and head that direction when

Jeff pulled up. He rolled to a stop and screamed at me that some crazy, drunk Indian was trying to run you off the road." Wheaton said, "I hollered back for him to get the hell back there. To try and cut you all off. I drove straight across some farmer's beet field. Good thing we haven't had rain lately. I'd be stuck out there in the mud and . . ." He stopped talking, leaned back in the booth and shook his head. "At least the kid had enough sense to listen to me."

They finished their meal in silence. After, Wheaton got in his cruiser and headed to the basement of the hospital to check on Doc Felix and his retrieval of the body. Cash realized she hadn't said anything about her visit with Shawnee. She got in the Ranchero and headed to the Casbah.

The sun rose quietly on the eastern horizon, bringing daylight to the dew-glistened prairie. Birds flew soundlessly through the air. A pocket gopher scurried across the road as Cash drove to the Borgerud field she was contracted to disc. She watched in her rearview mirror where the gopher dipped into a mound of dirt at the edge of the ditch on the other side of the road. She recalled how she made extra money one summer trapping pocket gophers. The county paid twenty-five cents for a pair of pocket gopher feet. The county was full of gophers and farmers who wanted them gone.

Cash had begged a foster brother to give her a set of steel traps. Each morning after her other chores were finished, she would walk the country roads until she found a gopher mound. She would set a trap down into the mound, attach a stick to the trap wire to prevent the gopher from dragging the trap back into the hole. She would walk around until she found the secondary mound. She knew pocket gophers lived a solitary life underground, so she would set another trap. She would get the little tunnel rats coming or going.

At the end of the summer, when she was moved to another home, another school, another family, she had to leave the traps behind, but Cash had made a killing for one summer.

Jeff was sitting in his pickup truck waiting for her when she reached the field with the John Deere tractor and disc ready to go. He jumped out and was at her door before she could shut the engine off.

He grabbed hold of the door ledge of the open window. "Jeezus H. Chriiist. What the hell was that about yesterday?" His faced turned red as he stared at her, waiting for an answer.

When Cash didn't respond, he continued. "Then you and the old man leave me to deal with a dead body and try to explain to Gus at the Standard station why there's a car in the middle of a field with a dead guy next to it and you and Wheaton run off to eat roast beef sandwiches someplace. What the hell." He slammed the flat of his hand against her car door.

"What did Wheaton tell you?"

"Not a goddamn enough."

"Calm down."

"Calm down? I thought you were going to run me over taking the corner like that. Or go flying off the road. Then that . . . that . . ." Jeff sputtered, drops of spit escaping from between his teeth. "That guy, his car flew off the road. Fuck me, bam, fucker flew right through the windshield. Looked like a scarecrow flying through the air." His eyes were wide. His face red with anger. His hands clenched her window frame. "I'm gonna have nightmares for the next twenty years. Goddamn scarecrow flying through the air."

"Can I get out?" Cash wiped a bit of spit off her cheek.

Jeff backed up enough for her to open the door and step out.

"This is the right field, right?"

Jeff stared at her. "You're scary, you know that?"

Cash lit a cigarette. Blew the smoke in his face. "What are you doing with Jean Borgerud?"

"What's that got to do with the price of wheat? That guy was trying to run you off the road . . ."

"Kill me." She blew more smoke at him.

"Now he's dead and you ask me about Jean?"

"What are you doing sleeping with someone old enough to be your ma?"

Jeff's angry red face turned to red with embarrassment. "Who said I'm sleeping with her?"

Cash stared at him until he looked away.

"Shit. . . She chased me."

"So you killed her husband?"

"Hell no!" He backed up to the end of the Ranchero. Stared at her. Looked ready to run.

"So what's going on there? She made you manager pretty damn quick after her old man was killed. And you're sleeping with her? Which came first? Killing someone? The job or the lay?"

"I didn't kill anyone. Jeezus Christ. After the funeral my dad told me to stop by, see if she needed any help. Next thing I know, I'm in bed with her. And she gave me a job. I don't even know her. 'Cept from church and stuff."

"Stuff?"

"You know, seeing her and her old man at the fair each year. Seeing them at the DFL picnic." He looked around the field and surrounding area as if searching for a place to run, to hide. Everything, for as far as one could see, was wide-open prairie. His eyes swung back to Cash. "People have been talking for years about her sleeping around on her old man."

"And?"

He held his hands up by his shoulders, palms up. "But I swear to god I just got lucky once he was dead."

Cash gave a sad shake of her head. Lit another cigarette. Tried to put pieces together in her mind. Whether from Nodin chasing her down and ending up dead or a grown woman sleeping with a guy Cash's own age, it was all too much for her to process.

"And what's with the guy in the field. What'd you do to piss him off?"

"Nothing."

Jeff stood still, continued to stare at her, clearly waiting for an answer.

"Pretty sure he killed a girl," Cash said.

"So why come after you?"

"I beat him at a game of pool."

Jeff gave a forced laugh, still uncomfortable with what he had witnessed but without the wherewithal to know how to handle it. "Sore loser, huh?"

Cash dropped the cigarette butt. Crushed it out with the heel of her shoe. "I guess. I'm gonna get to work. Gonna be a hot one. Would like to finish early." She walked to the tractor, climbed up. The tractor chugged to life. She leaned around, yanked the lever to drop the disc and moved the tractor slowly down the field.

She turned around once and saw Jeff standing by his pickup, watching her. She sensed more than heard him when he finally drove off. She wondered briefly if he was going to the Borgerud farm but chased the thought out of her head as she turned her mind instead to the two bodies at the old homestead. A middle-aged man and a young man.

She ran scenario against scenario through her mind as she drove the tractor up and down the field. Arlis killed Nils. Nils killed Bud Borgerud. Arlis did. Borgerud killed Nils. And what of all this killing did Shawnee witness? Cash had enjoyed scaring him, but Jeff didn't have the depth of character to pull off a killing. The chug of the engine, the steady rhythm of the tractor wheels going round and the sun's heat increasing as the morning wore on lulled her into a dream state.

Once again, she saw a young Indian woman walking down a gravel road. The woman again turned and said, "I'll be back." Immediately after she vanished, the young Indian man appeared, his hair combed back like Elvis's, flashed the peace sign and said, "See you on the flip side. Tell my main snag hi." And he evaporated like the steam that rises off a paved road on a hot summer day. She saw Wheaton eating lunch in a booth at a café with a woman whose face she couldn't see. Shawnee sat on the bedroom floor in the Borgerud house. A lone skinny doll with a big chest and long legs lay on the rag rug she sat on. She looked at Cash with her big brown child's eyes. From her mind to Cash's mind she said, "I saw that old man get shot." And in that second, in that image, the little girl threw the plastic doll across the room, curled up in a ball, her body shaking with sobs. And then the image flashed like the blue bulb of a Nikon camera and vanished.

Cash looked across the field. Black dirt surrounded her. Strips of short green weeds lined the ditches of the road on two sides of the forty acres. Another bare field edged the one she just finished. She pulled the disc next to her Ranchero, shut off the tractor and sat. She listened to the quiet that surrounded her. Heard a bird chirp in the distance. Saw a hawk fly overhead. Zoom down to pick up what appeared to be a mouse from the ditch down the road. Off in the distance she could hear what sounded like a grain truck driving down one of the county roads.

As Cash looked around at the section of land with no farmhouses in sight, she thought back to the killing of Borgerud and Nils.

As she thought through it, Nils had to have been killed first. There was nothing in the house to indicate he had been killed there. His body had been gnawed by wildlife. Had he been killed somewhere else, then brought back to the farm and stuffed under the corncrib? Where was Arlis when all that was happening? Where was Shawnee during all this?

Cash shook the thoughts from her head. Climbed down off the tractor and got into the Ranchero. A strange knock-on-metal sound came from the engine. Cash quickly turned it off, got back out, opened the hood and peered inside. Although she couldn't see anything, she could smell oil. She checked the dipstick. Empty. She got down on her hands and knees and looked at the ground under the engine. The smell of oil was stronger. She felt the ground and when she pulled her hand back it was covered in oil-soaked dirt.

Shit! That damn car chase messed something up. She looked up and down the road. Not a car in sight. She visualized the surrounding area in her mind, figured she was about three miles from the main county road that would take her into Shelly.

Three-quarters of a mile later, a farmer headed to town for sparkplugs picked her up and gave her a ride the rest of the way into town. He dropped her off at a service station, where a phone booth stood on the edge of the driveway. The four glass walls of the booth acted like a greenhouse. She propped the door open with her foot to let the hot air out and some cool air in. A skinny phone book hung on a metal chain inside the booth. It only served the surrounding Norman County communities, not Moorhead in Clay County.

Inside the gas station, she gave the attendant two dollars and asked for change for the phone booth.

"You break down?" he asked, counting the change into her hand.

"Yeah."

"We got a tow truck. Could get you in here. Slow day today."

"Nah. Gonna call a buddy. See if he can help." She stopped by the chest fridge, put in a dime and got a cold Coke. She popped the lid and took a drink. The fizzy sweetness burned her throat.

Back at the phone booth, she drank some more pop. She

hesitated a good minute before she dialed the operator, asked for Al's Auto Shop in Moorhead.

Al answered after five rings. "Hello?"

The operator told her to deposit fifty cents for the first minute. Thirty cents for each additional minute.

"It's Cash."

From the short silence that followed, she could tell Al was surprised by the call.

Cash felt her stomach tighten. She wasn't used to asking anyone for help. Didn't know how to ask. "My Ranchero broke down. I'm in Shelly."

Al didn't hesitate. "Take me a minute to close up there, but I'll be on my way."

Not knowing what else to say, Cash hung up. Took a swig of pop. Walked over to the metal bench outside the gas station and sat down to wait.

About an hour later Al pulled up in his pickup. Cash climbed into the cab. Gave him directions back to the field she had been working.

Halfway to the field, Al, without taking his eyes off the road, said gently, "You know, most people say goodbye before they hang up the phone."

"Hmmph," was her reply.

Back at the field, Al ran through the same process Cash had. Turned on the vehicle. Shut it off. Checked the oil. But instead of just looking under the Ranchero, he laid on his back and scooted himself under it. Came out with an oil stain on the back of his shirt.

"Can't tell if the oil pan is loose or has a leak. I'll tow

you back to my shop." He backed his pickup up to the front end of the Ranchero and pulled a heavy-duty tow chain out from the truck bed. He hooked it to his tow hitch, then fiddled around before hooking it to the front bumper of the Ranchero.

"Get in and steer. Keep it in neutral. We'll just take it slow. I'll get us over to Highway 9, see if there's a garage in Ada that might be able to do a quick fix."

Cash nodded. It was a slow ride from Shelly to Ada. Al stopped them at the Co-op on the edge of town and went in to talk to the attendant. When he came back out, he stood beside the Ranchero's open window. "He said we may as well tow it to my shop. Everyone's busy getting things running for field work. Could be days before anyone could even look at it."

"Let's go then. I need it fixed sooner than later."

"Thought so."

Al got back into his truck. The Ranchero jerked forward as he pulled back on to Highway 9.

As they passed through town, Cash glanced down the main side street. Parked diagonally in front of the hotel was a two-toned car covered in dust. Like it had driven across an open field. From a barn to be exact. *Like the barn at Borgerud's old farmstead.* Instinctively, Cash slammed on the brakes. The Ranchero jerked hard against the chain connected to Al's pickup. Cash hit the horn while at the same time she jumped from the Ranchero and ran down the street to the hotel.

She didn't stop to notice the desk clerk's reaction. Took

the stairs two at a time. Didn't knock, just tried the door-knob to room 204. It swung open. Cash wildly scanned the room, looking for Arlis. The only person in the room was Miss Dackson, gagged with a pillowcase tied around her mouth and a white hotel sheet securing her to the chair. Papers were strewn across the floor. The telephone knocked off the desk.

Cash untied the pillowcase from around the woman's mouth. "What the heck happened here?"

"Arlis." The woman gasped for air. Licked her dry lips. Turned her head from side to side as if the woman might still be in the room. "Arlis is trying to steal back Shawnee. The woman's crazy. Untie me!"

A momentary thought to leave her tied up crossed Cash's mind. Instead, she worked the knotted sheet loose while Miss Dackson continued. "I didn't tell her where she is. I didn't. She dug through all my papers. Told her all my paperwork's at the courthouse." Tears formed in Miss Dackson's eyes. "All my private letters. How can someone just come in and snoop through stuff that isn't theirs?"

Yeah, I wonder. I wonder how people can take kids who aren't theirs, Cash thought as she finally worked the big knot loose. Miss Dackson's struggles had only tightened the knot.

"She ran out just seconds before you came in. Didn't you pass her?"

"No." Cash ran out of the room. Looked down the dark hallway. She knew from exploring the hotel when she was a child that outside the window at the end of the hallway was a metal fire escape that stopped about five feet off the ground. The window was open.

Cash started down the stairs. Al met her halfway up. "What the hell is going on? You coulda ruined both trucks jumping out like that!"

Cash pushed past him. "Did you see a woman run out of here?" When she got outside, the two-toned car was gone from its parking spot. She whipped her head back and forth as she scanned the street.

"A woman got in and drove off just as I got here," Al said.

"Which way?"

He pointed east.

"Indian woman?"

He nodded.

"Where'd you park?"

"Same place you jumped out."

"Young?" Cash was already walking back toward their trucks.

"Yeah." Al walked fast to keep up with her. "What's going on?"

"She's crazy. Wanted for murder. I thought she was going to kill me," another voice added.

Miss Dackson had caught up with them on the sidewalk. Cash turned her head to Miss Dackson but didn't slow her walk. She noticed the woman's skirt was twisted around her waist so the side zipper was now in front, over her stomach. "I'll track her down. Least we know what she's driving."

"I didn't tell her where Shawnee is. Maybe I should warn Jean just in case."

"No! Arlis is going to think you placed Shawnee at the other end of the county like you always do. You think you're slick when you get the kids as far away as possible from the parents. 'Cause you know they always try to find their kids. If you didn't tell her, she's not going to know where to look, right?"

Miss Dackson smoothed her hair. Smoothed her skirt and noticed the zipper. Self-consciously twisted the skirt around her waist while struggling to keep up with Cash and Al. "I suppose."

"Best leave it be and let Wheaton or myself handle this."

"The woman's dangerous."

"She wants her kid. Wouldn't you?"

Miss Dackson ignored the question. "You know, you're right. I might need to think about placing Shawnee in a home in a different town. Jean wanted to do the right thing. Help the family. But with Arlis breaking the law, maybe it would be best to move her in spite of what Jean wants."

Cash stopped and stared at the social worker. "I'll handle it." Her voice so firm Miss Dackson took a step backward before turning and walking back toward the hotel. Cash took off at a fast pace toward the trucks.

Al hurried after her again. "You gonna tell me what's going on?"

"I need my truck."

"That's not gonna happen until after I get a chance to see what the issue is. Drive it now and you'll ruin the engine for sure."

Cash looked both ways down the main highway. The only vehicle in sight was a red Massey Ferguson tractor plodding north down the road. "Shit."

"Talk to me, Cash."

"Long story short. Arlis, the woman in the car, is wanted for questioning. Everyone but me thinks she killed two guys. And her kid Shawnee is in a white foster home. That's why her mother went after the social worker. Her mom wants to find her. Now Dackson is talking about moving Shawnee to another home. She doesn't care one way or the other about what's best for us."

"For us?"

"For us Indian kids. She just peddles us off to farmers to do their work for them. Shawnee's mom wants her kid back. I don't think she hurt anyone." Cash raised her voice. "I need my truck."

"Shouldn't you talk to the sheriff about her tying that woman up?"

"Nah. She'll run to him right away."

Cash led them to his pickup and her Ranchero, where they both climbed into their respective vehicles and continued the slow journey to his auto shop. Cash was ready for action, and being cooped up in the cab of her Ranchero with no control over the speed they were going drove her crazy. Her mind played out various scenarios where she caught Arlis and hauled her into Wheaton's jail. Where she caught Arlis after a road chase. Where Arlis rolled her car in a ditch and Cash had to pull her out of the tipped-over car. Cash caught Arlis and reunited her with Shawnee and they lived happily ever after. She smoked half a pack of cigarettes on the way back into Moorhead.

Once there, she spent the rest of the day pacing between the television in Al's living room and his auto shop that was attached to his house. She told him the story of Arlis, Shawnee, and Nodin in spurts on each walk out to the shop as she leaned on the cab of the Ranchero. She talked to his feet, which were stretched out from under the vehicle.

When she talked about Nodin, Al rolled out from under the Ranchero on his creeper, sat up and stared at her. He said "what the fuck" a couple times before lying back down and rolling under the vehicle without any other comment.

Finally, he emerged, wiped his grease-stained hands on a shop rag and said, "Should be good to go."

He held the car door shut as Cash immediately reached for it, eager to head out.

"You need to eat. It's late. Ain't nothing gonna get solved this minute. Come on. Soup and a grilled cheese sandwich?"

Al held the door shut even as Cash tried to open it. She side-eyed him, then finally let go of the door handle and walked back into his house.

In the kitchen, she scraped the chair loudly back from the table and sat hard on the vinyl seat.

Al opened two cans of tomato soup. Cooked them on low while he buttered bread and put cheese between two slices before putting the sandwiches in a frying pan. Cash's stomach growled as the smell of frying butter hit her nostrils. In an absent kind of way, her mind divorced from her body, she tried to remember the last time she ate. Gave the thinking up when Al placed a bowl of soup and hot sandwich on the table in front of her.

As she took a bite of the grilled cheese sandwich, she flashed on the first meal she had in a foster home. Mashed potatoes, corn and a pork chop. She had never seen so much food. She had mashed the corn into the potatoes and ate it in huge, scooped-up mouthfuls. The foster mother and father had laughed. They didn't stop the other children sitting at the table from making fun of her, either. Cash didn't care. She had picked up the pork chop with her bare hands and eaten it. She could hardly wait until the next meal.

Somehow, over the years, food had become something she rarely thought about. Sometimes she would eat. Often she just forgot to. It might explain why Wheaton was always hauling her off to some café for a roast beef sandwich or blueberry pie. One of the first things Al had done when they first met was make her some soup.

And now, before Al pulled out a chair and sat down with his own meal, he asked, "More soup?" He poured the remainder of the soup into her half-empty bowl without waiting for an answer. Then he sat down to eat.

"Don't suppose you plan on sleeping tonight?"

"Nah. Gotta head back out. Make sure Shawnee is safe. See if I can find her ma."

"Why don't you just call Wheaton? Let him deal with it."

"Shawnee trusts me. And I'm not convinced Arlis killed anyone. I think she just wants her kid back."

"So why's she hiding?"

Cash shrugged. Picked up the bowl of tomato soup and

finished it off by drinking the rest. "Outta here." She set the bowl back on the table and swiped her lips with the sleeve hem of her jean jacket.

As she stood up to leave, Al took her arm and pulled her onto his lap. "I worry about you." He held her close. "You can't save the world. You're just one small woman."

Cash squirmed out of his arms. "Not that small. Leave me alone. I gotta go."

"Whyn't you come back here and sleep, once you get done with whatever you're doing?"

"We'll see. Now lemme go."

AS CASH DROVE NORTH OUT of the small city of Moorhead, the pale white light of the Milky Way danced across the starlit sky. Cash eased back on the gas pedal and leaned forward over the steering wheel. As she gazed upward, the image of Jonesy shimmered into being on the passenger seat. She was dressed in jeans and a men's red plaid shirt. She was smoking a small pipe. Cash looked at her out of the corner of her eye.

"Keep your eyes on the road, my girl. That girl needs her ma. Her ma didn't do nothin' wrong." She puffed her pipe and blew smoke rings that drifted through the glass windshield up into the never-ending sky.

Eyes half focused on the road, keeping Jonesy in her peripheral vision, Cash followed the smoke rings up to the Big Dipper. And just like she had appeared, Jonesy shimmered back out of existence.

Cash didn't pass a single car on the road until she reached

the town of Ada. A station wagon and a couple pickup trucks were parked outside the local bar. Another handful were parked outside the hotel. Tire tracks left by field dust were all that was visible in the dull glow of the few streetlights along the main avenue. Cash turned off Main and drove slowly through the quiet side streets. TVs flickered in picture windows. Pale yellow light filtered from behind curtains on lone bedroom windows. The two-toned car was nowhere to be seen. Wheaton's cruiser was parked outside his house and the light over the kitchen stove was visible through the café curtains. She decided not to stop.

Instead, she drove out of town toward the Borgerud farm. Again, no other cars were on the road. As she headed down the road toward the farmstead, she realized she was a sitting duck. If Mrs. Borgerud happened to look out her window at this hour of the night, she would probably recognize Cash's Ranchero. The thought made Cash slow down, shut off the headlights, put the truck in neutral and drift to the side of the road as her eyes adjusted to the darkness. She didn't want to brake because the flash of red taillights would be a giveaway to anyone looking out a window at the Borgerud's. As the Ranchero crunched the gravel on the side of the road, Cash pressed the clutch in and shut off the vehicle, then rolled to a stop.

She lit a cigarette in the cup of her hand. Kept her hand over the lighted tip as she took a drag. She rolled down the window and blew the smoke out into the damp evening air as she acclimated herself to the surroundings. All was silent out here on the prairie. The stars and the sliver moon dominated the sky without making a sound. She tried to sense if Jonesy was around, but couldn't find the old woman's energy.

When Cash finally got quiet long enough, she could hear the nocturnal creatures going about their nightly hunting and gathering. She took a deep breath, held it and turned her head so both ears were more or less out the car window. A mouse or a gopher moved through the grass in the ditch. She pulled her head back in, took a breath.

Cash had decided a while ago to not drink and drive. With all the work she was doing for Wheaton, the last thing she needed was to get pulled over in some other county by some county cop for open bottle. Instead, she had taken to keeping a thermos of coffee to sip on; hot, warm or cold, it replaced the need to drink. But now she had to pee.

She saw the other vehicle before she heard it. Sure enough, she spotted headlights moving down the road on the crossroad opposite the Borgerud farmstead. A beam of yellow light swept the flat field as it turned in her direction and came down the road toward her. Cash knew that where she sat kept her out of the sight line of whoever was driving. But if they kept coming, country protocol would dictate that the driver stop and ask if she needed help. Cash rapidly ran various scenarios in her mind to explain why she was sitting in the dark on a back country road. She was stargazing, she stopped to check the air in her tires, she stopped to watch a family of skunks cross the road.

But the vehicle, a pickup truck, turned into the Borgerud driveway. "Jeff, I know why you're here," Cash said out loud as she watched him kill the headlights before he parked. Metal against metal sounded as he shut the door. Cash marveled at how every little sound carried on the prairie. She heard the creak of the screen door open and shut. Again, the silence of the night folded in on her, alone, in her truck a quarter of a mile away.

Rather than risk Jeff or Jean hearing the door open—which would require, once again because of country protocol, that they investigate who was on the road—she climbed out the rolled-down window and stepped to the other side of the Ranchero, pulled her pants down, squatted and peed in the ditch. Finished, she wiggled her butt, pulled her pants back up. She surveyed the flat fields all around the Borgerud house and Jeff's truck visible under the yard light.

Nothing to do. Nothing to see. She climbed back into the Ranchero. The engine interrupted the quiet of the night and the tires crunched on the road as she maneuvered the truck back and forth until she was facing the other direction. At that point, she turned on the headlights and drove away.

She was headed to the farmstead where Bud Borgerud and Nils were found. Where someone in a two-toned car had been sleeping in the root cellar. Might be someone sleeping in that same cellar right now.

"Wait! Damn!" Cash slammed her hand against the steering wheel while simultaneously slamming on the brakes. "That damn woman might try to move Shawnee tomorrow." The Ranchero skidded, snakelike, on the unpaved road. Cash quickly shifted gears: reverse, first, reverse, first, until she had the truck turned around and headed back in the direction of the Borgerud farm. She killed the lights and shut off the engine and again coasted until she was close to the homestead, where Jeff's pickup was still parked in the driveway. She crawled out the rolled-down window and ran into the farmyard. She stopped at the end of Jeff's truck bed to catch her breath, slow her breathing, and listened for any signs that anyone in the house had heard her. Nothing.

Cash eased herself slowly along the side of the pickup and walked softly to the screen door. No one appeared to stop her. She could hear soft sexual moans coming from somewhere in the house. She eased open the door and slipped inside. The yard light was bright enough that she could see vague shapes of furniture as she crept into the house and down the hallway toward the bedroom where, from her previous visit, she knew Shawnee slept. Bedsprings creaked furiously from behind the closed door at the end of the hallway. Cash quickened her pace and softly opened the door to Shawnee's room.

Shawnee, eyes wide open, was lying in bed with the covers pulled up to her chin. Cash put her finger to her mouth signaling silence. She grabbed what clothes she could see from the floor, picked up Shawnee, still in her nightgown, and carried her out of the house. Bedsprings still creaked wildly behind them.

Cash made sure the screen door closed quietly as they left. She shifted Shawnee over to her other hip and ran to the Ranchero, slid the little girl into the car seat through the open window and climbed in after her. No sense opening and closing a car door when they'd made it this far without detection.

Cash drove the speed limit all the way back into Fargo. She chain-smoked with the smoke drifting out the side window. Shawnee was silent as usual but halfway to town she laid her head on Cash's right leg and fell asleep. Back at her apartment, Cash carried her upstairs and laid her on the bed, covered her with blankets. Cash grabbed a beer from the fridge, her ashtray off the dresser next to the bed, then picked up the clothes from the overstuffed big chair that served as her makeshift closet and dumped them onto the floor before curling up in the chair. She smoked cigarettes, drank beer and stared at Shawnee.

This might be the dumbest thing you've ever done, Cash, she thought to herself. *You got her here, now what you going to do? You can't leave a kid alone all by herself while you go chasing down her mom. Didn't think this one through all the way, did you? Thanks a lot, Jonesy.* She blew smoke rings at the ceiling.

With the beer half gone, she got up and rummaged through a drawer in the kitchen and found the phone book for the city of Fargo. As much as she loathed the telephone, she figured she would dial up Sharon. Her hippie white friend would probably help her out, no questions asked.

Back in her chair, she ran her finger down the Ts in the phone book. The pages were thin, almost like the sewing patterns she used to use in home ec class. She finally found a Sharon Thompson at an address near the North Dakota State University campus. She placed the open page upside down on the floor, finished her beer and one more cigarette, then fell asleep, the armrest of the chair a firm pillow under her head.

Cash jerked awake from a nightmare where Mrs. Borgerud was silently screaming at her, the woman's face contorted in rage. She popped straight up, her heart beating rapidly in her chest. She glanced at her bed. Shawnee was sitting up, too, her back braced against the headboard, staring at Cash.

"Jesus, girl, don't stare at me like that. You okay?"

"I peed," she said in a tiny whisper.

"Oh man, you should of woke me up." Cash untangled herself from the chair and walked to the bed, where the air had an acrid scent. "Come on, you still gotta go?" She lifted the little girl off the bed and set her on the hardwood floor. "The bathroom's over here. If you gotta go, just go in there . . . or wake me up. Let me run you a bath."

While the water was running in the tub, Cash went back in the bedroom, opened the bedroom window and stripped the bed. She rolled the smelly sheets in a ball, stuffed them inside a pillowcase and put them by the kitchen door along with Shawnee's nightgown and some of her own clothes from the pile on the floor. "Guess I need to do laundry anyways," she said to Shawnee as she passed the bathroom.

When the girl was in the tub, Cash left the bathroom door open, opened the kitchen door to let some fresh air travel through the apartment from the kitchen and out the bedroom window. Her phone rang three times. Stopped. Rang twice. Stopped. And three times again. *Oh damn,*

Wheaton. Cash ignored the phone and retrieved the phone book from the bedroom floor. She stretched the cord from the phone in the kitchen as far as it would reach so she could just barely see Shawnee's head through the bathroom door as she dialed Sharon's number.

"What's crackin'? Sun ain't even up yet. Who's this?" Sharon's voice sounded groggy with sleep.

"Sharon, I need a favor. I ended up babysitting my friend's kid overnight but I gotta make a run to Ada to pick up my paycheck. Could you watch her for a couple hours here at my place?"

"Cash? You called me?"

"Yeah."

"I can't take care of a baby." Sharon sounded like she was sitting up.

"Not a baby. Maybe about five. And quiet. Good kid."

"Can you bring her to my pad?"

Cash looked at the top of Shawnee's head. Thought about the trauma the kid had been through. And now she'd been taken in the middle of the night from the home where she was staying. She didn't seem at all worried to be with Cash. "I bet she's hungry," Cash blurted out, forgetting for a moment that Sharon was on the phone.

"What?"

"Nothin'. Nah, I think she'd be better off here. You know, in case her mom comes back for her while I'm gone."

Sharon yawned. Cash could picture her stretching. "All right, let me throw on some duds. I'll have to hitch a ride over."

"What do five-year-olds eat?" Cash twisted the phone cord around her arm.

"Food."

"But what?"

"What do you have? Cereal? Milk?"

"No, I got bread."

"Make her some cinnamon toast."

"Hmmm, okay. Hurry up."

Cash hung up the phone. She unplugged the phone from the wall. Looked around her kitchen, then stuffed the phone behind some pots and pans in a lower cupboard. No sense risking Sharon answering the phone if Wheaton continued to call.

"Come on, Shawnee, you're shriveling up in there. Look at your toes, they're like brown raisins." Cash held out a towel for the girl to climb into. She helped her dry off and then pulled a shirt over the girl's head and pulled pants up over her hips. "Good thing we grabbed some clothes off your bedroom floor or you'd be wearing your nightgown all day."

Shawnee didn't seem to question what she was doing with Cash. She didn't ask why she'd been taken in her sleep. Didn't seem concerned. Cash could tell from the way she watched Cash's every move that the little girl was thinking about the situation, but she either didn't have the words for the questions she had, or she didn't care. But she did use her words to tell Cash she'd peed, and said yes or no a couple times, so Cash knew she was capable of talking.

Cash led Shawnee out to the kitchen and motioned her

to go ahead and sit on a chair at the table. "I got bread, butter and sugar. Guess you're going to get cinnamon toast without the cinnamon. That okay with you? You drink coffee? All I got to drink is coffee. You probably shouldn't drink coffee. Make you short like me. I wish you'd talk. I don't like talking either. Guess we can both be quiet, huh? You quietly eat your toast and I'll quietly drink my coffee. My friend Sharon is going to come watch you."

Shawnee's eyes darkened and opened wide.

"Don't worry. Sharon's a hippie. Peace and love and all that. She's just gonna watch you 'cause I gotta . . ." Cash searched for words. "I gotta run some errands. Throw the laundry in at the laundromat or we won't have sheets to sleep on tonight. I'll be back."

The girl slowly munched her toast, eyes downcast.

"Hey, Shawnee, look at me. I'll be back. I promise."

"Yoo-hoo. Anyone home?" Sharon came clumping up the outside stairs. "I was still talking to you and you just hung up on me. Gonna be a hot one out there today." She walked in through the apartment screen door. Platform shoes, paisley halter top and a denim miniskirt fit with the thin leather braid wrapped around her forehead, holding her fluffy hair down a bit. "Oooh, a baby Cash. Look how cute you are."

Shawnee wrinkled her nose and stared at Sharon. Cash also got a whiff of a heavy dose of patchouli oil.

Sharon looked around the bare two-room apartment. She tipped her head, gave Cash a questioning look. "Do you at least have a radio up here?"

Cash pointed at the table. "You could play solitaire. Got a deck of cards."

Sharon raised her eyebrows. "I'm hip." To Shawnee she asked, "Wanna play a game of slapjack?"

Shawnee just stared at her.

"She doesn't talk."

"Doesn't talk? Like, man, doesn't talk at all? Can't talk? What? You gonna just stare at me the whole time I'm watching you? You got me tripping now." She looked back to Cash. "How will I know if she needs something?"

"She's not gonna need anything. She knows where the bathroom is. Here, here's some paper and pencil. She can draw in this. Make her some paper airplanes or something." Cash grabbed a school notebook and pencil from the dresser in the bedroom and put it on the table by Shawnee. "She just doesn't talk. Don't worry about it. I gotta throw these clothes in the washer at the laundromat, run to Ada and I'll be right back, okay?" She ripped a piece of paper out of the notebook, folded it and put it in her jeans pocket. Grabbed a shorter pencil from a drawer and stuck that in her back pocket, too.

"I can tell you had a Beaver Cleaver childhood. Go on then. Hurry back. I ain't the babysitting type, you hip?" Sharon pulled out a kitchen chair, sat and began to shuffle the card deck. Shawnee stared at her, munching on her second piece of toast.

CASH THREW THE LAUNDRY INTO a washer at the laundromat just down the street and headed out of town.

Hope to god I don't see Wheaton, she thought more than once, constantly scanning the roads, hoping to not see his cruiser. Cash used back roads to head to the farmstead where she had first found Shawnee. The field grass behind the barn showed evidence that a car or other vehicle had driven into the barn, although no vehicle was in there when Cash peered into the dark interior. Cash walked twice around the house. The padlock on the house door was still secure and none of the windows had evidence of being broken into. The tamped down grass in front of the cellar doors also indicated someone else had been around.

Cash pulled the paper and pencil out of her back pocket, sat on the grass and wrote in cursive. *I have Shawnee. She's safe. I will bring her here tonight right after dark. You need to tell me how Mr. Borgerud and your husband were killed.* She approached the cellar doors. She gingerly touched the wood posts that held back the dirt wall and moved quickly down the stone steps. She picked an unopened can of sardines and placed it on top of the note with the words showing, so that when Arlis came down the steps—Cash knew with every fiber of her being it was Arlis camping out underground—she would immediately see the note.

Cash brushed the spider web hanging down from the rafters away from her face, then hurried back up to daylight. "Ok, Arlis, this is your chance," she said to the morning air, got in her Ranchero and headed back to Fargo.

AFTER PUTTING THE WASHED CLOTHES into a dryer and giving the machine enough dimes to cover an hour of drying, Cash went back to her apartment. Sharon and Shawnee were engaged in a wild slap-each-other's-hands game of slapjack. Shawnee was laughing, her eyes brightening with glee every time she whacked Sharon's hand and scooped the cards to her side of the table.

Sharon smacked another card down. Without looking up, she asked, "Get your errands done?"

"I have to run back in a bit to get the laundry."

Cash stood self-consciously in her own kitchen. It would never have occurred to her to play a game with the little girl. She made herself a piece of toast. Sprinkled sugar on it and stood at the counter eating. Soon, Shawnee had the whole deck piled on her side of the table.

Sharon exclaimed, "You won! Never been beat by a little kid before."

Shawnee giggled.

Sharon said, "Guess that's it. Time for me to book on home."

"Can you help me switch the mattress over first? And I gotta run back to the laundromat and get our clothes." Cash wiped her sugary hands on her jeans and moved to the bedroom, not waiting for an answer. The mattress stain was dry but the faint smell still lingered.

"Wait," Sharon said. She went back to the kitchen, rummaged through the bag she carried and came back with a small vial. She sprinkled patchouli oil on the mattress. "There you go," she said. "Good as new."

"My landlord will think I'm smoking pot up here."

Sharon laughed. "Might help you chill out. Come on, let's turn this over."

Both women took an end of the heavy mattress and flipped it.

"Just watch her another ten minutes and I'll run get the laundry." And with that, Cash ran back down to the laundromat, returned with the clothes and threw them on the bed.

"I thought you had a phone? I was going to call my main man and see if he could pick me up."

"Broke. I'd give you a ride but I gotta stay here with—"

"In case her mom comes for her?"

Cash glanced at Shawnee, whose eyes widened at Sharon's question. "I just need to wait here. Sorry."

"I got thumbs." Sharon laughed, miming hitchhiking with one hand.

Cash held the door open for Sharon. "Thanks," she said to her friend's retreating back.

Sharon lifted a hand in a wave. "Catch you on the flip side."

After she watched Sharon vanish around the corner of the building, Cash latched the screen door from the inside. Made the bed up, folded some clothes to put in dresser drawers and hung others over the back of the overstuffed chair she'd slept in. What was she going to do with a kid all day? She'd have to eat. And pee. And want to play with something. *You definitely did not think this through.* She sat on the edge of the bed, lit up a cigarette and looked at Shawnee still sitting at the kitchen table. The little girl's legs didn't reach the floor and her head was barely over the top of the table. *If her mom's not there tonight, guess I'll drop her*

off at Jonesy's since it was her bright idea to get her. Just have to
do something between now and sunset.

Cash stood, grabbed a spare blanket and said, "Wait up
here. I'm gonna run down to my truck." Downstairs, on the
passenger side of the Ranchero, Cash folded the blanket to
make a soft spot on the floor. She ran back upstairs, filled
a thermos with coffee, made four more pieces of buttered
and sugared toast and put them all in a black lunch box she
usually used to pack her field lunch in. "Come on, kiddo."
She scooped Shawnee up onto one hip.

Cash went down the stairs slowly, on the lookout for
anyone who might be walking on the sidewalk. No one. And
the drivers that passed on the roadway didn't look their way.
At the Ranchero she set Shawnee on the blanket on the
floor. "You'll be safer down here." She lied to the little girl.
"And if you want to take a nap, you can just curl and sleep."

She drove east out of Fargo, through Moorhead, and at
the edge of town pulled into a gas station she didn't normally frequent and told the attendant to "filler up."

She passed through Dilworth and Glyndon before
turning on the road that took them into Buffalo State Park.
The two spent the afternoon walking on paths. Shawnee
chased butterflies and crickets in the tall prairie grass.
Cash fed her toast at the edge of the pond that served as a
swimming hole and let her drink cold coffee from the cup
of her thermos. Cash found a place under an oak tree that
was partially shaded, the sun filtering through the leaves.
She spread out the blanket. "Let's take a nap after all that
running around." Cash lay down and crooked her arm for

Shawnee to rest her head and both dozed off in the warmth of the sun.

CASH WOKE TO A SLIGHT tap-tap on her left shoulder.

"I gotta pee." Shawnee said it so quietly Cash wasn't sure if she heard her or just read her lips. Either way, she quickly sat up and scanned the park ground.

"Come on, bathrooms are right over there."

Bathroom run made, blankets, thermos and shoes gathered, Cash put Shawnee back into the Ranchero.

"We got a few more hours to kill."

Shawnee jerked her head in Cash's direction.

"Oh, kid, poor choice of words. Just meant we have to find something to do for the next couple of hours."

Another soft squeak. "I'm hungry."

Cash looked at Shawnee. As a child, it would have never occurred to her to admit to being hungry. She ate when meals were served, that is, if she was allowed to. Often in the foster homes mealtime was battle time. Food a reward or a punishment. "We'll go over to West Fargo. You like Mexican food? I know a place."

CASH DROVE ACROSS THE MINNESOTA state line into North Dakota. Moorhead was in Clay County, directly south of Norman County, which was Wheaton's and the county Shawnee had just been taken from. Cash had worked with Wheaton long enough to know that transporting a minor across state lines amounted to a federal charge of kidnapping if caught. She wasn't about to get caught if she could help it. She drove to a section of the West Fargo suburbs that most residents called "the other side of the tracks," even though there were no railroad tracks in sight. The little restaurant, with an unpaved parking lot, sat next to the entrance of a worn trailer park. A strand of dried red chilis hung by the door next to a hand-painted sign in red and green that red PEDRO'S MEX-TEX.

The inside was cheery, south-of-the-border vibrant. Cash led Shawnee to a booth near the kitchen and sat across from her where she could watch the door. She had never seen anyone familiar to her in the restaurant, but you never knew. Two men wearing concrete-dust-covered jeans were in a nearby booth and a family with four kids sat around another table. With the exception of ordering in English, Cash and Shawnee fit right in Pedro's Mex-Tex.

"¿Qué te gustaría?" the waitress asked as she put a bowl of hot sauce and a basket of chips on the table. Thick black braids framed her face. She didn't carry an order pad.

"No hablo español," answered Cash. "Um, a couple tacos for each of us. I'll have a Coke. A Coke for her too."

The waitress nodded and disappeared into the kitchen.

Shawnee watched Cash pick up a taco to eat it and then followed suit. "Never had a taco, huh, kid? Yummy, huh?"

Shawnee nodded.

Cash debated whether to tell Shawnee she was going to try to take her to her mom. She thought back to the last time she saw her own mom. One minute they were riding in the car. Her brother was in the front seat. She and her sister in the back. Each of them had a job: to tell their mom if she got too close to the ditch on one side or swerved into the wrong lane on the other side.

Her mother had spent the day drinking with Cash's aunt over on the reservation and now, late at night, she was attempting to drive them home. Cash remembered standing, leaning into the front seat as she listened to her mom sing along to some country western song. The next thing she knew, Wheaton—although she didn't know he was Wheaton at the time—pulled her and the rest of her family from the car that had swerved off the road and rolled over in the ditch.

Cash remembered Wheaton carrying her beautiful, brown-skinned mama, with pitch black hair that curled around her always smiling, laughing face, into the jail cell. That was her last memory of her mother. That was just before Wheaton put Cash to bed on a wooden bench in the hallway.

Cash shook her head. Looked at Shawnee. The sadness in the little girl's eyes mirrored how she herself had felt at three.

She hoped beyond hope that Arlis would show. If she didn't, Cash didn't know what she would do. She wasn't ready to raise a kid, let alone deal with Wheaton's anger, or maybe his disappointment, if—when—he found out she'd kidnapped Shawnee. And she sure as hell didn't want to go to jail.

Cash lingered in the booth long after they both finished their tacos. They nibbled on chips, slowly drank their Cokes, took a trip to the bathroom. The construction men left and

202 · MARCIE R. RENDON

a table of other workmen replaced them. The first family exited and two other families entered. All spoke rapid Spanish. The mothers doted on the babies. The younger kids laughed at something funny their father said.

Finally, the window at the front darkened and the open sign was turned on. Cash gathered up Shawnee and put her in the Ranchero. She let the little girl sit up on the seat. No one would recognize her in the dark, she figured. She headed north of Fargo on Highway 29. She pointed out the tower to the Hector airport and an airplane landing. They went through the small town of Harwood, then through the lights of Argusville, Gardner and Granden. By the time she reached the turnoff to Highway 200, Shawnee had curled up on the seat next to Cash and was sound asleep. Cash drove east to Halstad, where she quickly turned off the main street to the side streets until she could reach another county road to head out of town. From there she took to field roads and back roads to approach the old Borgerud farmstead.

The farmhouse sat in darkness. No yard light illuminated the driveway or the front door. The barn, where Cash assumed Arlis had parked, was a dark, sagging presence in the empty cow pasture. Cash shut off the headlights and coasted to a standstill near the house. She shivered as she realized she was parked exactly where she had first seen Mr. Borgerud's car running the morning she discovered his body and Shawnee hiding under the bed upstairs.

Cash leaned out the car window and listened. It was silent. No crickets, no birds, no small creatures rustling through the grass. Someone was here. She put her hand on the key in the ignition, pushed in the brake and clutch and put the Ranchero in reverse. *Just in case*, she told herself.

"Who are you?" a woman's voice whispered.

Cash tilted her head to discern where the voice came from. Shawnee was still sleeping soundly beside her.

"Who are you?" the woman asked, a little louder.

Cash matched her tone and volume. "Cash Blackbear. Is that you, Arlis?"

"You have Shawnee?" The voice came closer.

Cash realized the woman was to her right, standing in the copse of trees not far from the corncrib where Shawnee's dad had been found. Cash's brain fired. *Shit, whyn't I grab the pistol before I pulled in here? Sitting duck, Cash, another one of your brilliant moves.*

As calm as she could, Cash answered, "Yes, she's here. I need to know what happened before you get her."

Before she finished the sentence, the passenger door cracked open and Arlis crawled into the cab of the Ranchero, scooping up Shawnee. The girl jerked awake. Broke into sobs, threw her arms around her mom's neck, crying, "Mommy, Mommy!"

Arlis clutched her tight, tears running down her face. "I'm here, baby, I'm here. Mommy's here."

Cash sat, unsure of what to do. She crossed her arms over the steering wheel and laid her head on it. Angrily, she fought against the crushing weight in her chest that threatened to explode out her throat. Then deep sobs racked her body. She wasn't able to control them. *What the fuck.* She gulped breaths and wiped her eyes with the sleeves of her jacket. *Get it together*, she admonished herself. She pulled out a cigarette, struck a match and inhaled. Held it in her lungs, felt the burn, and held it some more. She exhaled a giant swirl of smoke and quickly took another drag.

Arlis sat on the passenger seat, holding, rocking Shawnee, crooning "my baby, my baby" over and over, interjected with the occasional "Mommy's here, Mommy's here, Mama's so sorry, Mama's so sorry." Shawnee's crying had softened but she didn't loosen her grip on her mom.

"Where'd you go, Mommy? I wanted you," Shawnee said.

Tears slid down Arlis's cheeks.

Cash lit another cigarette off the one she had smoked down to the filter. In the brief moment of orange glow as she inhaled, she glanced at Arlis. The woman's curly hair, uncombed, was pinned back with hairpins. Her shirt wrinkled. No socks on her feet inside her tennies. After another puff, Cash's breath was steady. She was ready to hear whatever story Arlis had to tell her. She turned the key in the ignition and started the Ranchero's engine.

Arlis jerked. Pulled Shawnee in tighter. Looked wildly at Cash while reaching for the passenger door handle.

Cash grabbed her arm. "Nah, you aren't going anyplace. You need to talk to me, tell me what happened here. I think we're safer if I move the truck into that stand of trees. Keep us more hidden. Wheaton is probably out driving around looking for her, looking for me."

Arlis relaxed a tiny bit. "Oh." She kept stroking Shawnee's hair.

Reparked, lights out, Cash lit another cigarette. "Spill," she said.

"I didn't do this. I got scared and ran. She threatened to kill me, too."

"She?"

"His wife. The woman's batshit crazy."

"What?"

"I don't like to say too much in front of small ears." She pressed Shawnee's head against her chest and covered her other ear with her hand.

"I think she's already seen too much," Cash said as her cigarette smoke filled the pickup. *And Jean Borgerud had made sure Shawnee was placed with her.* Cash felt a wave of terror course through her body at the thought. No wonder the little girl wouldn't talk. Cash waved a hand to send the smoke out the window.

The words flew from Arlis's mouth. "I didn't know she . . ."

Cash finished Arlis's sentence. "She was sleeping with Nils?"

"I found out that morning. He just never came back from working the fields up north. He wasn't the most faithful type anyways, but with a woman almost old enough to be his mother?" Tears rolled down her cheeks. "We've been together since we were kids." She paused. Breathed deep. "He's a really good dad to Shawnee."

"So what happened?"

Arlis took a deep breath and pressed Shawnee closer to her chest. "Early that morning the old man came to collect his rent. Asked for Nils. I asked him where Nils was." She emphasized the word *him*. "Told him I hadn't seen Nils since the day he went to work in Crookston. That he should know where Nils was, not me." She put her hand over the little girl's ear that wasn't pressed against her chest as if to shut out her words. "The next thing I know his Jean comes storming in with a rifle. Screaming that she hated him. Hated me. Something about Nils being a better man in bed than he'd ever been. Her eyes . . ." She paused and stared into the dark. "I only met Jean a few times. She seemed like the perfect farm wife. Always in a housedress. Hair fixed. Nils told me that sometimes she would bring homemade cinnamon rolls out for the men working in the fields. But that morning . . ." Arlis trailed off, then inhaled sharply as if seeing the woman with a rifle all over again.

Another pause, deep breath. She smoothed Shawnee's hair. Rubbed her back. Covered her ear again. "Shawnee was standing on the stairs. She heard all this. Saw all this. I motioned like this," she gave a slight wave of her free hand, "for her to go back and she scooted right upstairs. The old man went to grab the rifle from his wife and she shot him. It all happened so fast." She looked directly at Cash. "I froze."

Arlis stopped talking. Cash looked at Shawnee, curled in her mother's arms. Her small body rose and fell with each breath her mom took.

Finally, Arlis continued. "It all happened so fast. Next thing I knew, she was laying on top of Bud, crying, then she half stood and pointed the gun at me, saying it was all my fault. I took off running. I figured she'd come after me.

I didn't think she'd seen my baby. She shot at me a couple times as I ran. I was scared for my life. I didn't mean to leave Shawnee. I would never leave my baby. I hid in some trees a few miles over."

"Did you see Jean leave?"

"No. Not sure. Looked up once and saw dust from a car but I don't know if it was her or not. I meant to go back and get Shawnee but by the time I got over being scared and snuck back, then you were there. I saw you put her in the cop car and drive off with her. And then the cop and the doc were all over the place. I couldn't get my little girl."

"Why didn't you come back?"

"I was scared. I hitchhiked to my sister's at White Earth, borrowed her car to come back to get Shawnee, but when I stopped at the gas station to fill the tank, I overheard some folks saying the cops were looking for an Indian woman for murder! They said a white guy and an Indian guy had been killed. I didn't kill anyone. Who's going to believe an Indian over a white, god-fearing, churchgoing woman?" She broke down sobbing again.

Shawnee patted her mom's cheeks. "Shhh. Shhh," she said, mimicking her mom's words. Arlis pulled herself together. Used the hem of her T-shirt to wipe the tears off her face. Then Arlis, with hands over both Shawnee's ears, looked at Cash over her daughter's head, bewilderment on her face.

"Did she kill Nils?"

Cash shrugged. She didn't know what to say given the situation. Mother and daughter reunited. Arlis claiming

Jean shot Bud. Who killed Nils? Did Arlis know? What had Shawnee seen? Herself wanted for kidnapping if anyone found out she had taken Shawnee.

Arlis broke down into tears again. She whispered "Nils" over and over as she rocked Shawnee on her lap.

Cash smoked another cigarette. Swatted at a couple mosquitos that weren't deterred by the smoke. She watched the headlights of a vehicle move slowly down a road that ran perpendicular to where they sat. A tightening in her gut told her to be on guard. "Listen, I think someone's going to come over this way. Would be better if you two went and hid down in that cellar." As she spoke, she watched the car on the other road make a U-turn and head back to the turnoff that would bring whoever it was down the road to where they were sitting.

Arlis swiped the tears from her face and looked to where Cash pointed at the slow-moving vehicle.

"Hide in the cellar. Hurry up. And don't you dare try to leave." Cash put her hand over the inside light as Arlis opened the door and slid to the ground with Shawnee. As soon as her feet touched the earth, she took off running around the corner of the house. Cash heard the cellar door squeak and close with a soft thud. As the vehicle got closer, Cash recognized the headlights. Wheaton's cruiser. She reached over, grabbed the blanket and stuffed it under the seat. She lit another cigarette as Wheaton pulled into the driveway. He parked right behind her, blocking her in.

Cash got out of the Ranchero and walked to the passenger

side of the cruiser, bent down to talk to Wheaton through the rolled-down window.

"What are you doing out here?" Wheaton asked.

"Trying to get a sense of where the girl's mom might be."

"I've been trying to call you all day. That little girl is gone."

"What?!" Cash appreciated the darkness of the night.

"She disappeared sometime last night. Wouldn't happen to know anything about that, would you? Lay down," he snapped at Gunner, who was pacing back and forth across the back seat of the car, ears perked up, nostrils widened, smelling the air.

Cash reached into the window and rubbed the dog's neck, which only seemed to confuse him more. She kept her head out of Wheaton's view and glared at the dog. "Yeah, Gunner, sit down." Gunner sat and took the petting but looked at Cash like he knew she was guilty of something.

"Mrs. Borgerud called me this morning in hysterics. Took me a minute to figure out what she was saying. She went to wake the girl up for breakfast and she was gone. Said she put her to bed right at eight and went to bed herself around ten."

Yeah, she sure went to bed, Cash thought. Out loud, she asked, "She didn't check on her before she went to bed herself?" Cash kept rubbing Gunner's neck. She could feel the tension in the dog. The dog's readiness to check out whatever was hiding in the farmyard.

"Said the girl was sound asleep at ten. I drove by here earlier today. Thought maybe by some chance the girl had come this way. Half expected her to be sitting on the front steps. Long ways for a kid to run, but been known to happen. Checked back with Miss Dackson. Thought maybe she had removed the kid. Nope. She told me about Arlis's visit to the hotel. Dackson was as shocked as me that the girl is gone. Said she was checking for homes on the other side of the county for the girl after the stunt Arlis pulled earlier today." They both watched a car's headlights travel across the flat land in the far distance. "What are you doing out here this time of the night anyways?"

Cash swatted a mosquito. Ignored his last question. "Miss Dackson doesn't know anything?"

"Nah. She believes that Arlis probably kidnapped her. You know how that woman went crazy on her, tying her up in the hotel and all. Thought maybe the woman had found out from someplace, or someone"—his tone was slightly accusatory—"where Shawnee was placed."

"Not from me, Wheaton. I'm looking for Arlis, like I've been doing. Thought she might come back here. Just one of them feelings I get, you know?" She leaned so Wheaton could see her face, or at least what was visible in the darkness. Gave the show of innocence. She hadn't lied yet. Not exactly. "Where else could the kid be?"

"We searched the land around the Borgerud farmhouse where she was staying. Pulled together folks from town. Quit when it got too dark. Guess we'll start again in the morning."

"When you gonna start? I'll come over and help out."

"Early. Sunup."

"Ok, I'll be there."

Wheaton tightened his grasp on the steering wheel, stared off into the distance. Cleared his throat. Turned to stare at Cash in the dark. "You don't know anything about her disappearing?"

"Swear to god, Wheaton, cross my heart and hope to die. I don't know why you think I'd have anything to do with it."

Wheaton drummed his thumbs on the steering wheel. Both were silent a good long minute. Gunner nudged Cash's hand, perked his ears back up. Cash squeezed the fur on his neck and gently shook him. The dog whined.

"Oh for Pete's sake, Gunner, sit down. Should have left you in the gunnysack." His impatience with the dog told Cash how stressed he was. She rarely, if ever, remembered Wheaton talking harshly to the dog or to herself.

"He probably just wants to go home. You look wore out yourself. Maybe time for you both to hit the hay?"

Wheaton sighed. "You aren't gonna sit out here all night, are you?"

"Nah. Maybe another hour, just in case. I'll be there in the morning to look for Shawnee."

Both went silent. The hum of the car engine filled the night silence until Wheaton put the car in reverse and said, "Ope, best be going then. Get myself some rest. You too. See you in the morning."

Cash stood and watched him back out of the driveway, head back down the road the way he'd come, then turn in the direction of Ada.

Cash slapped a mosquito on her neck. Stood and watched the car until she could no longer see the taillights.

Opened the Ranchero's driver's-side door, reached in and felt around in the dark for the pink purse. She took the money from the purse, left the handgun in it, shoved the purse back under the seat, shoved the money into her two back jeans pockets and walked around the house to the cellar door. She stopped and looked around the barnyard, down each road that ran anywhere near the farm. Not a headlight or taillight in sight. She bent down and lifted the door. It creaked on rusty hinges. "It's me," she called. "Can you shine the flashlight on the steps so I can see to come down?"

A pale beam of yellow light flickered on and Cash descended the steps. The air in the root cellar was damp and musty but a few degrees cooler than the air outside. Arlis stood in the shadows near the bottom step, flashlight in one hand and a can of food in the other.

Cash stopped midstep, almost to the bottom. "Put the can down."

Cash heard more than saw Arlis reach over and put the can on the wooden shelf. Cash continued down. Arlis backed up to the cot where Shawnee was curled up under a blanket. Stood between her daughter and Cash.

"You drove here?" Cash asked.

"Yeah."

"It's in the barn?"

"Yeah."

"You know you can't just take her."

"I'm taking her. No one's taking her from me. Ever again."

"That was Sheriff Wheaton. They were searching all day

for her. They're going to search again tomorrow for her at the Borgerud farm."

Arlis sat down on the cot. Stroked Shawnee's hair.

"Nils is dead, isn't he?" Barely a whisper.

"Yeah."

Arlis's shoulders slumped. She wiped tears from her face. Sighed deeply. "We'll go to White Earth."

"When they don't find her here, that's the first place they'll go looking for her. And you. You're wanted for murder."

"I didn't kill anyone." Arlis kept her voice soft as she touched her daughter's hair. Brushed loose strands off her sleeping face.

"You're saying Mrs. Borgerud shot her husband."

Arlis nodded. "I was right there. I saw her." She got a trapped animal look. Her eyes darted around the dark cellar as if looking for a place to hide. She dropped her voice to a whisper. "She probably killed Nils, too. Or maybe he did."

Cash thought about that for a moment. Remembered the conversation at the Drive-Inn. Jeff's comment about the community being a rural *Peyton Place.* "You should tell Wheaton."

"No one's going to believe me. They'll just lock me up."

Cash knew it was true. A churchgoing white woman's word against an Indian woman's desperate act. Arlis didn't stand a chance. Even if Wheaton believed her. Both women listened to each other breathe in the dank air of the cellar.

Finally, with desperation in her voice, Arlis said, "We'll go to Roseau River in Canada. We'll just live up there. My mom talked about working with some of the women from there who come down to work the potato fields."

"What's Roseau River?" Cash asked.

"A reservation. Just like we have here. Just let me take my girl and go. Please?"

Images of Cash's own childhood flashed through her mind as she stood in the cellar looking at Arlis and Shawnee. She remembered lying awake in the first foster home she was placed in. For months, she had fought sleep, certain her mother would come to rescue her. Each morning she would wake, still at the foster home. Each month she slipped further and further into despondency, although she didn't know that word at the time. She remembered that at some point anger replaced her deep sadness and she started to fight the other foster kids. Anything could set her off. She fought kids bigger than herself and kicked and scratched like a wildcat whenever the foster mother tried to discipline her. She shook the images from her head.

"You should drive up on the North Dakota side of the river. Shouldn't be anyone looking for you over there. Come on. Get her into your car." Cash turned and walked up and out into fresh air. Arlis followed. She carried Shawnee, the little girl's head resting on her shoulder. At the corner of the house right before the driveway, Cash put out her arm, signaled for Arlis to stop while she walked around the house and checked the driveway and roads. "Coast is clear. Come on." She led the woman and her child to the barn.

Once they reached the barn, Cash stepped back to let Arlis lead. They all three squeezed in through the front door that was stuck about a foot open and sagging on its rusted hinges. The smell of old hay and long-gone farm animals filled the air in the dark barn. Cash heard a mouse scurry across the hayloft. Arlis led the way by feel and practice.

The loud crack of the car door opening broke the night silence. In the dim glow created by the dome light, Cash watched Arlis lay Shawnee on a pile of blankets in the back seat. Gently tuck the blankets around her. The mother brushed loose strands of hair off the girl's forehead.

When Arlis stood up and closed the door, Cash reached into her back pockets and pulled out the wads of bills. "Here. There should be enough here to make a good start. You can't show back up this way ever again."

Tears streamed down Arlis's face. She grabbed a stiff Cash in her arms and hugged her tight. "Thank you."

Cash didn't return the hug. Endured the moment. Fought the tightness in her chest. Released a breath when Arlis finally let go. "I'll get the doors for you," she said as she walked to the heavy doors at the back of the barn. She pushed them open. Stood in the red gleam of the taillights as Arlis backed the car out, turned it around in the pasture grass, and drove across the field to the roadway. Like she had watched Wheaton drive away, Cash watched Arlis drive off in the opposite direction. Loneliness, although Cash didn't know the word to describe how she felt, enveloped her.

CASH STOPPED AT THE LIQUOR store in Halstad and bought a six-pack of beer. Drank three on the way back into Fargo. Thoughts of her own mother crept out of the corners of her consciousness again. Cash tried to remember her sister. Couldn't pull up a face or a name. Cursed her brother who had re-entered her life briefly before re-upping to Nam. Left her with a deck of cards to play solitaire with. She threw the empties angrily out into the ditch as she drove. Chain-smoked. With an hour before closing time, she stopped in at the Casbah. Downed more beer while she shot pool and pushed off farm boys' advances while taking their money at the table.

At closing time, she decided to drive out into the country. When she left Fargo, the streetlights were calling moths to the flame as well as one bat. She drove the speed limit and kept between the white lines. She drove through the town of Ada and saw Wheaton's cruiser parked outside his house. The blue light of a television screen snuck out around the edges of the curtains in his living room. Cash drove to Halstad. Drove slowly down Main Street on the slight chance that Jeff might be around. Nope. She headed out of town toward the Borgerud farm. Pulled into a turnoff to a beet field three miles from the farm. Shut off the engine and spread a blanket out in the bed of the truck. She lay on her back, smoking cigarettes as the stars hung in the sky. She floated between wake and sleep.

The sky was pitch black, except the stars that seemed within reach. The frogs in the ditches had decided she wasn't a threat and they called their mates in loud croaks. The crickets chirped.

Sunrise woke her. Cash pushed herself into a sitting position. Surveyed the farmland around her. There were no cars on the road, but in the distance she could see cars headed to the Borgerud farm. She sat a few minutes in silence. Then she crawled out of the pickup bed, peed in the ditch, then climbed into the Ranchero and drove to join the searchers.

Cash didn't know what the day would hold. She expected there to be a crowd of farmers, their oldest children, and a passel of farm wives. She also expected a group of church ladies to be there with breakfast rolls for the group. Some of the women might already be in Jean's kitchen making bologna sandwiches for the noon break.

Cash anticipated that Wheaton would ask her again if she knew where Shawnee went off to. But she didn't expect any of the other searchers to pay her any mind. Most farmers never expected her to talk. When you worked the fields, if there was conversation, it centered on the weather or machinery—did it work or what was busted? How were the crops doing, or not doing? In general, the town folks acted as if she didn't exist.

When she pulled into the farmyard, the first people she saw were familiar faces. Wheaton. Jeff. Mrs. Borgerud. Miss Dackson. And they all turned to look at her when she stepped out of the Ranchero. Wheaton, with a question on his face, anxiously rubbed his crew cut back, like a strand of hair might be hanging across his forehead. Miss Dackson, who wore a prim navy-blue skirt and white button-down blouse, looked at her with an expression that read, *You had to have something to do with this.* Jeff looked scared—like the barely-out-of-high-school boy that he was. Next to him was Mrs. Borgerud, hands on hips, a slight breeze blowing the skirt of her housedress against her legs. She might have looked seductive except her eyes, keenly focused on Cash, were filled with rage. Cash saw that clearly now. She stopped up short as she shut the door of the Ranchero behind her.

"What are you doing here?" spat Mrs. Borgerud at the same time Miss Dackson exclaimed, "If you know where that child is you better tell me."

The other searchers, who had been in conversation with each other as they drank steaming coffee from Styrofoam cups, all turned to look at Cash. Tension quickly filled the early-morning air. Even Gunner sensed danger and perked his ears up. Looked back and forth between the two women and Cash.

Wheaton brushed his crew cut back again. Took a step forward. Held up a hand. "Whoa, ladies, hold up there."

Cash said nothing. Didn't move. Looked from Wheaton to the women and back to Wheaton. Without thinking, she patted her leg and Gunner trotted over and sat on his haunches by her side. Ears pinned back. Black eyes focused on the crowd.

The two women looked to Wheaton.

"Everyone calm down." Wheaton was exasperated. "Cash doesn't have anything to do with this. We talked last night. Right now, our focus needs to be on finding the little girl." He turned to the rest of the crowd. "We'll line up like we did yesterday."

"We're going to cover the same ground again?" one of the men asked.

"We are," answered Wheaton. "All you adults form a line. Walk arm's length apart. Be sure to check the culverts. Good hiding place for a kid. You"—he pointed to a group of young men, who Cash recognized as the local high school football team—"I want you to search every building from top to bottom. Every nook and cranny. One building at a time." Jeff moved over to join that crew. "And you"—he pointed to the Ladies Aid group—"I know we've checked and checked, but go through the house one more time before you start making the lunch. Kids play hide and seek all the time. She might have found a hiding space we missed. The rest of you, go four miles out, scoot over the same width and come the four miles back. Hopefully"—and he swung his arms in a circle—"we'll get this whole area covered by two-three o'clock today. The ladies will bring sandwiches out to the field so you won't have to stop searching. Let's go." He motioned for Cash to join him.

The two leaned in silence against the hood of his cruiser and watched the various groups of people disperse. Gunner lay on the ground by Wheaton's feet. Cash lit a cigarette and blew the smoke upward toward the clear blue sky.

"It's gonna be a hot one." Wheaton used his sleeve to wipe the sweat off his forehead. "You don't have any idea where she is?"

Cash shook her head no. It was an honest answer, she thought. Maybe Arlis was somewhere in Canada by now. She blew a smoke ring and watched it float toward a nearby lilac bush.

"I kinda hoped you'd have a dream or something."

Cash shook her head no again. Ground the cigarette butt out under her heel. Lit another.

"Mrs. Borgerud is really upset. Miss Dackson too. Hope we find the girl," he said.

"The only dream I had was one where Arlis said she'd be back for her."

Wheaton looked hard at Cash.

Cash avoided eye contact. "It was when she first left. Remember? I went over to White Earth. I tried to find her. No luck. Never thought she'd actually come steal her back." She blew more smoke into the air. "I don't know. I'm thinking if we don't find her, she's probably with her mom somewhere." She ground out the cigarette and stuffed her hands in her back pockets. Shifted to a more comfortable lean on the hood. "I don't think Arlis killed either of those men."

Wheaton looked at her hard again.

"Just a feeling," Cash said, briefly glancing at him. She shrugged. "Where you want me to look today?"

"I'm going to check on the women. Whyn't you check on the guys in the barn. When they're done in there, tell 'em to check that pole barn next." Wheaton pushed off the hood and moved toward the house.

Cash assessed the barn as she crossed the driveway. Barn swallows flew in circles near the wide sliding door on the first floor. She could see two young men standing upstairs in the open doorway of the hayloft on the second floor. Hay dust filtered by the sun made them look almost angelic, especially the one with blond curls. *If you ignore the jeans and work boots*, she thought to herself. A wrought iron lightning rod with a copper four-direction arrow moved in the slight breeze atop the barn roof. Judging by the upkeep of the barn, Mr. Borgerud had been one of the more successful farmers in the Valley.

Cash stepped inside the barn. Barn dust, stirred up by the searchers, hung in the warm air. Three searchers turned to look at her but went right back to moving old milk cans as they checked one corner of the barn. Jeff wasn't one of them. She spotted the wooden ladder tacked to the barn wall that led to the hayloft. She was halfway up when a shower of hay stalks dropped down on her. She shielded her eyes with one hand and looked up to see Jeff peering down on her.

"We were just coming down," he said. Two towheads appeared beside him. "We've looked in every nook and cranny. Nothing up here except a litter of barn cats."

"All right," said Cash, backing down the steps. "Wheaton said to move on to the pole barn then."

Although Cash could tell Jeff was trying to avoid her, she positioned herself next to him on the walk to the pole barn. "Where were you that night?"

"No place." He quickened his steps, trying to leave her and the group of teens behind him.

Cash matched his pace. "Little more happening around here than just farm management. Figure more fields are getting plowed than Mr. Borgerud knew he had in acreage."

"That's crude."

Cash shrugged. "So you didn't hear or notice anything different?"

222 · MARCIE R. RENDON

"Who says I was here?"

"Let's just say that I know you were."

"I didn't see anything. Didn't hear anything." He looked scared as it dawned on him that maybe Cash was accusing him. "And I sure as hell didn't do anything to that kid."

"Two people in the house and no one heard anything?"

"Look, we were busy. And who says she disappeared while I was there?"

Cash kept her face stoic. She was enjoying his discomfort. As he talked, she looked toward the farmhouse. Mrs. Borgerud was standing outside, one hand on her hip, her chest seductively close to Wheaton. Then, as if she felt Cash's presence, she turned and met Cash's eyes.

Jean's eyes flickered to Jeff. Her face clouded and her hands curled into fists. She squinted, oblivious to what her face was showing Wheaton. Jealousy shot across the farmyard. Cash saw Wheaton notice the skin on Jean's face tighten with rage and then she watched him turn to see what Jean was focused on. He looked from Jean to Cash to Jean to Jeff and back to Cash again. Cash raised her eyebrows and looked from Jean to Jeff and back to Jean.

Unaware of what was happening, but reacting as if hit by the tension that was shooting back and forth between Jean and Cash, Jeff quickened his pace to the pole barn. Again, Cash quickened her steps to keep up with him. Cash was by his side, in step. When they entered, the only source of light in the pole barn came from the doorway. Cash could feel Jean's rage hit the space between her shoulder blades. Then she and Jeff were swallowed up in the dark, damp coolness of the pole barn. She exhaled, not realizing she had been holding her breath.

"I don't know what you see in her," Cash said, turning from the darkness to look behind them into the sunlit yard.

"Guess." Jeff shook his head as he stood beside Cash and seemed to relax slightly. Both of them appreciated the shroud of darkness they stood in. They felt safe knowing that Jean and Wheaton could only see their outlines.

Their preoccupation was interrupted by the captain of the football team barking orders. "We're going to form a line and start at the back of the shed. Everyone an arm's width apart. Check inside each piece of machinery and underneath. In the tire wells. Any place a little kid might think to hide." The group of young men brushed past Jeff and Cash.

"I better help," said Jeff, turning to follow the younger men.

"Guess I'll brave the storm and tell Wheaton no luck in the barn," Cash said to his retreating back.

Cash took a deep breath and walked out of the pole barn toward Jean and Wheaton. When Jean saw her coming, she went back into her house, slammed the screen door behind her.

"No luck?" Wheaton asked as she approached.

"No luck," Cash answered. They both went back to leaning on the hood of his car. Cash lit a cigarette. Wheaton leaned down and plucked a blade of grass to chew on.

"What was that all about earlier? Between you, Jean and Jeff?"

"The woman's nuts." Cash tried to think of a way to share that Jean and Jeff were sleeping together. Share what Arlis said about seeing Jean shoot Bud. But how could she say all that without letting him know she had taken Shawnee?

Before she could formulate her thoughts, Wheaton said, "That woman's worried sick." He scanned the area around them. "I'm worried, too. If Shawnee's out there by herself, poor tyke's scared out of her mind by now. And hungry. Jean said there isn't any food missing."

Rather than say anything that she had just thought, Cash said, "I'm still leaning more toward her mom got her somehow. I doubt Jean's worried about her. Probably more worried about what she might say if she decided to talk. Or what the neighbors think of her." She bent down and scratched the dog behind its ears. "Gunner doesn't seem to be too worried. Seems like if she were here, he'd be poking around. Like he did with Nils's body under the corncrib."

"Thought so too," Wheaton responded. He pointed at the line of searchers down the field behind the house, who were specks on the horizon. "Good to see so many come out to help."

The rest of the day passed in a summer haze. Humid Valley heat. Feathery white clouds across a clear blue sky. Barnyard animal noises. The smell of fresh dirt from a nearby plowed field carried on a barely discernable breeze. Small white moths flitted over the short white clover in the green grass. Bologna sandwiches and fresh baked chocolate chip cookies carried out to the searchers by apron-wearing housewives. Sweaty searchers, when they finally arrived back in the yard, complained of the heat, the pesky mosquitos, and the rash from ditch weeds on their ankles.

The young men crawled out of the dank farmyard buildings with the same layer of sweat, but itchy from cobwebs
and hay or straw dust. Everyone talked in subdued tones
as they stood around on the front lawn, smoking cigarettes
and drinking tepid coffee. No one wanted to admit defeat.
All felt remorse that they hadn't found the girl.

Cash felt a twinge of guilt that she couldn't tell them
what she knew. Just a slight twinge.

She left with the last of the stragglers. Left when
Wheaton called it a day. He headed to Ada. She to the Red
River just west of Halstad. At the bridge, she pulled off to
the side of the road. Checked for traffic in either direction.
Seeing none, she exited the Ranchero, reached behind the
seat and quickly pulled out the pink purse. Felt the slight
extra weight of the handgun in it. Stuffed the gun in the back
waistband of her pants. Bent down on the side of the road
and filled the purse with gravel. Tucked it under the front
of her T-shirt and walked to the center of the bridge.

The slow waters of the Red River ran twenty feet below
the bridge. The only time she remembered the river flowing
rapidly was during the spring floods. The rest of the time
it seemed to mosey on north. The water too muddy to see
the catfish that lived in it and grew to four feet in length.
Cash again looked both directions on the roadway. No cars.
She crossed to the other side of the bridge. Made sure no
fishermen were on either bank. Walked back across the
roadway to the bridge railing. She dropped the pink purse
into the water and watched it sink. She looked up and down
the road. No one. She reached for the gun tucked in her

waistband and dropped it in the water. Lost in the sound of the water, the buzz of mosquitos and the soft flutter of cottonwood leaves in the midst of hardwood oak, she watched the river flow for a good long time.

This time, this space, this solitude in nature. It was this land and this river that had fed her soul in the absence of her mother and the rest of her family. This river. These trees. These fields of black dirt, plowed broken fields, that lie flat thirty to forty miles either side of the river. This is what fed her soul. Kept her spirit alive.

Cash heard a car before she saw it. She stayed still, watched the car approach and lifted a hand to a farm wife crossing the bridge in a gray sedan. She had driven across the bridge herself many times and seen someone gazing down into the river. A not uncommon sight.

SIGNS OF HER RECENT COMPANY were evident throughout Cash's apartment. The cards from Sharon and Shawnee's game of slapjack were strewn across the table. Cash scooped up the cards, shuffled them and rapped them firmly on the kitchen counter so they were perfectly aligned to better slide into their paper case. Toast crumbs littered the other side of the table where Shawnee had sat not even forty-eight hours earlier. The towel she used to dry bath water off the little girl hung on the bathroom doorknob. If she breathed in deeply, she could catch a whiff of urine from the mattress in the bedroom.

It was late afternoon. The sun wasn't even close to the horizon. She cleaned up any sign of anyone being in her space. Pulled the phone out of the cupboard and plugged it back in. Turned the ringer to its lowest notch. Opened the bedroom window to let fresh air in. Ran hot water in the tub. Got a beer from her fridge. She set an ashtray on the floor next to the tub then sank naked into the hot water, her long hair tied in a knot on top of her head.

She didn't know what to make of the knowledge Arlis had given her. That Mrs. Borgerud shot her own husband. Had been sleeping with Nils. The prim and proper church woman, the wife who helped run her husband's farm. And she was now having sex with a guy young enough to be her own son. Cash shook her head, thought, *Just days, if not the same day, as when she buried her husband.* And the only people who could prove her guilt, who were eyewitnesses to the crime, were probably now in Canada. One a woman who would almost certainly be accused and convicted of the crime if caught. And a child, so terrified by the events that occurred she went silent.

Cash blew smoke rings at the ceiling. Relaxed her body and mind. By the time she stubbed out the cigarette, climbed out of the tub and wrapped herself in a towel, she had a plan.

CASH CHECKED THE ROLL OF bills in her top dresser drawer. If she asked Wheaton for some gas money, she had enough cash for rent, cigarettes and beer. She could go another week without a farm job to see her through. If worse came to worst, she'd have to hustle a few games at The Flame strip club. Take the men's money when their attention wasn't on the pool table but on the women gyrating on the pole.

She filled up the gas tank and drove to Jonesy's shack in the tamarack at White Earth. Summer sun shone down through the branches of the trees. Green foliage lined the road, from the ground right near the edge of the road to the blue sky barely visible through the coverage the trees provided.

Jonesy was outside tending to some plants growing inside a small square of dirt. She stood, hoe in hand, as Cash pulled into her driveway. She was dressed in blue jeans and a man's blue plaid shirt. One long braid, mostly black with some strands of gray, hung down her back almost to her knees. It was hard to tell how old she might be. The wrinkles on her face could be from years in the sun or from years lived. She nodded when Cash stepped out of the Ranchero. She motioned with her head that Cash should join her inside.

Between bites of venison stew, Cash told Jonesy about taking Shawnee and giving her to Arlis. About lying to Wheaton by not telling him about what she had done, by pretending to participate in the search for Shawnee. Jonesy listened without saying a word. Refilled their teacups and listened some more.

Jonesy chuckled. "Maybe that's what them Catholics mean by sins of omission. Don't be so hard on yourself," she added when Cash grimaced.

Cash moved a piece of venison around on her plate with her fork. "I think I've figured out how to catch Mrs. Borgerud. I just have to do it in a way that Wheaton is there when it happens, so there is no question in his mind. So maybe, sometime in the future, when this all dies down, Arlis will be able to return home with Shawnee. So Arlis can come back to her own mother here on White Earth. Come back to her own family."

Jonesy took a drink of tea. Sat quiet in thought before she spoke. "We are generations of grief. Children taken and placed in boarding schools. Parents and grandparents left to grieve, never knowing when or if their children would return. And then when they did return, many of us couldn't speak the language. Didn't understand the trees and the seasons. Couldn't hear the birds or understand the language of the plants. Then those children grew up to become parents themselves. But they hadn't been parented. They were raised by priests and nuns, who never had children of their own. Pile abuse on top of that and the children who came home and grew up and had children didn't know how to parent them."

Cash put the last piece of venison in her mouth and chewed slowly.

Jonesy continued. "It seems like Arlis is determined to be a mom. She protected Shawnee first by running away from evil. And then, it took courage and determination to get her back. I imagine there were many nights you laid awake, wanting your mom to come for you."

Cash couldn't swallow the food she had chewed. Her eyes stung and her right foot pushed against the floor, ready to stand and run.

Jonesy put her hand on Cash's arm. Cash felt, and in her

mind's eye she saw, a blue lightning current fly from Jonesy's hand into her own arm, through her own chest and out the top of her head.

Jonesy said softly, "There are some things we can never run from. We might try to, but the spirits move faster. We can't outrun them. We each have a purpose here." She made a sideways wave of her hand as if moving a curtain aside. "A purpose that was determined before we ever arrived here. We can run from that purpose. But it will always find us. And every time we run, there will be a hardship to face. Or we can learn from what life hands us, because the purpose will always find us before we leave this earth." As she paused, Cash felt another current run up her arm. Jonesy patted her hand and said, "You should just sit and finish your tea."

Cash did just that.

When she drank the last drop, Jonesy walked outside with her. The pink light filtering down through the trees signaled that the sun was close to the western horizon.

"I wouldn't worry too much about Wheaton," Jonesy said to Cash's back as she walked to the Ranchero. "Maybe next time you visit there'll be string beans from this scraggly garden to feed you."

When Cash looked in the rearview mirror, the old woman was bent over the plants she had been tending when Cash first arrived. Small blue and bright white flickers of light swept across the garden. *Not dark enough to see lightning bugs*, she thought, but after having experienced lightning pass from the woman to herself, she just shook her head, lit a cigarette and drove west.

Cash stopped at the café in Twin Valley and asked for a cup of coffee to go. She half expected, half hoped to catch Wheaton there, maybe find out once and for all if this girlfriend she heard talk of really existed. But no Wheaton. And their regular waitress wasn't working either. *Maybe they're on a date*, she thought as she waited for her coffee.

On her way out of the café, she stopped at the pay phone in the entryway. Thumbed through the phone book until she found a number for Jeffrey Johanson and ripped the page out, folded it and stuffed it in her back pocket when she realized she didn't have enough change to make the phone call.

ONCE SHE GOT INTO ADA, she pulled into the gas station where a phone booth stood out near the intersection. She ran into the station to get change to call the Johanson number. Back at the pay phone, out of habit, she checked the return slot for any loose change. It was empty. She dropped coins into the slots and listened to the inner workings of the phone. After three rings, she was ready to hang up when a man's voice said, "Hello?"

"Can I speak to Jeff?" she asked.

"This is," he said.

Cash paused. The voice was too old. "Jeff, manager for Borgerud's?"

"Just a sec." The man must have put his hand over the mouthpiece because his voice was muffled when Cash heard him yell, "Jeff. Phone. Sounds like one of your girls." Then unmuffled. "Just a sec."

Cash waited. Could hear the canned laughter of a TV show in the background. The operator told her to deposit another fifteen cents for another three minutes. Cash dropped a dime and nickel in the slots. Waited.

"Hello?"

"This is Cash."

"Oh."

"Thinking I'd stop by Jean's tomorrow around noon. Looking for work."

"Uh."

"Running out of change to talk. I'll swing by."

"Uh."

"I'll be there at noon."

The operator asked for another fifteen cents. Cash hung up.

From there she drove to Wheaton's. His cruiser was parked outside his house. His kitchen curtains were open and Cash could see him as he stood at his sink drinking a glass of water. He answered on her first knock. Held the door and stepped back for her to enter. "Come on in. What brings you out?"

Cash looked around his kitchen. Tidy as always. Pulled out a chair at the Formica-topped kitchen table. Gunner padded out from the living room, looked at her and padded back into the other room.

"I'm pretty sure Mrs. Borgerud is the one who shot her husband and Nils."

"Cash," Wheaton said in a tone that sounded an awful lot like, "Come on, really?" He put a cup of coffee in front of her and then sat down on a chair opposite her with his own cup. Pointed at the cream and sugar on the table. "Everything points to Arlis. Her running away. Attacking Miss Dackson."

Cash busied herself with the cream and sugar. As she stirred the coffee, she said, "I'm going out to her farm tomorrow at noon. Can you meet me there? I don't feel safe around her by myself."

"For Pete's sake, use your head. Why you going then?"

"Ask her about her husband. About Nils. I think she might go a little wacko on me."

"Cash, she's in grief. And upset about Shawnee missing."

"No. She's only worried about Shawnee missing because the girl knows the truth about what happened there that morning. And it scared her silent." Cash took a drink of coffee. "And I know when someone hates me and that woman hates me. I think she's the kinda woman that hates most women."

"If she hates women, why would she kill her husband? And Nils? Maybe the whole situation with Shawnee has you overreacting. Maybe reminds you of yourself?"

Cash scraped her chair back from the table. She was halfway standing when Wheaton reached out, touched her arm with just enough firmness to stop her. "Sit down. Come on. I didn't mean to upset you. I don't want to upset Jean either. She's been through a lot. Losing her husband. Shawnee disappearing."

Cash sat back down, but not as close to the table as before. Left herself some running room. "And you're a guy."

Wheaton raised his eyebrows in a question.

"I saw her flirting with you at the search."

"She was just being friendly."

"And you're dense. She was flirting, and I'm telling you, she's dangerous. And even if I am crazy, can you please come out there at noon tomorrow?"

Wheaton looked at her. Assessed her seriousness. "You're going whether I come or not, aren't you?"

Cash nodded. Finished her coffee. Stood to leave.

Wheaton walked her to his door. Held it open for her. From the Ranchero, Cash looked back. Wheaton, with Gunner by his leg, stood watching her leave. When she turned the corner at the end of the block, she looked in her rearview mirror. Wheaton and his dog still stood there.

CASH DREAMT OF SHAWNEE RUNNING barefoot in the woods around Jonesy's house. Arlis ran after her. Both of them were laughing. Shawnee hid behind a tree. "You can't find me."

Arlis said, "Yes, I can. I will always find you." When she got to the tree, she scooped Shawnee up into her arms and smothered her face with kisses. Shawnee laughed. She grabbed her mom's face between her small hands.

"Who's the girl who brought me home?"

And in that moment, Arlis's face became her own mother's face.

Cash woke with a start. Her pillow was damp with tears. She jumped out of bed, ran to the bathroom and threw water on her face, brushed her hair and braided it in one braid that hung down her back. Ate toast. Drank coffee. Checked the .22 behind the seat of the Ranchero. Made sure there was a shell in it. Kept the safety off. Regretted throwing the pistol off the bridge. Went to the Casbah.

Ol' Man Willie, from his bar stool throne, raised his glass in her direction. "Well, look what the cat drug in. Weren't we the last two to leave last night? Not that I remember leaving. Did I leave?" He turned to Shorty, raised his glass. "And now we're the first here? Least I know when I meet my maker, someone will be here to keep this barstool warm. Keep Shorty in clean underwear. Dirty job, but someone's gotta do it."

"Disgusting." Cash put a couple bills on the counter. "Quarters for the table and a beer."

Shorty shook his head. "Nah, Cash, I ain't serving you this time of the morning. Here's your quarters and I'll give you a cup of my coffee."

"That mud will put hair on your chest." Ol' Man Willie chuckled. "Them little titties will grow hair down to your knees." He laughed at his own joke.

Cash ignored him, took the coffee and quarters to the pool table.

Shorty sat behind his bar, close enough to the beer on tap that he could reach over and refill the old man's glass without getting up. He watched the black-and-white TV over the bar with the sound off and Ol' Man Willie drank his beers in silence. The clack of billiard balls kept everyone company.

Cash willed herself into the zone, that place where every

expert will tell they go to achieve perfection. Time and noise and other outside distractions disappear. It was Cash, her cue stick, the billiard balls and the pockets either side of the green to drop the balls into. Every so often Cash would exit the zone to look at the Hamm's Beer bear clock over the bar. She knew Shorty kept it running fifteen minutes fast so each night when he called "Last call" he was giving himself a few minutes' leeway.

When the clock said ten forty-five, Cash shot the remaining balls into any nearby pocket, hung the cue stick up on the wall, waved a hand at Shorty and left. As the screen door shut behind her, she heard Ol' Man Willie say, "Hair on her titties. Hang to her knees like that braid down her back." She could hear his laughter turn to a coughing fit as she walked to the Ranchero.

Cash drove across the river into Moorhead and north toward the farmland between Halstad and Ada. She passed fields where migrant workers hoed beets in the sun that already threatened temps in the eighties. She raised her hand in the farmer's wave at cars and pickups that were headed into Fargo–Moorhead for tractor parts or groceries. On either side of the road, fields were green with new growth: sugar beets, potatoes, wheat, corn, oats and a few fields where farmers had planted soybeans, a crop new to the area. The rich Red River dirt was doing what it had since the immigrants from the old world had arrived. It was growing food for the world.

Cash had driven the road from F-M to Halstad, from F-M to Ada, enough times in the last few years that she didn't need a watch to tell her how long a drive it was. At the Borgerud farmstead, she parked her Ranchero alongside Jeff's pickup.

Jeff must have been watching for her because he came out the screen door as soon as she stepped out of her truck. She walked to the back end of his pickup and waited for him to join her. From that vantage point she could see Jean Borgerud standing in the shadow of her house behind the closed screen door. Watching.

"I don't know," Jeff said he approached Cash.

"Don't know?"

"She"—he leaned his head toward the house—"she doesn't want me to hire you."

"Pussy whipped? Already?"

Jeff hung his head. He might have even blushed. Hard to tell with the farmer tan, which was really sunburn, on his face. He rested both hands on the tailgate, arms stretched out. He looked like he was holding on for dear life. "Come on, Cash."

Cash kept one eye on the door of the house. She moved close enough to Jeff that her chest was touching his upper arm and she put a hand on his lower arm. Smiled up at him and said softly, "I need a job."

The screen door banged open. Jean Borgerud, in a snug-fitting housedress that flared out from the apron tied at her waist, stood in the doorway, rifle in her arms. She pointed the rifle in their direction.

"Whoa!" exclaimed Jeff.

Cash pushed him behind the truck cab as Jean screeched, "Get off my property, you red-skinned piece of trash!"

Cash ducked down as the woman fired a shot that went

over her head. She screamed at Jeff as he started to crabwalk toward her. "Get back over there. She can't shoot us both if we stay in two places." Cash popped back up and hollered over the truck bed, "I found Shawnee!"

Jean lowered the rifle a titch. Reached into her apron pocket and inserted another shell.

"She decided to talk," Cash said loudly.

The rifle came back up. Pointed directly at Cash. "Where is she."

Cash, ready to duck back down by Jeff, scanned the roadways. No sign of Wheaton.

"Not going to tell you if you keep shooting at me. Put the rifle down."

"What did that little bitch say?"

"Whoa." Another soft comment from Jeff, who was scrunched down behind his truck.

Cash lied. "She said you shot your husband."

"Lying little bitch. You all are alike. Two-faced sluts."

"She's a child," Cash spat back angrily.

"Where is she?" Jean stayed on her front step. "Stand up, Jeff, where I can see you too."

Cash motioned for Jeff to stay down. She stood up. Ducked as she saw Jean raise the rifle again. Heard the bullet fly in the air above her. *Where the hell is Wheaton?* Cash thought as she scanned the roadways from her low vantage point. Saw a puff of dust farther down one of the roads. Heard Jean put another shell in her rifle.

"Did you sleep with her dad?" Cash hollered. "Kill them both?"

"Is that what she told you? Her mother ran. Missed her. Or she'd be under the corncrib too."

"Why'd you kill the men?" Cash hollered, still ducked down.

"One guy had too much dick, the other not enough."

"Shit." Jeff, still hidden, spoke softly. "People were talking about her sleeping around. I thought it was just gossip."

"Well, now they'll be talking about you," Cash retorted quietly.

Cash could smell road dust. She peeked up. It was Wheaton's cruiser. She glanced at the woman. She was frozen in her spot at the doorway to the house. Cash saw that Jean was hyper focused on where Cash and Jeff were. Cash knew the look. Jean was in the zone, the same zone Cash went to when she shot pool. Nothing existed outside the cue stick, the white cue ball, the ball that was destined for a pocket. The rifle had become a part of Jean. Cash was the ball headed to drop in a pocket. Jean was oblivious to the fact that Wheaton had pulled into the yard, driver's-side window rolled down.

Cash raised her voice and asked, "So you killed Nils? And your own husband? I'm gonna stand up and tell you where Shawnee is. She's talking now but if you shoot me, you'll never find her."

Cash stood slowly, ready to duck down at the slightest movement of Jean's hands. The woman's farm dress hugged her thighs and a slight breeze blew hair across her cheek that she didn't bother to swipe away. Except for the rifle in her hands, she could have been posing in *Good Housekeeping*.

Except her eyes, too. The woman's eyes were devoid of emotion. Cash lied again. "She saw you shoot your husband."

"I didn't know she was in the house. Her damn mother ran like a jackrabbit. Hip-hopping across the field." Jean laughed, repeating what she'd said earlier.

Jean's laugh let Cash know the woman was sliding farther from the edge of reality. "She's sleeping in the cab of my truck. I brought her here with me."

Without hesitation, Jean fired into the passenger door of the Ranchero. Cash was too stunned to move. She watched Jean rapidly load another shell into the rifle and fire again.

"Sic 'em!" From a far distance, like someone hollering down from the top of a grain silo to someone standing at the bottom, Cash heard Wheaton yell again, "Sic 'em."

Cash didn't see Gunner run but she saw the dog hit the woman, bite down on the nearest arm, heard the rifle drop, heard Jean scream. Saw Wheaton kick the rifle away, grab Gunner's collar and pull him off the woman.

Cash looked at the door of her Ranchero. The metal pierced by two bullet holes. The window shattered down into the insides of the door. Jeff, in shock, stared at her through the driver's-side window. He pointed at the empty car seat, the question, *Where is Shawnee?* in his eyes. Cash burst into tears. Leaned her head on the side of her truck and sobbed.

The next thing she knew, Jeff was patting her back like she was a baby. Angrily, she brushed him off and wiped the tears from her eyes. The whole yard seemed overbright. She had a brief thought about kryptonite glowing or god parting the heavens and angels streaming down. But there was only the harsh reality of Wheaton as he put handcuffs on Jean. Sun glinted off the rifle on the ground and the diamond ring on Jean's hand. Gunner lay in the grass, tongue out, ears perked. Cash squinted to block the brightness. The air vibrated around her like the hum of a thousand wasps.

"What the hell is going on here?" Wheaton hollered.

The brightness went out of Cash's world. She had never seen him this angry.

"She thought Shawnee was in my truck."

Wheaton was incredulous as he pulled a sobbing Jean to her feet. "You tried to kill Shawnee?"

"She said she killed her husband and Nils," Jeff piped up.

"What the hell are you doing here?" Wheaton shouted back at Jeff as he walked Jean to his cruiser.

"He's my new farm manager. And . . . a friend."

The tone of Jean's voice made Wheaton look between her and Jeff. Jeff avoided the question and looked down at his feet.

"Are you dumber than you look, son?" Wheaton asked, his hand tight on Jean's bent elbow.

"Sure is," said Cash.

Wheaton put Jean in the back seat of his cruiser, pointed at Gunner to get in and said to the dog, "Sit." Gunner couldn't have looked prouder. When the dog looked at Cash, she gave the dog the finger.

"What's that for?" asked Jeff.

"Dog gets on my nerves," Cash answered. "You okay?"

"I don't think I want to know you. Almost got me killed three times now."

"Thought it was two?"

He leaned his head in the direction of Jean. "She's like that black widow spider you hear about. Kills her husband, or eats him, after they, you know, do their thing."

"Do their thing. You did her thing." Cash started to laugh. "You're lucky I saved you, Mr. *Peyton Place*."

Cash sat down on the ground. Leaned her back against the bottom of the shot-up door. Both of them glanced at Jean in the back of the cruiser. Gunner standing guard. Wheaton still angry, glaring at them both. Cash pulled out a cigarette. Offered one to Jeff.

"I don't smoke," he said, taking it from her, his hands shaking.

Cash lit his cigarette, then hers. Jeff coughed on his first drag but kept smoking. Wheaton looked at the two of them. Shook his head. "Will need to talk to the two of you back in town. Gonna need a picture of that door for evidence."

After Wheaton drove away, Cash and Jeff finished their cigarettes in silence. The summer sun baked down on them.

Finally, Cash stood, brushed gravel off her butt. "Guess I better go talk to Wheaton."

"Me too." Jeff stood. "Cigarette made me dizzy."

Cash shook her head. "Kids."

Jeff, some of his old swagger back, stuck his thumbs in his belt loops and said, "Man enough for some."

Cash shook her head again.

———

THEY SPENT THE REMAINDER OF the afternoon answering Wheaton's questions. First, Wheaton made Cash wait while he took Jeff into a back room alone. When he brought Jeff back out, he told him to have a seat and wait on the oak bench that Cash thought of as hers. Then he motioned for Cash to go with him.

In the back room, Wheaton's secretary was sitting at a small desk off to the side, a Smith Corona typewriter and a stack of blank paper in front of her. Wheaton sat behind a large wooden table and Cash across from him. A tape recorder sat in the middle of the table. Wheaton had a small stack of papers in front of him. Cash realized they were rote questions, probably the same ones he had asked Jeff. He was seeing if their stories matched. Cash answered each question; Wheaton waited until his secretary was done typing before he asked Cash the next one. The only sound in the room was the *click-click* of the typewriter keys and the ding the return bar made when the secretary shifted to a new line. Wheaton barely made eye contact with Cash. After the last question on the last page, he asked, "Anything else you want to tell me?"

Cash shook her head no.

"You have to answer out loud," Wheaton said.

"No," Cash said.

As he stood up, Wheaton shut off the tape recorder that had been running throughout their time in the room. "That's it for today. Think you can stay out of trouble for a while?" It wasn't a question.

Cash nodded yes.

When she joined Jeff in the main office, she spoke under her breath. "I feel like a criminal and I didn't even do anything wrong."

"Can we go?" Jeff asked, just as quietly.

Cash shrugged. "He didn't say we couldn't."

Just then, Wheaton entered. "Jeff, Jean told me to tell you she wants you to stay on as her farm manager. She's in jail right now. But I should tell you, she's found a lawyer and will probably make bail later today or tomorrow."

Jeff paled. Stuffed his hands in his jeans pockets. Shook his head no. "Nah. Tell her I resigned. I'll work for my dad. Wait. Don't tell her that," he said nervously. "Just tell her I resign. Don't want her to come looking for me."

Wheaton sat down at his desk. Shuffled and restacked some papers. Tapped a yellow pencil on the wood. "Watch your backs," he said, then added to Jeff, "Go home, son."

Then he gave Cash a nod that said she too was dismissed. Gunner yawned and licked a paw.

Cash said to Jeff's retreating back in the parking lot, "I still need work."

Jeff answered without turning around, "I'll see what my dad's got," and gave a backhanded wave.

OVER THE NEXT FEW DAYS, Cash found work shoveling out grain bins for a local farmer and hauled a pickup load of hay from one farm to another for a different farmer. After an afternoon of helping one old-timer change the oil on his ancient car, she stopped at the Drive-Inn in Halstad when she saw Jeff's pickup parked there.

She pulled in alongside his car. "How's it going?"

He offered her a sideways grin. "Still this side of dirt. How's the air-conditioning?" He pointed at the bullet holes in the Ranchero passenger door.

Cash glared at him before asking, "Your dad got any work for me?"

He looked at her, all grin gone from his face. "I don't know, Cash. Trouble seems to follow you."

"Last I heard, trouble was locked in jail."

As soon as the words were out of her mouth, a carload of teenyboppers pulled into the open spot on the other side of Jeff. The four—no, six—girls in the car, the town's cheerleading squad, all called Jeff's name followed by behind-the-hand giggles. Three leaned out the car windows facing Jeff. All at once, the questions flew. "Did that crazy lady really shoot at you, Jeff? Jeff-y, hope you were shooting blanks. Is it true what they say about older women?"

Jeff tried to ignore the girls. Two of them got out of their car and leaned into his passenger-side window, showing lots of cleavage from their halter tops as they continued to torment him.

A car pulled into the Drive-Inn and parked on the roadway behind them.

"Jeff, look behind you," Cash said.

Jeff looked in his rearview mirror and turned pale. Mrs. Borgerud sat in her husband's sedan staring at him and Cash alternately.

Jeff unhooked the metal tray that held his burger basket

and dropped it on the ground. Told the girls on his door, "Get off." Sharp enough that they backed up, stunned.

He backed out of his parking spot. His car tires squealed and kicked up dirt as he left. Cash followed suit but backed out in the opposite direction and sped out of town. When she checked her rearview mirror, Mrs. Borgerud had pulled into the parking spot Jeff had left. She slowed and watched the carload of teen girls exit the Drive-Inn.

Cash circled around the streets of Halstad but couldn't find Jeff. She drove to the jail in Ada. Wheaton was at his desk.

"Why'd you let Jean go?" she blurted out before she was fully in his office.

Wheaton looked up from the *Fargo Forum* he had open to the sports page.

"She made bail. Hired some high-powered attorney from the Cities. Mortgaged the farm is what I heard."

"She just scared the hell out of Jeff and me at the Drive-Inn in Halstad. Pulled in behind us and just sat in her car and stared at us." She plopped down on the oak bench across from Wheaton's desk.

"She say anything?"

"No, just stared."

"We cleaned her house of guns."

"Doesn't mean she can't find another one. They're going to charge her, right? Why didn't the judge keep her locked up?"

"Innocent until proven guilty and all that. And like you said, a god-fearing white woman against whose word? Some guy lusting after her and an angry Indian? Even if you do work for me."

Cash slumped back on the bench. "You think she might get away with it?"

Wheaton paged through the newspaper on his desk. "I hope not."

"But you're not sure?"

"It's like me not seeing the crazy in that bank robber. Swayed by her youth and innocent looks. Put Jean in front of a jury of her peers with a good lawyer and who are they going to believe?"

"You heard her! You saw her! You're the sheriff! Your word has to count for something."

Wheaton looked at Cash. Brushed a hand over the sadness in his eyes. "All I saw was her shoot the hell out of your truck. You and Jeff were the ones who heard her talk about Bud and Nils."

"What the hell."

Wheaton continued. "Doc Felix says Nils was shot with a different gun. We didn't find a gun that matched when we searched the house. Doc thinks he was shot at a different location and then moved and stuffed under the corncrib. We don't know when she took the time to do all that. And she can look real fragile, like women around here are prone to do. Even if they can throw hay bales with the best of men."

Cash slumped even farther down on the bench. She had been right to let Arlis run to Canada with Shawnee. Had been right to give her the money to do so. After years in foster care with no escape, no respite from the abuse heaped on her, she had learned early where the power lay and who could and would get away with murder if push came to shove. She realized she had dared to hope for something else this time— and nothing had changed. After a moment, she slapped her thighs, and said, "Guess I'll go find some work, then."

"I heard from the school. They'll give you the work-study internship to help out here. Not much, but should cover gas. And running around money. Won't have to do so much field work."

"Maybe I don't mind the field work." Cash, halfway out of the office, stopped without turning around, clenched and unclenched her fists, then left.

AS SHE DROVE AWAY FROM the jail, Cash couldn't shake a feeling of doom. She knew the sun was shining. She knew, her intellectual mind knew, the sky was blue, the sun was bright, the grass and trees were green. But the world outside her windshield flickered like the black-and-white TV screen behind Shorty's bar. The entire Red River Valley appeared in shades of black and white. When she blew cigarette smoke out the window it was indiscernible from the gray, humid air. She looked at the sky, searching for the black thunderclouds that foretold a soaking rain and potential tornado. There wasn't a cloud in sight. *Blue*, she told herself. *The sky is blue.*

She drove out of Ada in the direction of the Borgerud farm. Five miles out of town, about a half mile ahead, she spotted Jeff's pickup, nose down in the ditch. She stepped on the gas. Pulled alongside the still running truck and jumped out, hollering, "Jeff! Jeff!"

Cash peered into the rolled-down window on the driver's side and saw blood smeared across the passenger seat toward the open passenger door. "Jeff!" she hollered, already moving around to the other side of the truck. Jeff was not in the ditch. The flattened grass was soaked with a dark liquid. "Jeff!" Cash called again, looking wildly up and down the ditch and into the nearby field. She shook her head, tried to shake the television static out of her mind, tried to bring color back into the world. She heard a groan. Froze. Tried to get her bearings. Tilted her head to hear better. Heard the muffled groan again. It came from under the truck.

She dropped to her knees and looked under the pickup. The ditch grass touched the underside of the truck bed. She crawled forward toward the cab. That's where Jeff lay, curled in a ball, his arms wrapped around the upper half of his body. "Jeff?" Cash said softly.

He groaned in response.

Cash stood and ran up into the road. There wasn't a car in sight. Shit. She ran back down into the ditch. Using every ounce of strength and every ounce of willpower she possessed, she grabbed Jeff's ankles and pulled him out from under the cab. Jeff screamed in pain. "Sorry, man," she said as she pulled him, feet first, up the ditch to the road beside her Ranchero.

By the time she had him out of the ditch, Jeff's arms had loosened from around his midriff and Cash could see where blood seeped out his left side around the area of his rib cage. Cash looked at his face. Even with his sunburn, his skin was pale white. She put her hand under his nose to see if he was still breathing. He was. Barely. Cash opened the tailgate of the Ranchero. Without thinking, without determining whether she could or couldn't, she picked Jeff up under his armpits and pulled, shoved him, and dumped him into the truck bed. She scanned the road again. No help in sight. But also no crazy lady. She got the blanket she had used to make a bed for Shawnee. She climbed into the bed of the truck and rolled Jeff in it like a sausage. Back in the cab, she whipped around and raced to the hospital in Ada.

AFTER GETTING JEFF INTO THE emergency room, Cash drove to the jail. Cash's black-and-white world turned red when she glanced at the want ads page open in front of Wheaton on his desk.

"That crazy woman tried to kill Jeff," she screamed at him as she grabbed the entire newspaper, crumpled it into a ball and threw it across the room.

"Whoa, slow down. What happened?" Wheaton was already standing.

"She shot him. Left him lying for dead in the ditch. He's at the hospital. He's half dead. Maybe he's already dead!"

"Come on." Wheaton grabbed Cash by the arm and led her out to his cruiser. Put her in the front seat and opened the back door for Gunner.

JEFF SURVIVED. FROM HIS HOSPITAL bed, after surgery and a blood transfusion, he told Wheaton how Jean Borgerud had been parked at the crossroad north of town.

When he drove past, she opened fire on him. Yes, he was sure it was her.

Wheaton, by himself, with Cash standing guard in her Ranchero up on the road, knocked on the door of Jean's house and arrested her without incident. Put her in handcuffs, moved Gunner to the front seat of the cruiser and put Jean in the back seat. Retrieved what looked to Cash from a distance like a brand-new hunting rifle from the back seat of Jean's sedan and transferred it to the trunk of his car.

Jean's attorney got her transferred to the Clay County jail in Moorhead. According to Wheaton, who refused to tell Cash where he had learned the information, Arlis was visiting relatives at White Earth with Shawnee when Jean and Nils had rendezvoused at the farm. Jean admitted she shot Nils and stuffed him under the corncrib. Jean, according to the story she told, had lost her mind when Nils tried to dump her before he was to head north to work the fields near Crookston. After three months in jail, the same attorney arranged a sweet plea deal. Jean pled guilty to the attempted murder of Jeff and was cleared of any charges in the murder of her husband and Nils Petterson. She was sentenced to Shakopee women's prison for a short stint of five years.

Cash was pissed. Afraid of the rage caged in her chest, she avoided Wheaton. While she knew he wasn't to blame, she feared she would lash out her anger at him. Instead, she worked the fields. Did menial farm work for any and all who would hire her. Drank and shot pool at the Casbah until closing time and fell into bed alone each night.

Toward the end of summer, Cash got a job throwing second crop hay bales on the Klock farm. She was reaching for a bale coming off the baler when Klock turned around, yelled and pointed down the field to where Jeff stood next to his pickup, waving at the tractor to stop. As the John Deere sputtered to a halt at the end of the row, engine still running but with the baler shut down, Jeff motioned to Cash to come talk to him. She jumped off the wagon and walked toward him, brushing hay off her sweaty arms. Now that she paused working, she felt the itch of hay dust that had seeped into her cotton shirt and was running in rivulets of sweat down her spine.

When she reached Jeff, he looked at the ground, hid his eyes behind the bill of his hat, kicked a clod of dirt before he looked back up to meet her eyes. "You know Jenny? She was homecoming queen a couple years back?"

Cash shook her head no.

Jeff looked back at the ground. Kicked another clod of dirt. He took his time talking, with long pauses between each sentence. "She's knocked up. We're getting married in a couple weeks. At the Lutheran church in town. Didn't know where to mail an invitation."

Cash gave him a startled look, not understanding what he was saying. He looked like a little kid offering to share his candy. Then it dawned on Cash he was inviting her to his wedding. "Oh, I don't think I can." Her eyes swept across the wide-open fields surrounding them. She pictured women and girls in church dresses and high heels. Men in suits. There was no place to hide in the expanse of land around her. "I can't." She looked around the prairie again. Looked back at Jeff.

He looked a little disappointed but said, "Thought I'd ask. After everything we been through."

"Just not my thing," she finally said, then added, "Had enough of the soap opera lifestyle have you? Stay away from the teenyboppers and old ladies." She gave him a small smile. "I'll get you beer next time I see your truck at the bar in town."

Jeff touched the bill of his farmer's cap, turned and walked back to his truck.

Cash motioned to Klock she was ready to get back to work. She walked to the hay wagon and climbed back up. Jeff waved again as he drove off.

Hours later, arms and legs sore, sweaty and itchy with hay dust, Cash left the field. A cold beer in the dim light of the Casbah was the only thought on her mind as she drove south toward Fargo–Moorhead. She was deep in a mental daze, cigarette smoke blowing out the driver's window, when a siren broke through the fog. She looked in the rearview mirror. Wheaton was behind her, lights on, siren on. "What the fuck," she said out loud as she pulled over to the side of the road. She sat, forearms across the steering wheel, and watched Wheaton walk up to her window.

"Hey, Cash."

She nodded.

"Let's go grab a bite to eat over in Twin Valley."

Cash stared at him.

"Look, I know you're mad at me. Come on. I'll get you a sandwich. Blueberry pie."

Cash looked at the road ahead. Gray highway. She knew the lines were white. Knew the sky was blue. The fields green. Her shoulders dropped in acceptance. "I'll follow," she finally said.

In the Twin Valley café, Wheaton led Cash to a booth where they could look out on to Main. A lone man sat at the counter drinking a cup of coffee. Two men dressed in oily coveralls were eating a meal in a nearby booth. The waitress brought two cups of coffee and, with pen and order pad in hand, stood stiffly by the booth, and asked, "What can I get you?"

Wheaton said, "Shirley, you know Cash, right?"

"Of course. You're the hot roast beef sandwich and blueberry pie girl. Haven't seen you in a while," she said, pen already scribbling the order.

Girl, my ass, Cash thought.

"And you know Shirley, right, Cash?"

Cash just looked at him.

"I know you've heard the gossip about me, um, dating someone." After a sip of coffee, with Shirley looking steadily at him, he continued. "Shirley and I have been seeing each other." Another moment of silence. Things were so quiet Cash heard the man at the counter put his coffee cup down on the saucer in front of him. Heard the men in the booth scrape forks across their plates. She could smell the hay dust emanating from her shirt.

"Ok," she finally said.

Shirley's face softened. Her shoulders relaxed. Wheaton said, "I'll have the same."

Shirley scribbled and walked behind the counter to slide the order through the kitchen window.

"Should have told you," Wheaton said.

Cash nodded.

"I'm sorry I couldn't do more with the Jean Borgerud situation."

"I'm sorry Jeff almost got killed before she finally got locked up."

"Cash. Things don't always work out the way we want them to."

Cash looked at him. "Tell me about it."

Shirley brought their hot plates over, asked, "More coffee?" and filled each of their cups without them answering. Went back behind the counter. Busied herself with filling salt and pepper shakers.

"How do we get things back on track, Cash? School's going to start in a few weeks, you've got the work-study. They'll expect you to come to jail. Help me out."

"I kept that bank robber's purse."

Wheaton barely raised his eyebrows.

"I threw the purse and the gun in the river."

Wheaton said nothing.

Both ate their roast beef sandwiches. Chewed their food, looked out the window when cars drove by instead of at each other. Ate some more.

The food threatened to stick in Cash's throat. She drank coffee. Sipped water from a plastic glass that smelled faintly of bleach.

"I kidnapped Shawnee," she blurted out.

"I know."

Cash looked at him. Tears threatened to spill from her eyes. The tightness that had gripped her chest for weeks loosened.

"I can sense some things too, Cash. I'm not as dumb as I look."

Cash blew air from her lips. Shook her head. Wiped her eyes with the paper napkin. "Never said you were dumb." She gave him a crooked smile.

"Like I said, life isn't always fair."

"You gonna lock me up?"

"Nope." He took another drink of coffee. "When you swear to uphold the law, you swear to do the right thing. Do what's right according to the law. When you're doing this work-study, you'll have to agree to that. You be straight with me, I'll be straight with you. From now on. Deal?"

Cash looked at another car that passed on Main. A woman with three kids. A teen in the front and two younger ones in the back. A family. She looked at Wheaton. Looked at Shirley, who was still busily ignoring them, but now filling ketchup bottles. She thought of Jeff with a wife and a baby on the way. She didn't know what to do about the gray TV static that currently clouded her vision. She didn't know what to do about the emptiness that filled her soul. She looked at Wheaton and the coffee cup on the table in front of him was white. The small jukebox attached to the wall at the end of their table was silver and red. The rest of the world was still enveloped in a fog. But she looked at Wheaton and said, "Deal."

ACKNOWLEDGMENTS

Miigwech to the many people who helped me get this from idea to manuscript including my agent, Jacqui Lipton of Tobias Literary Agency, and the team at Soho Press—Erica Loberg, Rachel Kowal, and Alexa Wejko. And Steven Tran for guiding me through the Heartland Fall Forum. As always, to my friends Danny and Eileen, L'Jeanne's Grand Marais Writer's Residency and my fellow writers of the Women From the Center writing group. My daughters, grandchildren and greatgrands are the driving force of my life and the multitude of reasons why I write; they give me the space and time to do so. Also a shoutout to Midwest farmers who live and work in the "breadbasket of America"—thank you for feeding us. All you Native writers out there rock-starring it through the publishing world—thank you for being role models, inspiration, and support on this journey.